I0563266

THE Setting Sun

THE Setting Sun

Compiled in the year 499 A.A. by
Archwizard Garth Septimus Simon

by Brighton Greet
& Joshua Hillman

THE SETTING SUN

Cover art by stacherdesign

Wise Man's Work (page ix) by Pavel O.

Editing by Oren Eades

Published by Brighton Greet & Joshua Hillman, Edmonton, Canada

ISBN:
Paperback	978-1-77354-569-1
Hardcover	978-1-77354-588-2
ebook	978-1-77354-589-9

Publication assistance by

PUBLISHING
PageMaster.ca

for Alex, Chris, Jacob, Josh, Nigel, and Rylee,
who brought this world to life

Uncharted North

Baharon Sea

Dufaire

Lorath Hills

Tribus Terras

Gornak Ranges

Garm

Wishbone Wood

Holm Tagor

The Father's River

Vokmar Pines

Tann

Yamizal

Biz Shalom

Ma'an

Tung Tameel

Tung Empire

Samiz Bizbee

Biz Sahlo

Dahk

Dargor

The Pocket

Seat of Rygar

Takkar Hills

Hildar

Charming Sea

Dorsal Sea

Westerton

Hylete Province

Dunn

Hylete

Stathmore

The Manor

Ager   Balor

Bridge of Unity

Alexander

Borderland Hills

Arcane Province

Arcanlodge

Arcanan

Tal Taro

Feldin

Moorlu

Elden Wood

Ophlto

Cornerstone Province

The Mouths

Wolfdale

Oxcommon

Prairieland Province

The Crown Lands

Cogton

Stone Haven

Franklin's Bay

River of the Setting Sun

Port of the Setting Sun

Kraken Sea

N

W   E

S

Glistening Sea

Contents

A Brief History of the Glorious Realm... 1

The Great Voyages of Alexander III 12

The First Tungish War: The Justice of Grant I 34

Plots and Paranoia: The Reign of Jacob II.................................. 52

The Royal Schism and the Rise of the Sunspots 80

The Second Tungish War: A House Divided 115

The Second Tungish War: The Zehiram 127

The Last Tungish War 154

The Great Gluttony: The Bloated Reign of Oliver II 188

The Fair and The Mad: The Sons of Oliver II 198

The War Under the Sun 207

Appendix A: Kings of the Glorious Realm 238

Appendix B: The Pike Family Tree... 240

THE
SETTING
SUN

A Brief History of the Glorious Realm

(9 BA—278 AA)

A Foreword by Archwizard Garth Septimus Simon

"A Glorious Realm." The words were first uttered by Lord Jacob Pike, who wistfully gazed o'er the Glistening Sea north of the Kingdom of Blumenkranz. For before the Glorious Realm, before the Dynasties of Pike, Leon, and Rygar, and before the House of Xhumevar sailed the Charming Sea and ruled the Realms of Men, the stars withdrew their lights, the sky went black as death, and all Hell broke loose. This was the age that became known for long after as The Doom, a time of great desolation that ravaged the once-fruitful land called the Kingdom of Blumenkranz.

Said to be covered in fresh summer grass as green as emeralds, and heralded each morn by a brilliant sunrise of amber, magenta, and gold, the land of Blumenkranz was as full of splendor as it was of bliss. Unspoiled by war, famine, strife, or plague for centuries, the people of the land were contrite and peaceful as lambs. The houses were painted in dazzling blues, greens, yellows, and reds, and the rooftops were overgrown with fragrant flowers. The people awoke each morning to the cheerful noises of children playing, goats braying, and faithful praying.

King Johannes VI of the House of Schwarzburg ruled stably as a benevolent monarch, taxing his people fairly and protecting the lands from the roaming Giants of the East. The white daisy of the Holy Order of Blumenkranz adorned the banners of the Paladins who protected the esteemed Faith, which was established long before by Gutenberg the Wise. As the saying went, "Peace is both a journey and a destination." Following Gutenberg's Holy Tenets, the Paladins vowed to keep the peace, to maintain that Blumenkranz was virtuous, pure, and holy, and to carry out this boon for many prosperous generations.

And so it was that the Kingdom of Blumenkranz was completely, utterly, and irrevocably blindsided when the one known only as the Ruby King took the Schwarzburg throne with little to no resistance to be spoken of, singlehandedly plunging the world into an Age of Doom never since forgotten.

The changes wrought by this Ruby King were subtle and innocuous in the beginning. The people of Blumenkranz had been for so long accustomed to peace and frivolity that they were quick to trust and charitable to the extreme. Yet many a Blumenkranzian felt a great disturbance when the Ruby King took their throne. Still, they did not take up arms or resist his rule in any tangible way. And so it was that the Holy Order was tasked by their new liege to collect taxes from the people of the land at a price tenfold the original amounts laid out by the gracious Johannes VI. Many Blumenkranzians surrendered their coin to the Holy Order's collectors, but others were less so inclined. Their defiance sparked the Ruby King's ire. He decreed, "Any and all citizens who cannot provide the required sum are to give up their firstborns in service to my armies."

Taxation was not the only policy to which the Ruby King brought great and unprecedented changes. He forsook the ongoing war against the Giants of the East, instead repurposing the Paladins for other, less-chivalrous tasks. Taxation was among them, but also subjugation of the citizens and preparation for a grand event the king referred to only as the *Inoculus Inversion*. To this day, none know or understand what the king's words meant, but they saw its dreadful effect take hold shortly thereafter.

The Kingdom of Blumenkranz was in despair, its citizens grappling with this newfound tyranny and assault upon their rights and livelihoods. With Johannes VI displaced and powerless, hysteria overtaking serenity and malaise a pox upon the land, it seemed as though nobody would make a stand against the Ruby King and his corrupted Order of Paladins, which had all but abandoned Gutenberg's Holy Tenets and the Faith.

But then, there were the Eight.

The circumstances of their gathering are lost to time and history, yet their brief and inspiring time on this earth is not easily forgotten. For many peoples of the time, the Eight were considered to be the bastions of chivalry and good virtue who embodied the Holy Tenets better than any before or after. Heralded by Old Lavvy, the aged storyteller of the Jolly Badger—an inn with a history older than Blumenkranz itself—the Eight rode through the streets of the capital upon steeds as white and pure as innocence, and the sun broke through the blanket of stormy clouds above, a sign of their presence and a beacon of hope for one and all.

The true heir to the throne, Prince Johannes Schwarzburg—eldest son of Johannes VI—bowed before the Heroes and imparted a Holy Blessing upon their Quest. They received his Holy Blessing with humility and grace, and vowed to return the throne to its rightful ruler, continuing the righteous line of the Schwarzburg kings. Multitudes of downtrodden peoples of all ages crowded the streets and cheered exuberantly for the Eight Heroes, and some say Gutenberg the Wise himself descended from the Heavens and placed a Holy Hand upon their heads to exalt their inevitable victory.

The Eight galloped with urgency and purpose toward the Ruby King's gates. The Ruby King's corrupted Paladins in garrison of Castle Blumenkranz fell swiftly to their immeasurable prowess. The crowds watched eagerly from without the walls as the Heroes disappeared beyond the courtyard of the castle to confront the evil Ruby King himself.

Alas, it was not to be.

The people did not accept the dreadful tidings at first, but soon enough, the reality was clear: the Eight Heroes had fallen, each and every one of them. For the Ruby King was not the haggard, withered man that the land had believed him to be.

It is said that after the Heroes were slain, the Ruby King emerged victorious from Castle Blumenkranz cloaked in their blood and holding his ebony staff aloft, its scarlet light blazing brighter than the sun itself. Thereafter followed a great darkening of the skies. The Castle's gleaming walls were scorched and blackened by the Hellfire that rose up from below. Its flames licked the towers and citizens alike, and its hunger could not be quenched by water nor prayer. The earth below split asunder with a thunderous crack, swallowing the livelihoods and memories of a thousand generations. A deep crevasse spread across the entire kingdom from north to south, forming a hideous canyon leading into Hell itself. The earth quaked, its foundations threatened to crumble, and ash rained down from the skies—a grey snow that covered everyone and everything who remained.

Any hope that lingered from the time of the Eight Heroes was snuffed out as Blumenkranz surrendered to The Doom.

It is now time to introduce the first of the House of Simon, from whom all chroniclers of this history are descended: Ethzar Simon. A mage in service to King Johannes VI Schwarzburg before the Ruby King usurped the throne, Ethzar was a man who laboured over matters of the Arcane, a subject of which little was known and less was understood. Yet Johannes VI saw value in the mage, and funded his research with the Crown's own reserves. Surely he faced opposition for this "evil" act, for the piety of Blumenkranz, noble and well-intentioned as it was, cultivated a deep aversion to such godless crafts. Whether or not the research was beneficial or detrimental to the Crown in any way was not revealed in Ethzar's writings, but his learnedness in the Arcane arts would play an important role in the time of exodus to come.

Many lords ruled the provinces of Blumenkranz as vassals to its king; among them were the four Great Lords of Pike, of Leon, of Hylar, and of Oxer. They each held control over significant territory within the kingdom, and each was shaken in turn when calamity struck. Lord Jacob Pike, mystified by the writings of Ethzar Simon during the time of Johannes VI, journeyed valiantly into the heart of the kingdom to beseech the mage as The Doom wracked the land, for he had a plan that, if successfully executed, could perhaps save multitudes of Blumenkranzians from the Hellfire the Ruby King had wrought.

Whilst ash continued to rain and tremors shook the ground, Lord Jacob rode into the capital on his dappled grey stallion, his striped violet cloak billowing behind him as he searched the ruins for the mage upon which his plan relied. In a crumbling tower beset by fire and smoke, Jacob discovered Ethzar poring over his findings, uncon-cerned with the ailings of the world around him. It was on that fateful day, three years Before-the-Arrival, that Lord Jacob Pike spoke of his great plan to Ethzar Simon, saying, "I and others of mine Province of Pike have heard whisperings of great promise regarding thine inquiries into the mystical phenomenon of the Arcane. I, having travelled across tumultuous lands to reach you here, in the hopes that thou mightest offer aid to me and mine people, beseech thee to do as such. If ye shall accept—and I pray that ye will for our sakes—we could bring to pass great providence to the displaced and fear-stricken peoples of this forsaken land. For I plan to venture where no man of Blumenkranz hath ventured before: across the Glistening Sea and to lands yonder off, where we mayest find solace in these times of darkness, where we mayest form a kingdom as glorious as Blumenkranz once was."

And so it was that the fruitful partnership between the Lord of Pike and the mage of Simon had begun—a friendship to last a lifetime, and a coalition that would remain for centuries, informing many events to come. Amid the smouldering remains of the once-beautiful realm of Blumenkranz, the lords of Pike, Leon, Oxer and many lesser lordlings (Lord Hylar had sought alternative passage across the Glistening Sea) gathered thousands of their remaining subjects and made for the northern coast. Their journeys to follow are well-documented, beginning with a Great Voyage that would herald the sunrise of a new era.

Upon arrival, the lords who had travelled alongside Jacob Pike crowned him King Jacob I, and his striped purple-and-black banners were renewed to include a golden crown complete with an amethyst gem in the centre—the Royal Banners of the Pike Dynasty. The site of his crowning would later blossom into the great city known as the Port of the Setting Sun.

In what became known as the Age of Exploration, forty thousand then followed him further north to explore the new lands. Jacob I was adamant about finding a suitable site for his new Royal Capital. While some of his followers, led by Lord Arthur Oxer, remained behind in the vast prairielands early on in their journey, and others, led by Lord Redfyre Rygar, split off to continue north to the twin lakes of Ophite and Moor'lu, Jacob I's party continued westward where, eventually, the city of Arcanan was founded in the northwest corner of the Mouth.

Jacob I reigned long, and saw the construction of his great city, as well as the White Keep and the College of Sorcery, built at the behest of Ethzar Simon. Jacob I died in the forty-ninth year After-the-Arrival, or AA, and the throne passed to his grandson Jared.

Following the ascension of Jared I, the realm found itself divided. In the northeast Rygar Province, Lord Redfyre Rygar seceded almost immediately and formed the Rygar Kingdom, crowning himself King Redfyre I, and following that first betrayal of fealty sworn to King Jacob, a second one came in the Prairieland Province, where Lord Argyle Oxer seceded from the Realm as well, forming the Prairieland Kingdom and crowning himself King Argyle I.

A war council was formed, and Jared I got to work with Archwizard Quiros Simon in mustering an army that would unite the Realm and crush the separatists.

By 54 AA, Redfyre's Host had annexed Tal Taro, and was on the march to Feldin to meet with Argyle's Host, but by 55 AA, the siege of Feldin went awry, as Redfyre and Argyle's hosts did battle with each other rather than joining forces. The Rygars were betrayed by the Tals, and Redfyre's Host went to rout. To put the nail in the coffin, King Jared I arrived in Feldin with a new army of immortal soldiers summoned through Quiros' Arcane powers, and the city was saved.

To chase down the two separatist hosts and end their treason, Jared I formed the Quenching Host and the Branding Host. With the former, he marched to the Seat of Rygar to defeat Redfyre. With the latter, Lord Geralt Leon marched on Oxcommon to force Argyle into submission.

Neither feat was easily accomplished. While the Branding Host eventually conquered Oxcommon, the siege was years-long and arduous, and Argyle was ultimately betrayed by his own wife rather than succumbing to Geralt's siege. In the north, King Jared was slowly gathering allies among the Hill Dwarves of Hildar and the Islander Dwarves of Dargor, peoples who both had reason to hate Redfyre Rygar. After liberating Dargor from Rygar slavers and their own corrupt king, Jared sailed to the Port of Rygar and, with help from the Hill Dwarves, burrowed underneath the walls of Castle Rygar to reach the Archpyre's tower. However, Redfyre had already brought his kingdom to ruin through dark Occult magick and experiments, and he himself was naught but a husk by the time Jared found him.

With the Founding Wars ended, Jared I returned to Arcanan, but left the majority of his rule to Lord Geralt, as his mind was never quite the same following what he had witnessed in Rygar. He died in 78 AA, and his throne passed to his son Murth.

During the Founding Wars, when Lord Geralt returned successful to Arcanan following the siege of Oxcommon, he ruled the Realm in the king's place. But his stewardship was a point of contention for Prince Murth, who had long desired the throne, and multiple attempts were made to undermine or even murder the Lord Commander. When Jared I finally passed from this mortal coil and Murth Pike was crowned Murth I, he conspired further to eliminate Lord Geralt, whom he viewed as the utmost threat to his reign. But now, he had the might of his father's immortal army, the Sworn Swords, behind him.

Murth's first plot as king to bring about the death of Lord Geralt was overheard by his court, and so numerous executions, even of Murth's own uncle Jacob, were carried out. One of the executed was also Lord Kasper Rohe, who had built tunnels beneath the White Keep at the king's behest. Kasper's death incited a great outcry from Stone Haven, and the king responded with force. He dispatched a Host of Sworn Swords to the Cornerstone Province to capture Stone Haven, but greatly underestimated how difficult an endeavour that would prove to be. Using the natural terrain, as well as guerilla warfare and ambushes, the Rohes' fighting force, known as the Oclor, protected their lands from Murth's armies until they were forced to retreat.

Later, in perhaps Murth's most heinous act, he declared war on the Mountain Dwarves of the Gornak Ranges, angling to "complete the Realm." This act proved very unpopular, but the Sworn Swords were sent north nonetheless—with Lord Geralt, in an attempt to remove him. Lord Geralt saw through this plot and slipped through the battle lines to escape to Arcanlodge. While the Dwarves fought viciously in defence of their lands, Murth caught wind of Lord Geralt's whereabouts and personally marched on Arcanlodge with a retinue of Sworn Swords. It was there, in the year 84, when Lord Geralt laid a trap of his own and outsmarted the king, leading to Murth I's long-overdue demise.

Murth "the Menace" was succeeded by his nephew Alexander, who went on to reverse much of Murth's damage, bringing the Realm into a Golden Age.

In his first act as king, Alexander I destroyed the majority of the Sworn Swords by sending them into the Mouth to rust and disintegrate over the ages. He sealed away the rest deep underneath the White Keep, only to be opened again by the power of a Simon. Throughout his storied and prosperous reign, he went on to establish the Glorious Council, to build great roads that served both to connect the great cities of the Realm's Provinces together and to promote trade, and also to discover the Hylete Kingdom to the west, past the Father's River, and to bring it under the rule of Arcanan diplomatically.

Under his rule, he also resolved the Second Dunn Rebellion—a crisis that was instigated when Lord Harrison Hylar bent the knee to Arcanan—and oversaw the construction of the Bridge of Unity, as well as many other grand construction projects within his Realm. He had many children, and greatly expanded the House of Pike, though all but one of his children were daughters, and many tragically passed before he did.

During the later years of his reign, a great scandal erupted in the Royal Family when it was revealed that the king's daughter Jenna had married a man who turned out to be Redfyre Rygar's own grandson—or perhaps a reincarnation of Redfyre himself, a popular belief held at the time—in a Rygar plot to regain control over the Glorious Realm. That scheme came to a bloody end in 140, when it was thwarted by Archwizard Ormus Simon and Lord Commander Lucas Leon, but the Royal Family was never quite the same afterward.

Alexander I passed away in 153 AA, and was succeeded by his eldest grandson, Christopher. The reign of King Christopher I was one marred with great tragedy and circumstance, permanently implanting the cursed nature of the Topaz Crown that he wore into the collective memory of the Glorious Realm. But then followed Tomas I, a king who became known as "The Root," for he greatly expanded the Royal Family in prestige, wealth, and indeed numbers, as he had many, many children and heirs over his long life. He also expanded the use of the Royal Navy and continued many of the infrastructure projects begun by Alexander I, such as the building of a great road leading from Arcanlodge all the way to the Port of the Setting Sun.

However, the Realm was left with King David I, or David the Abomination, after Tomas's death in 236. David I was a cruel, vindictive king who, like Murth the Menace, was drunk with power. The offspring of a scandalous affair and remarriage within the Royal Family, David I's reign began already marred by controversy, and in less than a year, he had established a reputation for himself as one of the worst kings the Glorious Realm had seen up to that point. His reign was cut short by a poisoning at an anniversary feast commemorating his first year as king.

Next was Alexander II. Crowned in 237 with the Crown of White, Alexander II cared more for tourneys, jousts, and festivities than ruling, and left the bulk of his administrative responsibilities to the Glorious Council. He spent heaps of the Crown's wealth on opulent celebrations for seventeen years until he was fatally injured in a joust he insisted on participating in. After a year-long coma, during which his fate was uncertain and the Realm was stewarded by his Lord Commander, Aiden Leon, he finally perished in 254.

The throne passed on to King Samuel I. Now, Samuel I was no doubt a merciful and just king who strove to be honourable and gracious to all his subjects, but his reign was unfortunately compromised by famine, plague, and winter. While he tried earnestly to keep morale high and keep amenities flowing from the rich to the poor, he was tragically killed in 276 during a Royal Demonstration when a terrible riot broke out in Arcanan.

His successor, Jared II, did not fare much better. A young king who took to the throne at twenty years old, Jared II was born sickly and was greatly susceptible to illness. He contracted a flux in 278 and passed away a fortnight later, leaving no issue. His reign was another example of the Topaz Crown granting ill luck to its wearer.

Following the deaths of Samuel I and Jared II, however, history brings us to the reign of Alexander III. Wearing the Crown of Purple originally worn by the first of the Pike Kings, Jacob I, Alexander's coronation coincided with the end of the Great Famine at last. It was a hopeful time for the Glorious Realm, and many believed that this new king would usher in a new Golden Age, much like the reign of Alexander I.

And thus ends this brief history and begins the chronicling of the Seven Voyages of Alexander III and the three Tungish Wars that would inevitably bring forth the downfall of the great Pike Dynasty.

The Great Voyages of Alexander III

(278—291 AA)

COMPILED FROM THE CHRONICLING WORKS OF ARCHWIZARD XENAGOS NOVUS SIMON

It was late autumn in the 278th year After-the-Arrival.

Upon the glistening snow-white dais where ten kings had sat before to rule the vast kingdom known as the Glorious Realm was Alexander of the House of Pike, Third of His Name, clad in gold-and-silver armour embroidered with amethyst garnets. Upon his shoulders was draped a billowing cloak of a deep purple.

Xenagos Novus Simon, the Royal Archwizard, climbed the wide marble steps that led up to the Arcane Throne bearing a small pillow upon which sat the Crown of Purple, the crown worn by King Jacob I. Upon that Holy Day, anointed by High Elder Tyful'singrir of the West Church of Gutenberg, Alexander was crowned King of the Glorious Realm before kin and court.

Years of famine, plague, and toil had wracked the Glorious Realm since the age of Samuel I, and hope had dwindled in the hearts of many of the Realm's peoples. Jared II, a king who appeared outwardly as frail as the collective peoples felt, had reflected this weakness to many. The plague took him, as it had taken countless thousands of fathers, mothers, grandfathers, grandmothers, children, and babes.

So, when the Crown of Purple was carried out by the Archwizard Xenagos, it was seen as a sign of hope once again rekindled—a reminder that the sun had not yet set on the Glorious Realm.

And so, the famine's end did come. As if by Divine Will—a notion handily perpetuated by the High Elder and his flock—the coronation of King Alexander III marked a great subsiding of the hardships and suffering by which the Glorious Realm had become so terribly afflicted. The harvest that year was plentiful, and the rot did not take so many crops as it had the years prior, overturning many peoples' expectations for another meager winter of starvation and death. The Realm at last had enough sustenance to go around. Throughout the 270s, when winter came, the sick, old, and infirm would forego food to ensure their younger, healthier counterparts would survive. At long last in 278, they needed not go hungry. 279 was further hopeful, as it seemed the plague had at last run its course after nearly ten years. It was a time of gratefulness and a time of rebuilding for all peoples, rich and poor.

With a new king came a new Glorious Council. King Alexander III summoned forth those who had faithfully served his predecessors Samuel I and Jared II, and they were judged accordingly. The Lord Commander was Louis Leon, who had held the title since 255, and was sixty-seven years old—quite aged for a Lord Commander. The Royal Admiral was Lord Dominic Dunn, who had served since 260. The Royal Accountant was Archibald Oxer, who had served since 267.

The office of Royal Defender had changed like a courtier changes their clothes during the reigns of Samuel I and Jared II, as the frequency of Arcanian riots and demonstrations had increased dramatically, considering the conditions. Many a Defender had been cut down during routine surveys of North Arcanan, the Mudpits, the Gutters, and Dregs, and even occasionally in Tomas' Square or the

Kingsroad Marketplace. Arcanan was not safe for the City Guard, who were often the nearest targets for downtrodden—or vengeful—townspeople to direct their rage.

As it stood currently, the latest Royal Defender, a man named Hatwell Flum, had been found dead in the Windmaker's Inn; his death was first attributed to the patrons of the inn in an act of foul play—the Windmaker's Inn was a known haven for gamblers and scoundrels—but, following an autopsy conducted by Archwizard Xenagos, it was ruled that the late Defender's cause of death was actually due to plague. The Inn was quickly cleared out, and all patrons who had been there when Flum was discovered were put under strict quarantine. Hatwell Flum, as it were, happened to be one of the final victims of the plague during its ten-year rampage.

Nonetheless, when Alexander III took the throne, a new Royal Defender was in need of appointment, and so he promoted the late Flum's second-in-command, Lemmon Frost, who gladly accepted the title.

The Royal Architect was Taron Rohe, who had been recently appointed by Jared II upon a recommendation from Lady Tamina of Stone Haven. The Warden was a man named Jack, who was cousin to the new Royal Defender, and the Executioner was a one-armed former blacksmith called Ironstump by friends. All was in order, and so the new king got to rule.

With the coming of the new year, the king's priorities were first to set the Realm's finances in order, accounting now for the new influx of produce and harvest from across the land. Many farms were back in business, having suffered losses from starvation and plague in the years prior, but now finally finding their footing once again. It would suffice to say Lord Archibald Oxer was busy at work balancing the budget and allocating subsidiaries from the Crown during this time. But once these matters were handed over to his Councillors, the king could return to what he truly loved more than anything: sailing the seas.

Ever since he was a young lad, Prince Alexander had been enamoured by the open ocean. He had heard tales of his ancestor Jacob and the Great Voyage he had ventured upon when he and his fifty thousand crossed the Glistening Sea to escape the Doom. Alexander longed to complete a voyage of his own and explore lands further yet beyond the Glorious Realm; he pored over maps in his youth that were charted during the reigns of his namesake Alexander I and also Tomas the Root. Always disappointed by the lack of true knowledge regarding what lay west of Dunnland or east of the Elden Wood, Prince Alexander frustrated his mentors—namely the Archwizard Xenagos, who was his tutor throughout much of his youth—to no end with his constant barrage of questions.

So, it is perhaps no surprise that by the age of eleven, Prince Alexander had asked the Royal Admiral of the day, Dominic Dunn, if he could train him in the arts of seafaring. Dominic Dunn did indulge him—how could he deny a Royal Prince such a request?— and took him out upon the Mouth during the summers. This all was much to the displeasure of King Samuel I, who also happened to be Prince Alexander's father. "If I hear one more tale of how you nearly drowned, or were assailed by pirates, then you shall never set foot inside a boat again until you come of age!"

Lord Dominic did attempt many times to quell the king's anxieties, stating, "The boy can hold his own at sea, my liege. I see in him a better sailor than I was at his age, and that is no small feat, considering I was raised in Dunnland and had all the greatest mentors in the Realm."

Samuel I did allow these outings to continue, but stressed that "If anything happens to my son, it is on your head!"

By the age of eighteen, when Prince Alexander did indeed come of age, he and Lord Dominic had sailed to Paradise Isle, Stone Haven, Cogton, and even as far as Hylete Square and Dunnland. The prince impressed many of his peers as a capable—if overly ambitious— captain, and was undeterred by storm or strife.

It was during one of these voyages that he revealed to the Royal Admiral thus: "I shall sail to the lands beyond before I die; for while my ancestor foresaw a Glorious Realm, I see a great coast of ice, fiery mountain isles, and exotic lands where the finest cuisines and delicacies reside."

Lord Dominic supported the prince in all these dreams, and confided in him that one day he would have the means to do so— he would just need to find a crew with a similar vision. For Prince Alexander did not expect that one day he would be king and bear the responsibilities that lay therein, though perhaps he ought to have considered the possibility more in earnest, as his elder brother Jared had been born sickly and small, and oft fell ill for long spans of time during his youth, as if he was more vulnerable than most. Compared to the healthy, lusty babes who Alexander and, to a lesser extent, his younger brother Avery were at birth, Prince Jared was a cause of concern for House Pike, as it was whispered in the absence of his presence among the court that he would not make it to the Arcane Throne on account of his poor health and frail nature. Prove his detractors wrong Jared II did, but alas, he only reigned a year before the worst happened anyway.

Another such matter that plagued the king's youth was that of marriage. After his fifteenth birthday, he was hounded on the daily by ingratiating, ambitious lords and ladies of the White Keep, who marketed their daughters to him and his father behind thin veils of courtesies and pleasantries. Lord Archibald Oxer attempted to offer his own daughter, Amanda Oxer, on many occasions, but failed to mention that his daughter had already been promised to five other suitors—unbeknownst to one another—and was seven years Prince Alexander's younger, besides. Other offers trickled in from great and noble Houses such as the Leons, the Hylars, the Whits, the Felixes, and the Rohes, though all were coldly ignored by the young prince, who was wholly uninterested in such matters. That year, during a feast in the Great Hall before all the lords and ladies of the court, he controversially blurted, "Why do I need a princess when I have my ships? Will she follow me out on my Great Voyages, or simply remain home and large with child? I do not want anything to anchor me to Arcanan, as my world is grander than one city. I mean to witness wonders beyond most men's wildest dreams, not be bound and chained to a life of matrimony."

This, needless to say, was troublesome for the court, and especially to the prince's father, King Samuel. "You *will* wed, and you *will* father heirs. Forget this business out at sea; you are a prince first, and a sailor second!" Samuel I forbade his second son from any further seafaring adventures with the Royal Admiral, and thus confined him to the White Keep to study statecraft and literature.

This proved to be a fool's errand, as Prince Alexander was wont to trick his tutors often and sneak off toward the port anyways, leaving a servant or friend in his place at the castle to pose as him while he was off at sea on another adventure, usually alone. By 271, Archwizard Xenagos had given up on trying to tutor the prince, as any attempt left the Archwizard frustrated or humiliated by another one of Alexander's schemes. He largely turned his efforts toward tutoring the prince's brother Avery instead, for Avery appreciated his birthright as a Royal Prince and joined the Archwizard in scoffing at Alexander's peculiar fascination with all things exotic and strange.

Meanwhile, Prince Alexander embarked on his first Great Voyage that summer in 271, having gathered a crew of similarly minded sailors from Arcanan's docks and taverns to accompany him.

Alexander's first Great Voyage, which he embarked upon at the age of sixteen, took him south and east along the coast of the Prairieland Province and the Elden Wood until he reached a smattering of stony isles among a great expanse of open ocean. But more impressive a sight than these uninhabitable, empty islands was the sea life that the prince and his crew did spy: great whales of immense scale; their fins the size of sails rising above the waves and crashing back down with such force that they nearly overturned the prince's ship. Believing himself to be the first sailor ever to bear witness to such a beast, he had one speared and brought aboard the deck to inspect; the act nearly cost the prince his life, as well as his crew's, for the creature proceeded to explode gore and blood all over the ship with a magnitude that nearly burst the hull. Still, Prince Alexander retained one of the creature's giant fins, and had it kept in a massive saltwater basin for the duration of the trip home in an attempt to preserve it. By the time he returned to the Port of Arcanan at summer's end, the fin had largely succumbed to rot, but was still a sight to behold at court.

The prince's Great Voyage—first of eight, so Alexander proclaimed, in honour of The Eight—was hailed as a success, much to the chagrin of his father Samuel I, his former tutor Xenagos Simon, and his brother Avery, who hotly approached the prince to deride his actions. "While you were off gallivanting upon the open seas, hunting fish, *I* have been preparing myself for rule."

But at this, Prince Alexander merely laughed. "Brother, if you have opened a book or two, you would surely know that the line of succession passes down by order of birth, does it not? The Arcane Throne will go to our brother Jared, not I, and *especially* not you. Perhaps instead of wasting your time poring over old manuscripts with Xenagos the Archwrinkle, you could find yourself a hobby or two? Or better yet, a woman?"

This, among other similar encounters between the brothers, added further oil to the flames of rivalry that had been slowly burning in the years since the princes' youths. But that selfsame year, perhaps to spite his brother, Prince Avery did indeed find himself a wife in the daughter of Lord Cillius Stock, a lithe maiden named Rachel. The fact that Prince Alexander remained unmarried during this time did further stoke the whisperings at court, and King Samuel I became more adamant to secure a marriage for his second son thereafter—to similar success as before.

Despite a harsh reprimand from his father and further chastisement at court, Prince Alexander meant to follow up his first Great

Voyage immediately with a second. In the summer of 272, he snuck off in the night to board a galley he'd had his crew prepare for him beforehand. His ship, which by that point he had officially named *Horizon Sun*, had left the Port of Arcanan by the time the first rays of morning light had broken through the clouds. For his second Great Voyage, Prince Alexander meant to sail yet further and discover what other lands lay to the east of the isle he'd discovered on his first voyage, which he dubbed Whale Reef.

But what he and his crew found was beyond anything they had imagined—another entirely populated continent.

Across what he called the Charming Sea, Prince Alexander landed his ship on the west coast of the land he named the Charm. They laid their anchor and embarked. Before them lay a fertile prairieland bordered by a sparse woodland. The prince and his crew found passage through the lands and journeyed up a river to set their eyes upon the vast city of Zealodin. Towering structures that glittered like diamonds, great castles with hundreds of turrets and entranceways, and legions of Paladins clad in shimmering silver armour greeted them. The city overlooked a large inland sea called Turtle Lake due to its irregular shape.

Prince Alexander sought an audience with the leader of Zealodin, a man named Alvon Amozeth. Here, the people followed an ancient religion that glorified a Silver Scale of an Elden dragon, and the leader of said religion was called the Keeper. The army of Silver Paladins was known as the Holy See, and they were charged with the protection of their lands and the proliferation of their Faith.

While the people of the Charm spoke a different common tongue than those in the Glorious Realm, there were similarities in the vernacular that perhaps had origins tracing back to the common speech of the Far East, where the people of Blumenkranz first lived long ago. As such, one of the prince's crewmates could roughly translate their speech, or enough as to be passable for simple conversation.

Keeper Alvon Amozeth was intrigued to hold an audience with Prince Alexander, and they discussed—as much as they were able—trade between their two realms. Upon the conclusion of their stay in the land of the Charm, Prince Alexander humbly requested of Keeper Alvon a token to bring home in commemoration of their visit to this Sacred Land. Keeper Alvon understood his request, and as a token of good faith and charitability, he donated a suit of armour for the prince to return home with—a beautiful, silver-blue set crafted by the finest smiths in Zealodin using a rare metal ore native to the Charm. Prince Alexander accepted this gift with great thanks and set off back to the west to return to the *Horizon Sun* and make the journey home.

News of Prince Alexander's second Great Voyage and the evidence of the Platinum Armour did wonders for his reputation back at home. For once, his father King Samuel seemed duly impressed by his second son, and at once sent forth Dominic Dunn and seven ships of the Royal Fleet to follow the prince's coordinates and set eyes upon the Charm for themselves. Prince Alexander was praised as an adventurer among the likes of Ethzar Simon or Ethan the Swordfish.

As a result, many more lords and ladies put forth their daughters as a suitor that year. Just as before, Prince Alexander curtly denied all attempts and remained unmarried, while his brother Prince Avery and his wife Rachel delighted in the birth of their firstborn son Jared Pike. The enmity between the brothers had only grown since Alexander's return, as the newfound admiration for his voyages had further cast Prince Avery to the wayside—not only in the eyes of the court of the White Keep, but also in the eyes of their father, Samuel I. "I bet on one of these excursions, my brother is like to marry some exotic whore and forever dilute our proud House of Pike with foreign blood. Mark my words: it will happen, because my brother cares as much for the honour of our House as he appreciates the Arcane Throne!"

In 273, when Prince Alexander made plain his plans to embark upon a third Great Voyage, his father was less inclined to inhibit him. In fact, in an act of great penance for his prior harshness, the king gave leave for his Royal Admiral, Dominic Dunn, to accompany Prince Alexander as First Mate.[1] And thus, Prince Alexander set out upon another great adventure that summer, this time to journey south of the Charm and discover what lay beyond.

The voyage took Prince Alexander and Lord Dominic past Whale Reef and among many scattered islands until they eventually landed upon a large circular island with a great bay in its centre. There, they discovered a lush rainforest teeming with life—much of it deadly, including fire-red ants that moved like a carpet of fury upon the ground, eerie birds that mimicked the speech of the prince and his crew, and spiders the size of their faces that scuttled along the tree trunks and spun webs as thick as twine.

As dangerous as these forests were, there were plains as well near the cliffs of the island's north face. There, Prince Alexander founded Tybolt, a camp named after one of his crewmates who died in the island's forests when he was lost to quicksand while taking a piss.

By the summer's end, the *Horizon Sun* returned to the Port of Arcanan with a collection of plants, shells, and the carcass of a giant spider. By the shape of the isle, Prince Alexander named it Crescus. For weeks, many peoples of the court gathered voraciously around the prince and listened to his tales of the journey there and his crew's adventures in those rainforests.

Meanwhile, Archwizard Xenagos studied samples of the spider's venom for use in alchemy at the College of Sorcery. It was this discovery that led to the creation of the School of Anatomy—a school of magick formerly considered to be Occult—as a subject to be taught

---

1   Lord Dominic Dunn's own voyage to the Charm was a resounding success; trade between the Port of the Setting Sun and Teslora, a city in the Charming Bay to the west of Zealodin, had been established, and rare spices, fruits, and textiles had begun importation—along with a minor influx of the Keeper's religion, much to the disapproval of High Elder Tyful'singrir of the West Church of Gutenberg.

at the College thereafter, with Xenagos being the first professor of the craft.

The next Great Voyage that the king planned was to be in an entirely different direction than his previous three. This time, he meant to travel north to the Tung Empire, a land that had been discovered by Redfyre Rygar in the early days of the Rygar Province's founding, but had never been visited by a Pike. For years, the Rygars had done trade with the Imperial Capital, Samiz Bizbee, as well as with the Dwarves of Holm Tagor. Prince Alexander had questioned many times why Arcanan had not sought the Tungs for trade in all these years since the Glorious Realm's founding, and the answers he'd received were all severely disappointing. As such, he took it upon himself—and Lord Dominic Dunn—to sail there next and see the desert oases of Samiz Bizbee, Biz Shalom, Biz Sahlo, and Tung Tameel for himself.

Then, during the year 274, remarkably little was known about the history of the Tung Empire. Today in 499, it is known that the Empire was founded somewhere around 1500 BA, and the original capital was located where presently the wastes of Alkharabu reside—the region also known as the Land of the Damned. Alkharabu was formerly a centre of civilization in the North, a beacon of prosperity and plenty. If the Eldtales can be believed, it was a land of clear rivers, imposing waterfalls, lush valleys, and high cliffs all carpeted in green summer grass, and it saw neither winter nor storm. This lasted for over 600 years, during which the early Tungish people settled and built the grand city of Alkhalidu.

But, after a zealous faction known as the Believers stole away the sacred Eye of Wahid Eazimun, the lands were cursed by that god and fell into ruin. The vast grasslands were corrupted into endless desert sands, blistering hot in the summers and equally cold during the winters. All the rivers ran dry, and the waterfalls became landslides of cold, dead earth and bones. The Believers were buried deep beneath the sands. Foul, accursed creatures descended from the twisted grey skies and began to make the land their new home, roaming its oncesplendorous expanse and devouring anyone and anything in their path. All semblance of life other than these new, alien creatures had been stamped out or erased, and the once-great city of Alkhalidu was left a crumbling ruin, half-buried in dunes of sand and later lost to time.

Those who fled the wrath of the Wahid Eazimun and the Ruin of Alkhalidu made their way south through the harsh deserts of Kodarsh. The leader of this great exodus, Samiz Biz-Bee, founded a new city for his people on the southeastern coast by the Baharon Sea, and from there, a new capital began to flourish. However, many still believed that the wrath of Wahid Eazimun would follow them to their new city and punish them for trying to evade Him.

One such man, a renowned alchemist named Alkemy, who is said to have first founded the art, gathered more men of similar mind together to plan a great defence of Samiz Bizbee, their new haven. It was 874 BA, or the 21st Year of the Wrath of Wahid (YWW). Their eventual consensus was to build a ward of ancient magick that would stand around the walls of the city and defend it from the divine wrath of their god, whether from sky or earth. Therefore, the only entrances or exits from Samiz Bizbee became the few designated gates. Samiz Bizbee's gargantuan walls would otherwise protect it from invading armies, as attempting to scale them was futile. Still, though, despite the walls and the ward, some remained wary of the Wahid Eazimun's wrath, and maintained that "the arrogance of the alchemists will not protect us forever, for the prophecy of Torak Benesha claims that one day our Holy City shall fall, and the Wahid Eazimun will have his way, just as he did with the Lost City of Alkhalidu and the foolish thieves who stole his Eye."

By the year 274, the Tung Empire—a misnomer in many ways; as their lands do not spread overseas, but rather are isolated to the northeast corner of the continent, entirely encased in desert and dry heat as a result of the Wahid Eazimun's Curse—remained exceptionally poor. Where there were once lavish orchards growing upon those fertile lands, now there were only endless rolling dunes of sand and stone.

However, the few cities built along the relative oases by the coast of the Baharon Sea: Samiz Bizbee, Biz Shalom, Biz Sahlo, and Yamizal, had become hubs for civilization. Dense populations of Tungish peoples reside there, as well as in the city of Tung Tameel, which was built along the Bay of Ma'an. Many of these cities became centres of trade, first with the Dwarves, then later with the Rygars. Trade items include rare spices found only in the deserts of the Empire, as well as intricate textiles such as robes and tapestries depicting moments of legend. The Tung Empire also long involved itself with trade with other foreign kingdoms and empires off the continent to the far north and east.

Culturally, the Tungish are a highly religious people, and their dominant faith is that of the Khatiaton. It is believed to be over 1600 years old, and consists of a pantheon of gods underneath a paramount one, the Great One, called Wahid Eazimun. Ancient scrolls record the Tiakon Revolution during which Khatiaton was enforced as the state religion of the Empire. Enemies and detractors of the Tiakon fled west of the Tungish Dunes and across the inhospitable Lorath Hills to found the city of Tribus Terras betwixt three biomes of tundra, desert, and grassland; the rest were slain by the Tiakon Emperor's Holy Army of Tung-Junud.

One might ask why the Tungish people never sought to leave the arid deserts of the North and flee south beyond the Gornak Ranges to the lands that are now the Glorious Realm. Well, the clearest reason, according to Scholars of the College of Sorcery, is simply that after over a millennia spent living in those lands, the people had grown accustomed to its harshness and could not imagine themselves abandoning their Sacred Land. For a more religious angle, some Tungish peoples believed that to try and settle somewhere else, such as to the south or across the Baharon Sea, would simply call down Wahid Eazimun's wrath; their ships would sink far from the coast, or their crops would fail or spoil in the south. In short, the overwhelming belief was that to leave the desert would be suicide for their people at best, or sacrilegious at worst.

During the summer of 274, when the *Horizon Sun* landed in the Port of Samiz Bizbee, Prince Alexander was impressed beyond measure. The Tungish ships were larger and more magnificent than any in the South—even the great galleys of the Dunnish Fleet, Lord Dominic did admit—and the bazaars and markets of the city were rife with rich smells and foods. The tapestries and carpets sold by many a merchant of the city told tales of triumph, turmoil, and terror. The people were as kind as they were proud.

But the greatest treasure Prince Alexander found during that summer in Samiz Bizbee was *love*. The prince had long pushed away any potential romances at court in Arcanan, but now, during his fourth Great Voyage, he had found a spark at last. The lady Mahya Biz-Ramya, daughter to the Emperor Amir IV, caught the prince's fancy while he attended an Imperial feast to honour his visit to Samiz Bizbee.

One of the Emperor's personal protectors, the Kaulkaan, caught Prince Alexander abed with Princess Mahya one night, and immediately rushed to inform the Emperor. Lord Dominic Dunn witnessed this occur, as he was secretly on guard on behalf of the prince to ensure that his nightly exploits were not spied upon, and so he surreptitiously informed the prince that it was time to leave the city at once.

While Prince Alexander was saying his goodbyes to his beloved with a heavy heart, the Emperor surprised each party in turn by endorsing his daughter's proclivities. Summoning her to court along with a captured Prince Alexander and his crew—at which point Lord Dominic and the prince were certain that they would face their deaths—he announced that he would give his Imperial Blessing unto Princess Mahya and Prince Alexander as long as they were wed that selfsame day. Elated, the prince and his beloved did agree.

Thus, during a boiling summer day in 274, inside Samiz Bizbee's Great Palace of Biz Eazima, Prince Alexander Pike took Princess Mahya Biz-Ramya to wife, and she became the future Queen of the Glorious Realm.

By the time Prince Alexander returned to Arcanan in late 274, reactions to his consort were greatly varied within the White Keep. Some praised the union as great news, as it was a binding alliance between Arcanan and Samiz Bizbee and a way to wrest the Tung Empire from its solitary trade alliance with the Rygars—who were long-time enemies of Arcanan. Others were less enamoured, remembering Prince Avery's words spoken years before now in a new light. King Samuel I himself was simply happy that his son had finally found himself a woman, for he had been beginning to worry that it would never happen. Naturally, scores of lords and ladies from the White Keep's court were furious that the prince had denied their daughters' hands in marriage only to marry a Tung in their stead, but Prince Alexander paid them no heed, for he was deeply in love, and would never let anyone deride his lovely wife or deny them their affection for each other.

Prince Avery Pike, now outspoken in his stance, continued to preach of Princess Mahya's "unwelcomed presence" in Arcanan, and even went as far as to call for High Elder Tyful'singrir to annul their marriage, as it was officiated by an elder of a foreign religion rather than the legally recognized West Church of Gutenberg. However, the High Elder's response was instead to conduct his own wedding ceremony for the prince and his consort, this time in the White Keep's Great Hall, at the behest of King Samuel I.

A son came not too long afterwards; by the spring of 275, Prince Alexander and Princess Mahya welcomed Prince Grant Pike to this world. A large, healthy boy with dark hair and an intense stare, he was beloved by the king and his heir, Prince Jared, but detested by much of the court, in particular Prince Avery, who often and loudly noted the babe's "Tungish features."

The years that followed saw many major events already mentioned: the deaths of King Samuel I and King Jared II, the ascension of Prince Alexander to King Alexander III, and the end of the Great Famine and plague that had wracked the Glorious Realm for years. Alexander, now King of the Glorious Realm, was plagued instead by a great deal of responsibilities of rule that he had long hoped would never rest upon his shoulders. Alas, his plans for future Great Voyages were delayed time and time again.

Additionally, during this time, in 279, the Realm saw the death of the aged Lord Commander, Louis Leon, and so his son and heir Sir Marcus Leon ascended to the role that year. An esteemed knight— though with a thirst for blood and a streak of madness in his eyes—Sir Marcus was perhaps not many peoples' first choice for the new Lord Commander, but as was precedent throughout history, the title was always passed down to the eldest living Leon heir, and Alexander III did not wish to further add to the controversies his life and reign had already provided. Many believed that Lord Marcus would jump at a chance for war, and were careful to keep him on a close leash during the years he sat upon the Glorious Council.

In the year 283, Alexander III finally had the chance to embark upon a fifth Great Voyage, as many matters of state were either being managed by his council or had not yet boiled to a point where the king need worry. Once again enlisting his lifelong friend Lord Dominic Dunn, he brought the *Horizon Sun* out of retirement to set sail once again o'er the Charming Sea; however, this time, he meant to head further northward than he had before.

Unfortunately, unbeknownst to the king, his queen Mahya was with child. Though she did not show any signs when Alexander III set out upon the *Horizon Sun* with his crew, during the months of his absence, she grew large of belly and eventually gave birth, but without her husband present. Thus, Prince Jacob Pike was born by the end of 283, and was surrounded not by his father and fellow Arcanian nobles, but rather by the queen and her own Imperial kin.

Alexander III, meanwhile, had sailed as far north as the *Horizon Sun* would take him: all the way to the lands he called the North Coast. A frozen tundra at the very edge of the earth, the North Coast was a frigid landscape teeming with gargantuan mammals and ferocious winter beasts such as the Wooly Mammut, the Giant Vitten-beorn, and the Enoy Storrtroll.

After braving the extreme colds of the North Coast, and after Lord Dominic Dunn slayed an Enoy Storrtroll with his own blades, Alexander III ventured further beyond the icy wastes to come across some modest holdings and villages further inland. However, they were hostile to the king and his crew, and a deadly skirmish followed. With most of his crew injured and two slain, the king retreated to the *Horizon Sun* and promptly decided to leave.

Frustrated by his perceived failure at the North Coast—besides discovering it for the Glorious Realm, he did wish for a more peaceful venture, and greatly bemoaned the losses of his crewmates—and unwilling to return back to Arcanan just yet only to suffer further years of "arduous rule and insufferable courtiers," he instead elected to head straightaway into his sixth Great Voyage. This time, he desired to head as far south as the *Horizon Sun* could go, as a direct opposite venture to his last, for he wished to lay eyes upon the land of his fore-fathers, the Land of Blumenkranz, which was now called The Doom.

However, his long ventures at sea did have their implications for the Glorious Realm back home. The sitting Steward of the Realm, Lord Marcus Leon, was of the character many would fear in a king, for in his time at the helm of Alexander III's kingdom, he sought war. During the long years of the Great Famine and the plague that had followed, there were scant few battles to be fought, and fewer opportunities for a knight to prove their valour with a sword. Lord Marcus desired this and more, and the most sure-fire way to start a war was to reignite the conflict that had wracked the Realm during the Holy Schism of 264.

The circumstances of this conflict within the Church of Gutenberg are extensive and need not be recounted, but suffice to say the schism resulted in the formation of two separate churches, each governed by a High Elder, with one in the West in Arcanan and one in the East in Farcross. To reopen old wounds, Lord Marcus met with High Elder Tyful'singrir to discuss rumours from the East that they planned to undermine and overthrow the West Church's leadership through heinous acts of subterfuge. "It has come to my attention that the Heretics of the East have been planning this for a long time now, and I fear that they shall take this opportunity to strike while the king is at sea. But as your sitting monarch, I shall not let this come to pass."

At once, High Elder Tyful'singrir got to work informing the Faithful of this coming threat, and bade them all to stay vigilant for "heretical heathens" within their congregations. Meanwhile, Lord Marcus sent the Keeper of the Keys, Julius Tals, to distribute posters across the city of Arcanan warning the populace of the East Church of Gutenberg's intentions. *In their heresy and their ignorance, they have done away with one of Gutenberg's Three Holy Tomes: The Book of Absolution*, the poster did—fictitiously—state.

Almost inevitably, war came. By the spring of 285, the Faithful—peasants from Arcanan and the Vale of Arcanlodge, devoted to the West Church—pre-emptively invaded the Prairieland Province with the intention of marching on Farcross, bringing Gutenberg's Judgement to their doorstep. Naturally, the East Church had no inclination that the West was going to attack, much less that they had been provoked. High Elder Fal'spa'ghort of the East Church of Gutenberg rallied his own Devout at once, and there was a bloody, gruesome clash in Farcross between peasants on one side of the faith and the other.

Meanwhile, Alexander III and his crew aboard the *Horizon Sun* had landed upon an isle north of the Whale Reef as a brief stop along the way during their voyage to The Doom. This small isle was pleasant, though treeless and bare, and the king called it Arvon, misremembering the leader of Zealodin's first name.

By the year 286, the *Horizon Sun* finally reached the lands south across the Glistening Sea. What the king, his Royal Admiral, and the rest of their crew witnessed that day, they did not record, nor did they speak of it to kin and court upon their return to Arcanan afterwards. It can be presumed that what they had seen in the ruins of Blumenkranz's desolation—the land of their ancestors that they had heard so many tales about in their youths—was so terrible that they wished they had never set foot upon those accursed shores.

King Alexander III returned during the spring of 286, and when he saw what had become of his Glorious Realm during his absence, he was not amused. Hundreds—if not thousands—of peasants had slain one another in the town of Farcross, and the West Church of Gutenberg was in disarray, with neighbour accusing neighbour of being an "eastern heathen." There were many stonings in the streets of the city and many homesteads burnt for one sin or another.

And at the root of this disaster was none other than Lord Marcus Leon, the Lord Commander who sat the Arcane Throne. Alexander III learnt of this plot from Keeper Julius Tals, who admitted to it all once questioned by the king. The king then sought out his old tutor, Archwizard Xenagos, who was dissecting a corpse in the bowels of the College as part of his research. "Archwizard, I know we have had our disagreements in the past, but I am calling upon you now to set the Realm straight. It appears my Lord Commander has gone rogue during my absence and started a war of folly without my leave."

It is said that Xenagos Simon rose from his laboratory and removed his spectacles. "You wish me to aid you in the deposition of Lord Marcus?" This, the king confirmed. "Then I will help you. Long have I awaited that fool's downfall. Finally, dear Alexander, I do see the mettle of a true king within you."

A battle then was fought within the White Keep's own Throne Room. Lord Marcus, who refused to leave the throne despite the king's return, stood to defend it with sword and shield against Alexander III and Xenagos Simon. He could hold his own against the king, who was admittedly not the most capable swordsman, but few could boast to have battled an Archwizard of the House of Simon and live to tell the tale. A rain of spectral, silver arrows descended upon the Lord Commander and pinned him to the Arcane Throne, where he expired.

Having removed the Lord Commander from office—and this mortal coil—the king then called upon the High Elder Tyful'singrir to end the assault upon Farcross, though the damage was done, and many by then had already died. And, to make matters worse, the Faithful had surrounded the Eastern High Elder Fal'spa'ghort and stoned him to death with many small rocks.

King Alexander III was forced to treat personally with Lord Amon Oxer regarding the war Lord Marcus had rekindled, and attempted to resolve matters diplomatically, offering three thousand Crowns from the Royal Treasury, which would have been distributed directly to Oxcommon's coffers had the Lord of Oxer not angrily told the king to "Keep your blood money and your debts! You care not what I want." With this, the Salting of the Wound—as it became known—concluded, though the Crown and Council remained wary of Oxcommon and pondered the nature of Lord Amon's words.

The next two years were largely consumed by the king necessarily setting matters of state back in order following the disastrous, albeit brief, stewardship of Lord Marcus. As another was needed to claim the title of Lord Commander from that lord's cold corpse, Alexander III appointed Sir Gerric Leon, a cousin of the late Lord Marcus, to the role. Sir Gerric was of much better character than Lord Marcus, it is said; he was a noble knight with a valourous heart and a just nature. To do this, the king did pass over Lord Louis' second son, Sir Landron, much to his ire. But Alexander III believed that "the grape did not fall far from the vine," and that Sir Landron could prove to be as disastrous as his brother if he were to take the mantle of Lord Commander next.

And in the year 288, there was another death in the Royal Family. Prince Avery Pike, the third son of Samuel I, perished in the winter when he choked during a Royal Feast in commemoration of the king's wedding to Queen Mahya. It is said that the dishes prepared that day largely consisted of Tungish cuisine, which contained spices much harsher than those consumed in the South, for Alexander III had developed quite a taste for Tungish spices, and was eager to spread his affection for such tastes upon the others at court. But alas, Prince Avery did choke upon the meal, and did perish after many attempts to dislodge the food from his princely throat. A festivity that began with high spirits and laughter ended with sorrow and heavy heads.

Avery Pike was buried in the Royal Cemetery later that week. Quite curiously, Lord Amon Oxer and his entire House arrived to be in attendance at Prince Avery's funeral, though scant few words were spoken by any Oxer to any Pike other than Avery's wife and son. Near the end of the rites, Archwizard Xenagos arose and spake, "No pupil of mine was as bright nor as capable as he was."

And, after a long-winded speech, High Elder Tyful'singrir blessed Prince Avery, stating, "Though a prince in life he was, let Gutenberg elevate him from death to a Saint of Honour."

Prince Avery's son Jared lived on thereafter with a heart full of blame, and swore never to eat any food laden with Tungish spice again.

However, on much happier news for the Royal Family, the king's third son, Prince Jaron Pike, was born unto him in the year 290. A small but infectiously happy babe, the little Jaron was a delight to all at court—especially so, perhaps, because the sour Prince Avery's endless commentary about the king's sons and their appearances had ceased.

At last, in 291, after numerous matters at court had been put to rest, King Alexander III set out once again for another Great Voyage—this one being the seventh. Bringing along Lord Dominic Dunn and a third of the Royal Fleet to accompany him—as the king knew not what dangers might await him—he stepped foot upon the deck of the *Horizon Sun* and breathed in the salty ocean air. Of his planned eight Great Voyages, this one was toward the west, where he meant to discover what lay beyond the Dorsal Sea, which Lord Dominic's ancestor Ethan the Swordfish had bravely navigated when he brought the Hylars, Wayns, and Voyants to the Glorious Realm.

His plan for his eighth and final Great Voyage was a secret known only to him and the crew of the *Horizon Sun*, to be revealed to the Realm once he had returned from his seventh.

Alas, it was not to be.

The First Tungish War: The Justice of Grant I

(291—306 AA)

COMPILED FROM THE CHRONICLING WORKS OF
ARCHWIZARD XENAGOS NOVUS SIMON

With the tragic loss of King Alexander III at sea came a frightful new era for the Glorious Realm. For three years, Lord Gerric Leon sat the Arcane Throne, waiting steadfast for Alexander III, Lord Dominic Dunn, and the great portion of the Royal Fleet that had accompanied them to return, but when the trees began to take on hues of yellow, red, and orange for the third time, Queen Mahya went forth to Lord Gerric and expressed her deepest despair. "Lord Leon, I feel it in my heart—it weighs upon my soul—and I know it in my mind of the truth of my life." (This, she called her husband regularly.) "My dream showed him to me, adrift and alone at sea. My seafaring husband is gone, and never found that Nothing he was searching for."

With a heavy heart—for Lord Gerric had his doubts about the king returning at all—he descended from the throne for the natural order of kings to continue and to comfort the queen in her anguish.

Grant Pike, the son of Alexander III and the Queen Mahya, ascended the Arcane Throne in that autumn of 294 and took his father's place as King of the Glorious Realm. He was bestowed a new Crown of a fine burnished silver inlaid with emeralds—the Crown of Green. The Royal Coronation of 294 was conducted by the Archwizard Xenagos Novus Simon in the White Keep, and was attended by prominent nobles of the Glorious Realm and the Tungish Imperial Family alike—although the Lord of House Oxer, Amon Oxer, as well as his noble family were conspicuously absent. The only member of House Oxer to attend the Coronation was the Royal Accountant, Archibald Oxer, who remained quite tight-lipped regarding the absence of his kin, according to the Court Fool Tickelman.[2] Though many of King Grant's court were certain, or near enough, that the House of Oxer's coldness could be attributed to the effects the Holy Schism and the Salting of the Wound had upon their Province, it didn't quite explain their presence at Prince Avery's funeral.

During his time as king, Grant I garnered a considerable reputation for himself as a harbinger of justice—a wise king who treated all matters with equal precedent and judged them all with careful consideration. He was, above all, deeply rational and unwavering in his commitment to uphold fairness at court.

On one such occasion, King Grant I demonstrated his virtues when two Arcanian noblewomen approached the Arcane Throne in the winter of 295 with a matter of utmost concern. The king listened carefully and attentively when Lady Tabitha Swan accused Lady Nicole Portman of "commandeering [her] most lavish and irreplace-

---

2   This particular Fool, Tickelman, made it his business to personally pester the Royal Accountant during the entirety of the coronation, tourney, and feast, eager to get to the bottom of his House's absence. Tickelman's "aggressive" tactics grew so unruly—in particular, the thing that Tickelman did with the Cherry Tarts—that afterwards, Lord Archibald never voluntarily visited the Throne Room without assurance that the Fool was absent first.

able silverware." The king, naturally, lent an ear to this dispute—and doubly so when Lady Swan added that the silverware was—allegedly—"inherited from the famed Lady Marisha Steward's own personal set!"

When the Ladies had laid out all the facts of the matter before the Arcane Throne, the king furrowed his brow and stroked his Royal Chin in deep contemplation. And then, he spoke. "My Lady of Swan, and my Lady of Portman; wouldst thou be so kind as to send for thy servants to retrieve these silverwares and present them forth for my court to bear witness?" At once, the servants were summoned and sent off to the Nobles' Quarters, where they collected the silverware—forks and knives and spoons and ladles and butter knives and sporks and salad-tongs and dessert-spoons and soup-spoons and steak-knives and pea-pickers and cake-scoopers and potato-mashers and apricot-slicers and corn-handles and many, many more—from the manors Swan and Portman and carried them carefully to the court.

When all devices were laid upon the marble stone floor of the Throne Room, the king sent for the Royal Blacksmith, Humphrey Higgums, to "come at once to the Throne Room," for a "matter of extreme urgency calls for his immediate presence!" The Ladies Swan and Portman were united in their confusion toward Mister Higgums' summoning, but they held their peace. Before the court, in a dazzling display of his Wisdom, King Grant I bid Humphrey Higgums to "scoop up those cake-scoopers" and "pick up those pea-pickers" to "bring them into the royal smelting pot!" For, the king continued, the "only way one may verify the integrity of said silverware is to reduce the metal to its primordial stage. Only then would it be possible to compare its molten form to that of Lady Marisha Steward's own craft."

Before the Royal Blacksmith could but lay a finger on a single pea-picker, Lady Swan burst into tears. She knelt before the throne and confessed, for she had uttered a severe untruth before King and Court. "I admit," becried the Lady of Swan, "that I hath borne false witness and hath spoken a lie to my king's Royal Ear! This silverware presented here toward thee is *not* inherited from Lady Marisha Steward!"

It was said then that Lady Nicole Portman revealed upon her face a smirk of satisfaction, for she had won. With Lady Swan's admittance of guilt, the matter was settled, and—as the bards like to say—"the jig was up." The silverware of no renown was henceforth re-collected, re-sorted, and re-carried back into Lady Swan's possession, and the noblewomen departed from the king's Royal Courts.

This, and many, many other similar cases, went on to demonstrate Grant I's unfailing wisdom and justice at court, and contributed to his eventual earning of the title The Just. In fact, his actions went so far as to imbue the Crown of Green with a specific significance: it was to symbolize a reign defined by a steadfast commitment to all that was Just.

Notwithstanding this truth, and being noticeably half-Tungish himself, King Grant I faced his share of prejudice at court. There were undeniably those present in the White Keep—and the Realm at large—who regarded King Grant with malaise. The king was not a fool, however; he sensed the reason behind these peoples' unease: the presence of the Tungish Imperial Family in the courts. Many Arcanians were ambivalent toward the Tungish folk and their "strange customs," "curious dress," and, most notably, their "foreign religion." King Grant, however, did not wish to stoke these flames of prejudice, but he recognized that the Tung Imperials were now as much a part of the Royal Family in Arcanan as the Pikes were. He, after all, was one-half Tungish Imperial and one-half Pike Royalty. And so, after the Royal Coronation, he invited the Tung Emperor and his wife the Empress to remain in the White Keep as cherished guests, along with their court, family, servants, knights, and any subjects who had travelled from the Tung Empire to Arcanan for the occasion.

During the reign of King Grant I, the Glorious Council was such: the Lord Commander was Lord Gerric of the House of Leon, holder of the title since 286 and sitting Steward of the Realm since 291, until King Alexander III was officially declared dead by Archwizard Xenagos Simon. The Royal Admiral was newly appointed to be Lord Zachary of the House of Dunn, as the previous Admiral—Lord Dominic Dunn—had so tragically been lost aboard the *Horizon Sun* alongside King Alexander III. The Royal Accountant was the afore-mentioned Lord Archibald Oxer; the Royal Defender was replaced by a certain lowborn noble named Gregory Gore, formerly a knight of the City Guard; the Royal Architect remained Lord Taron Rohe; the Keeper of the Keys was still Julius Tals; the new Royal Warden was a man named Kurtz, and the new Executioner was his brother Kraven.

Grant I assembled the Council in early 295 to discuss the matter of ships. One third had followed the king on his seventh and final Great Voyage, and another third besides were in no further shape to be seaworthy, by Lord Zachary's estimates. Therefore, new ships needed to be built—and fast. The king put the Royal Accountant up to the task of raising swift coin, and the matter was dealt with by means of taxation and a supplementary loan from the Stronghold until the rewards of the new taxes would be reaped. Lord Zachary Dunn returned home to Dunnland to meet with his brother Lord Alec— who currently ruled the Isles from Sharktooth Keep—to discuss the matter of shipbuilding. The king sent a thousand builders with Lord Zachary to the Isle of Dunnland, and by the summer of 296, progress on three hundred ships was underway. The King and Council were duly pleased.

However, during these fruitful years of shipbuilding and recon-struction, another matter cropped up in the south that demanded King Grant's attention. The River of the Setting Sun, which winded from the Port all the way north past Oxcommon and into the Lakes of Ophite and Moor'lu, was suffering from a series of blockades. In fact, the matter was brought to the Glorious Council's ear by none other than a courier from the Stronghold, a certain Max Jarr, who had travelled to Arcanan on behalf of his masters at the bank to demand repayment of the loan Lord Archibald Oxer had taken out for the

Crown of Arcanan in the previous year. While the tax laws that Lord Archibald had instated upon the citizens of the Realm were indeed paying dividends, the Crown was not nearly ready to repay their loan at that time, but Max Jarr claimed that his masters demanded it—"and *now*"—or they would risk a denial of future loans for ten years or more from the Stronghold. Naturally, the bank of the Port of the Setting Sun had been a valuable resource for the Crown of Arcanan since the time of King Alexander I, and so King Grant and the Council were very much in agreement that they must meet their demands.

However, Keeper of the Keys Julius Tals then informed the king of the reason behind the Stronghold's woes: Oxcommon. For the Lord of House Oxer, Amon Oxer, had instated the blockades upon the River of the Setting Sun—both the fork leading north to Lake Ophite and the fork leading west to Stone Haven—and had placed great tariffs on any goods travelling to and from Feldin, Stone Haven, or the Port of the Setting Sun that were not of the Prairieland Province. Such a boldly provocative move from Oxcommon was received with scorn and frustration from the Council, and many accusations were hurled at the Royal Accountant, Archibald Oxer, who swiftly denied his involvement in any such schemes. "Why would I conspire to place pressure upon the Stronghold? Was it not I who took out this loan for the Crown? Why, I am deeply ashamed of my cousin Amon, for he has made matters dire for all of us!"

King Grant asked his Council what should be done. Lord Gerric Leon suggested that they summon Lord Amon Oxer to Arcanan so he might personally explain these blockades and tariffs upon the river. Others on the council—namely Lord Archibald—resisted this notion, suggesting that Lord Amon would sense a threat and refuse to make the journey.

Grant instead turned to the Keeper of the Keys. "Lord Tals, send a letter to Oxcommon bearing my Royal Seal, and ask Lord Amon about his reasoning in the most polite of terms. I wish not to provoke him, only to understand. Perhaps this can be settled in terms of policy, and things need not escalate any further, and then Max Jarr and his masters of the Stronghold will need not demand our repayments at this time, and we can continue with business as planned."

And so, it was done. In the summer of 296, Lord Julius Tals sent a courier to Oxcommon bearing the king's message, and the Glorious Council—as well as Max Jarr, who insisted to remain at the White Keep as a pampered guest "until all matters are squarely resolved!"—waited on Lord Amon's response. Suffice to say, it was not a pleasant one.

In his lengthy and impassioned response, Lord Amon of the House of Oxer, Lord of Oxcommon and the Prairieland Province, made his intentions quite clear. He angrily decried the presence of "Tungishfolk" in the Glorious Realm and demanded that King Grant send the Tung Emperor and his House, as well as all Tungish servants, knights, and subjects currently lodged in the White Keep, the Nobles' Quarters of Arcanan, and the City at large, "back to their native desert at once and forevermore." For Lord Amon and the rest of House Oxer—on whose behalf Lord Amon spoke—believed that the Tungish presence and influence in the Glorious Realm would lead to Jacob Pike's kingdom turning into a colony of the Tung Empire and a theocracy within which all peoples would be forced to follow the Religion of the Wahid Eazimun and Tungish Law. All of this he wrote, and as a closing statement, added, "Oxcommon will not stand for this blatant war upon our storied culture!"

Upon reading Lord Amon's letter, the Council deliberated for days on a proper response. Many eyes were turned once again toward the Royal Accountant, who remained adamant that he was not involved in Amon's schemes and that he "disagreed vehemently" with Amon's views. Regardless, the scrutiny of the Council and nobles at court befell him, and the Keeper of the Keys made it a priority to keep tabs on Lord Archibald's comings and goings at all times.

King Grant I refused any suggestion of appeasement toward Lord Amon's demands. "The Tungs are family; they are *my* kin, and they are part of this Glorious Realm's ruling House. This is an immutable fact, and has been since my father took my mother as his queen. Therefore, the Tungs shall remain. It is not us who must change our thinking, but rather, those of House Oxer, who nurse harmful prejudice and fear toward my own family. The Glorious Realm shall remain the Glorious Realm—he need not fear us joining the Empire. Lord Amon must accept my word and end this petty resistance so our kingdom may move on from this foolishness!"

Naturally, Lord Amon was not pleased by this response, and refused to lift any of his blockades and tariffs. As such, King Grant had to look toward other means of raising coin so that the loan could be repaid. Lord Gerric suggested sending the Royal Armies to the south to force the Oxers to end their defiance, but King Grant refused to escalate the conflict to warfare. He instead sent Lord Archibald to Hylete Square to request the aid of Lord Lawrence Hylar, for the province of Hylete was home to many fine gold mines and mints, and it was time for the Crown to seize production until the time at which the loan could be repaid. Lord Lawrence was at first quite angered by the assumption of King Grant that he would be compliant with this "complete and utter takeover of our province's gold," but when the king promised him a third of the newly built Royal Galleys as recompense, the Lord of Hylete backed down.

Naturally, Lord Alec Dunn was quite furious with this proposition, as the last thing he wanted was for the Hylars to get their hands upon Dunnish ships, and so he arrived in Arcanan in the spring of 297 to drop his anchor on the king. King Grant calmly explained to the angered Lord of Dunnland that these ships were not *truly* to belong to the Hylars, as they were still ultimately part of the Royal Fleet, only in service to Hylete Square, for the Royal Fleet would always remain that of the Dunns, and no matter where they were stationed, the Lord of Dunnland need not worry that they were not his property. The Royal Admiral, Zachary Dunn, confirmed the king's words, and was able to quell his brother's fury somewhat. However, before he left, Lord Alec demanded that Lord Lawrence receive the lesser third of the fleet—those that were smaller, weaker, and with more defects in their construction—and of this, the Royal Admiral was able to convince King Grant to accept. Mildly satisfied—mainly due to the slight he was able to direct toward the Hylars, regardless of how subtle—Lord Alec Dunn set out from Arcanan and returned to Sharktooth Keep.

And so it was that by the end of 297, the loan that the Crown had taken from the Stronghold of the Port was finally repaid—just in time for the Royal Fleet for which the loan was originally taken to be completed. Max Jarr returned to the Port of the Setting Sun with the funds loaded onto a fine Tungish galley, and his masters at the Stronghold were satisfied. However, the resistance put up by Lord Amon Oxer of Oxcommon still stubbornly remained, as the Tungish Imperial Family were still present in Arcanan.

And then, to make matters far worse, King Grant chose a wife.

King Grant I Pike had been offered many potential suitors in his time, though none caught his fancy much like the Tungish Princess Salma. Born of a major Tungish household, Salma Biz-Qadri was beautiful beyond ordinary measure, with flowing hair the colour of raven's feathers and eyes that reduced any man who gazed into them to a blubbering fool. In the winter of 298, King Grant I took Princess Salma as his wedded wife and made her his queen. The Tung Emperor returned to Arcanan for the occasion, joining the remainder of his family, who had been living in the White Keep since 294, for a visit. Once again, the nobility of Arcanan, as well as prominent nobles from beyond the city, attended the ceremony and the following feast—save for the House of Oxer.[3]

---

3   Lord Archibald Oxer *did* also attend the wedding, though he kept at least a room's distance from the Fool Tickelman at all times. Cherry Tarts were also not present at the tables for the feast.

When news reached Oxcommon of the king's choice in marriage, there was a great outcry of fury heard within the Oxhead Hall. Lord Amon Oxer was said to have been so irate that he personally had his servants shorn and whipped bloody and imprisoned his wife and children in the Silo for a fortnight. A tense silence had fallen upon Oxcommon, and the Lords of the Prairieland Province did not know what Lord Amon was wont to do next.

But soon, all in the Realm were made aware of Lord Amon's plans for retaliation—for in the summer of 298, a great Host from Oxcommon marched its way north up the River of the Setting Sun into the Lakeland Province with only one destination in sight: Feldin.

The Lord of Feldin, a certain Phineas Felix and nephew to the late Queen Patricia, had known peace for many years; it was not since the Founding Wars that Feldin had been the site of a great battle. Alas, in 298, they were the centre of attention once more; Lord Amon's Host not only raided and pillaged all the fertile lands south of Feldin within the Lakeland Province, burning crops and slaughtering livestock anywhere within sight, but also rounded up peasants and serfs and forced them into the army's ranks as fodder for the front lines.

By summer's end, the Host had surrounded Feldin from the south and west. A siege had begun.

Lord Phineas immediately called for the aid of the Crown, but Grant I was busy enjoying his newly married life and did not want to jump into war. He still maintained—to the chagrin of the majority of the Council, and particularly Lord Commander Gerric—that matters could be resolved diplomatically between Arcanan and Oxcommon, and so he sent the Keeper of the Keys to parley with Lord Amon instead. Suffice to say, Julius Tals was not thrilled with this task, but he carried out his duties nonetheless.

By autumn of 298, a small envoy from Arcanan carrying the Pike standard and fortified by knights of the Royal Armies approached the Lord of Oxcommon's emerald-green tent, which stood well behind the siege lines. While Feldin continued to starve without trade or access to the outside world, Keeper Julius Tals approached Lord Amon Oxer to discuss terms. The Lord of Oxer, however, was not content with diplomacy. In his words: "The time for talk has long passed. The king has gone too far with his unashamed fornication with these Tungishfolk, and Oxcommon calls for war!"

Keeper Julius maintained negotiations regardless of the Lord of Oxcommon's stubbornness. He promised Lord Amon that the king would order that the Tungish nobility would send their subjects and servants back to the Empire, but that was not enough. Lord Amon demanded that *all* Tungish peoples return north to their "desert wastes," and would not settle for less.

Julius Tals sent a message back to Arcanan communicating the terms, and with a heavy heart, King Grant decided that it was necessary to oblige. Over the course of the following month, the Tungish side of the Royal Family left Arcanan for Samiz Bizbee with a legion of the Royal Armies alongside them to journey north to Tal Taro and take a ship from the Pocket, which would take them across the bay to the deserts of the Tung Empire. Even Queen Salma's own family returned with the Host. It is said that she barely spoke with King Grant for the remainder of their matrimony afterwards; despite a warm and friendly start to their relationship, she missed her family, and felt incredibly isolated in the South without their presence.

But King Grant was confident that now that Lord Amon's demands were finally met, the siege of Feldin would end and matters need not escalate to war under his reign.

Alas, it was not to be.

For, in the autumn of 298, when Lord Amon Oxer heard the news from the Keeper of the Keys that the Tungs had been vacated from the White Keep and sent back north, he verified with Lord Julius that *all* Tungishfolk had returned. When the Keeper expressed confusion over this question, the Lord of Oxcommon said it plainly instead. "The bitch wife of his still remains in his bed, does she not? She is Tungish, so why has she stayed while the rest of her kind have gone?"

Keeper Julius, with a resolute sense of failure in his heart, conveyed this message back to his king.[4] When Grant heard of Lord Amon's demand, it is said he wept and gnashed his teeth in anguish, for he did not wish to part with his wife, even if she had grown colder toward him as of late. The king would not let the Lord of Oxer take *her* away from him, too. The time for diplomacy was reaching its end.

King Grant sent a simple reply back with Lord Julius Tals: "It will *not* be done. My Queen remains in the White Keep. Our *friend* of Oxer has overstepped the boundaries of reasonable negotiations."

When Lord Amon received the news, he revealed that he "expected no less" of King Grant. He then ordered his knights of Oxcommon to seize the Keeper of the Keys, and announced that he would be sending a message of his own, directly this time. One by one, he had Keeper Julius' hands and legs tied with sturdy rope to four large oxen, which were then branded on their backsides by hot irons and provoked to charge—each in a different direction. The loyal Keeper of the Keys was therefore quartered on that day, and his screams were heard all across the camps when his limbs were forcefully torn out of their sockets and dragged across the fields of Feldin. Julius Tals perished mercifully soon thereafter from the pain and heavy loss of blood, but Lord Amon was not done with the Keeper of the Keys yet: he ordered his guard to collect the remains of Julius' limbs and had them sent back to King Grant as a "gift" for his wife the queen.

Needless to say, when the gift arrived at the White Keep, King Grant was beside himself with rage. By this point, Lord Commander Gerric was adamant that the king send the Royal Armies east to Feldin to confront the Oxer Host and punish Lord Amon for his crimes, but King Grant still maintained a level head, and replied that he would simply be playing right into the Lord of Oxer's hand—that Lord

---

4   While the general message of Lord Amon's thoughts was conveyed to the king, it goes without saying that a certain few choice words were omitted.

Amon *wanted* war. And so, despite Lord Phineas Felix's ever more frequent requests for aid—reminding the king of their cousinship— the Royal Armies remained behind the walls of Arcanan.

In the autumn of 300, Feldin fell. It is said that when Lord Amon Oxer took the city, he set his most brutal knight, Sir Crugus the Cruel, after Lord Phineas Felix and his family. In a display of gratuitous malice, Sir Crugus killed Lord Phineas' family before his very eyes, then proceeded to drag the Lord of Feldin—naked as the day he was born—through the city behind his horse, finally stringing him up, split open down the middle like a caught lakefish for good measure, upon the walls in place of House Felix's banners.

When King Grant caught wind of these cruel obscenities, and of Feldin's fall at large, he finally conceded to the Council[5] that it was time to act. That day, the Royal Armies were mustered. By the fortnight's end, they were marching on Feldin to wrest it back from Amon Oxer's clutches.

By the spring of 301, the Royal Armies arrived west of Feldin. Lord Amon Oxer had established himself as the Lord of Feldin and Oxcommon, and ruled the trading capital with an iron fist, forbidding any citizens out of their homes past curfew and rounding up dissenters to throw them into the dungeons of Castle Felix. The most egregious rebels against his rule were given over to Sir Crugus the Cruel, and unspeakable acts of violence and sadism were committed unto them.

When the Royal Armies surrounded Feldin, the Lord of Oxer enacted his plan of defence. Catapults cast out the flaming corpses of various livestock into the ranks of the king's armies to shower them with rancid flesh and spread disease. The corpses of dead Felix nobility were also cast from the catapults to terrorize the king's men

---

5   Upon which, it should be noted, that the Royal Accountant was
     absent. Reports claim that Archibald Oxer had fled the city during the
     night when the truth of Feldin's fall was confirmed, but perhaps only
     Tickelman the Fool ever knew for certain.

and shatter morale. Archers loosed arrows tinged with manure to rain hell upon the Royal Armies, killing a noble knight and infecting three times as many with festering bloodrot. The king's armies were in disarray, and the sentiment by late 301 in the camps was overwhelmingly to return home and abandon this dreadful siege.

But King Grant had made up his mind: if Lord Amon Oxer wanted war, "War he shall have."

The siege raged on for five long years.

By the year 306, Feldin appeared insurmountable. The majority of the Royal Armies had deserted or died of either battle, starvation, disease, rot, or flux, and King Grant had few options remaining to him. He could abandon the siege at last and retreat, tail between his legs, to the City of Arcanan and offer Lord Amon a victory, or he could rally his remaining troops and try to storm the walls of Feldin. To his dismay, over these five years, the Oxers had found a way to smuggle in food and resources in and out of Feldin, so the siege had been practically rendered pointless, and only truly harmed the Royal Armies. Add to that the vast numbers of dead on the king's side, and the Host perpetrating the siege of Feldin had been reduced to a mere annoyance rather than a proper cause for concern. Feldin was hardly starving nor suffering in the slightest despite King Grant's efforts. Capture of the city seemed years away, if not impossible altogether. In time, the king would be left with no further forces. It was time for drastic action, or to give it all up and fold.

King Grant chose action.

Within his Royal Tent, the king summoned his Council, as well as his two brothers, Prince Jacob and Prince Jaron, noble knights both. Jacob was now twenty-two years and Jaron had reached sixteen years a week earlier. In the summer of 306, Grant I revealed to them his final plan: to smuggle in a small army through the walls of Feldin via the supply lines that came in from the Lake of Moor'lu. They would hide amongst the cargo and pass through the gated portcullis of Feldin's east, and once inside, raise the drawbridges to the west and south, letting in the remainder of the Royal Armies to flood the city and capture it. It was their only hope, and their last chance of success.

After a fortnight spent ironing out the final details of the plan, it was finally time to set it into motion. Lord Commander Gerric Leon led a force to the lake and captured a nearby trading vessel, stowing away inside it and posing as traders headed into Feldin. The king and his two brothers did the same, each with their own small band of soldiers.

The Lord Commander's vessel passed through without a trace, but it was the second group that alerted the guards. Prince Jaron was still wearing a royal heirloom around his neck—an amulet gifted to him by his great-grandmother, Queen Elise—and it was noticed by one of Lord Amon's knights, sabotaging the entire operation. The prince was brought before Lord Amon—but not before Gerric Leon was able to raise the southern drawbridge. The Royal Armies flooded into the city via the southern gates, and battle raged inside Feldin at last.

During the chaos, Prince Jaron broke free from his captors and took Lord Amon's firstborn son, Andrus, hostage. Lord Amos sent out Sir Crugus after the prince, with strict orders to bring back Andrus alive and slay any who tried to hold him.

Prince Jaron tore through the alleys of Feldin with the boy Andrus at knifepoint until he was cornered by Sir Crugus and his band of brutish knights: The Dreadful Dozen. When they surrounded Prince Jaron, it was revealed that Andrus was not with him; he had been swapped out for a commoner with a similar likeness. The *real* Andrus Oxer had been passed over to Lord Commander Gerric.

Following his Lord's orders, however, Sir Crugus and the Dreadful Dozen gutted Prince Jaron in that alleyway and spilled his bowels upon the muddy ground. And so it was that King Grant's youngest brother perished upon that Dreadful Day. He would not be the last.

When Lord Amon Oxer learnt that Sir Crugus had been following the wrong captor, he ordered the knight to lead a sortie outside Feldin's walls to find Andrus and reclaim him. And so the

Dreadful Dozen made their way toward the lakeshore as fresh corpses littered the streets of Feldin.

Sir Crugus' sortie met Lord Gerric upon the west bank of Lake Moor'lu, where King Grant, Prince Jacob, and the remainder of the Royal Army were stationed in preparation for a final stand against Lord Amon's forces.

Sir Crugus the Cruel and his soldiers clashed with the king's, and the Battle of the Lakeshore had officially begun. The song of swords rang out into the air as the battle raged on for the rest of the day and into the night.

One by one, whilst the battle raged on, King Grant, Prince Jacob, and the Lord Commander bested many knights of the Dreadful Dozen, and their bloodied corpses lay upon the sands, cleft in twain among hundreds of fallen.

At last, when the crescent moon illuminated their swords, the battle gave way to allow the king to challenge Sir Crugus himself. Their duel was truly glorious to behold. However, while King Grant fought valiantly and with honour, his opponent did not. The brutish knight exploited the king's every weakness, until he was worn down and kneeling, covered in his own Royal Blood.

Upon learning that his most precious knight was doing battle with the king himself, Lord Amon Oxer rode out toward the lakeshore to watch the events unfold. Seeing that King Grant was near defeat, he called out to him among the din of swords. "My king! It appears that we have reached an impasse! My knight has beaten you. Seeing you in this sorry state, I will extend a hand and offer you a way out. Give me back my son, and I will order my knight to spare you, so you may retreat behind your *brave* soldiers and live another day. What say you?"

King Grant replied with vitriol in his voice. "Amon, I am through with your insolence. You know nothing but violence and cruelty, and I have no reason to believe that words will accomplish anything further. I shall accept my fate, as you will yours."

Lord Amon Oxer gave the order. Sir Crugus swung his sword.

And so King Grant I Pike, known as Grant the Just, perished on the west shore of Lake Moor'lu in the three hundred and sixth year After-the-Arrival during the height of the long and bloody Battle of the Lakeshore.

But the king had anticipated his own death, and planned accordingly. With firm, steady resolve, Prince Jacob took the Crown of Green from his brother's severed head, splashed it in the waters of the Lake Moor'lu, and placed it upon his own head. Moments later, the Archwizard Xenagos galloped toward him, shouting the Rites of Coronation from horseback.

And so it was that, during the midst of the Battle of the Lakeshore, and mere minutes following Grant I's death, Prince Jacob Pike became King Jacob II and took charge of the Royal Armies alongside Lord Gerric Leon.

And without a moment wasted, King Jacob rallied the remaining knights of the Crown and charged Lord Amon. Lord Gerric Leon confronted Sir Crugus and engaged him in deadly battle while knights clad in the silver, gold, and purple of House Pike pushed back with all their strength against the Oxer Host. Weakened by his duel with the former king, Sir Crugus the Cruel was no match for the Lord Commander. When Lord Gerric swung his silver sword and crushed his helm, Crugus fell backward and impaled himself upon the spear of a fallen comrade. And so it was that Sir Crugus the Cruel joined the mounting piles of the dead upon the sandy shores of Lake Moor'lu.

Realizing his ranks were breaking, Lord Amon attempted to rally his men, but perhaps they could sense the panic in his voice, for the Oxer Host scattered and fled. Those who remained were crushed by the emboldened Royal Knights, inspired by King Jacob II.

Finally, King Jacob reached the Lord of Oxcommon himself and drew his sword. While Lord Amon was undoubtedly a cunning commander and a shrewd tactician, he was worth little as a soldier on the battlefield. The king made short work of him, and upon Amon Oxer's decapitation, the Battle of the Lakeshore was won at last.

The Prairieland Host was routed southward, and Feldin was reclaimed for the Crown. As Lord Phineas and his family had perished, the rulership of Feldin passed to Phineas' cousin Francis, who never in his lifetime had expected to become Lord of Feldin. While he was naturally grateful, Francis Felix could not help but feel a sense of ennui, considering the circumstances by which he'd received the title.

King Jacob II then ordered his men to collect the bodies of his brothers, King Grant and Prince Jaron, to be returned to Arcanan and buried in the Royal Cemetery beside the White Keep. With his return to the capital, he was greeted by a grand reception of peasants and nobility alike, though with the news of King Grant's noble sacrifice and the death of Prince Jaron, the mood in Arcanan shifted to one of deep lamentation.

When the time was right, and the pain of grief for their king had lessened in the hearts of the Realm, King Jacob II was given a second, more official Royal Coronation in the White Keep. Once again, Xenagos Simon was present to perform the rites, and the Crown of Green was formally bestowed upon the new king. King Jacob II vowed to uphold his elder brother's legacy and rule like Grant did, with an unwavering commitment to justice and a prioritization of diplomacy over war.

Jacob II's ascendancy to the Arcane Throne brought forth a time of unsteady peace for the Glorious Realm—but all who study their history know that during such times, the seeds of war are sown.

Plots and Paranoia: The Reign of Jacob II

(306—336 AA)

COMPILED FROM THE CHRONICLING WORKS OF
ARCHWIZARDS XENAGOS NOVUS SIMON AND
LUCAMIRUS TRINIUS SIMON

Following the ascendancy of King Jacob II Pike during the Battle of the Lakeshore, the Glorious Realm settled into an era of uneasy peacetime. After the new king's Second Coronation, this time in the White Keep before a grand audience of commonfolk and nobles alike, he summoned forth the Glorious Council to survey the state of the Realm, but alas, there were two absences upon the Council that were in need of immediate addressing.

The first was the Keeper of the Keys. As Keeper Julius Tals had been unfortunately quartered by Lord Amon Oxer during the siege of Feldin, he was no longer fit to serve upon the Council. However, as Lord Julius was undoubtedly a capable servant to the Crown, Jacob turned to his firstborn son, Kiaron Tals. Kiaron was a quiet, mild-mannered youth of seventeen who was well-liked in Tal Taro, especially among the maidens of his age.[6]

Secondly, ever since the disappearance of Archibald Oxer, the Realm was in dire search for a new Royal Accountant. Due to there only being one Master Key to the Royal Treasury, the Crown was also scouring the Realm for the "Taker of the Keys"—a new title for Lord Archibald coined by the ever-clever fool, Tickelman.

In time, the former Royal Accountant was indeed found and captured by Lord Gregory Gore's men. He was discovered in a seedy brothel in the bowels of the Port of the Setting Sun, clad in naught but the Master Key around his neck. Suffice to say, the ladies of the brothel were henceforth shooed away by Gore's men. The Taker of the Keys was seized and dragged through the Port's muddy streets for all to witness with revilement.

Archibald Oxer was afterwards returned to Arcanan and thrown to the dungeons to languish under Warden Kurtz's knives. During his torment, he revealed that he had stolen one tenth[7] of the wealth of the Royal Treasury, and had squandered nearly all of it indulging in his "base desires."

Needless to say, a copy of the Master Key was pressed and poured so that such an event would never again transpire, for there were never *two* Royal Accountants at one time, after all.

When the matter of the Treasury was at last resolved in early 307, Jacob II had found himself a suitable replacement for Royal Accountant. Naturally, since the House of Oxer had so recently

---

6   Although, if the court gossip of Tal Taro can be believed, few of these girls could claim to be *maidens* furthermore after becoming acquainted with the adventurous young Kiaron—for few could resist his charms.

7   While he had made this claim verbally in torment, further investigations of the Crown's ledgers suggest it to be closer to one *ninth* of the Crown's wealth. Regardless of the true number, the riotous spending of Archibald was one not to be surpassed.

rebelled against Arcanan and instigated the First Tungish War, the precedent of selecting an Oxer for appointment was discontinued. One must also remember that the deaths of both of the king's brothers—direct results of Lord Amon Oxer's war—still weighed heavily on his mind. And so it was that during his long and storied reign, King Jacob II never forgave the Oxers, and kept them a great distance away from any claim to power in Arcanan. Instead, Clarence Hylar, the second son of the aging Lord Lawrence of Hylete was appointed by the king.

The bookish and astute Clarence Hylar was overjoyed when he received the king's letter inviting him to serve upon the Glorious Council. He was thirty-five years old, unmarried, and balding. Being dreadfully averse to swordplay and afeared of horses, he had struggled to find a place for himself in Hylete Square. All his life, he endured mockery and scorn toward his perceived "lack of manhood"—but he did not mind, for his passions lay in numbers, writing, and poetry, much unlike his father and brothers. When Clarence Hylar did depart from his home to answer his new calling, it is said that nobody in Hylete Square cared. Even the servants of High Hall never noticed his departure. Some claim that during dinner no less than a fortnight past Clarence's departure, the eldest of Lord Lawrence's sons noted that he had "not seen that wimpy brother of [his] for some time now." And that was the last time Clarence crossed his brother's mind.

Once the new Royal Accountant had arrived in Arcanan, the Glorious Council was whole once again, and the reign of King Jacob II began in earnest. His first act as king was to impose heavy sanctions upon the Prairieland Province. It was no secret that the king held the Oxers in great contempt and meant to put this distaste into law. During one contentious council meeting, the king declared that he wished for the Prairieland Province to face high tariffs on all trade flowing through the River of the Setting Sun, north past Oxcommon, and into Lake Ophite. This policy prioritized profits for Feldin, where, in the king's mind, the people had been victims of Amon's war and deserved reparations—to be paid out in full by the House of Oxer.

The king's furious demands were quelled somewhat by Lord Commander Gerric Leon, who had served since the dawn of King Grant's reign. Lord Gerric raised concerns with the king's approach and warned that "such a steep punishment will not be taken in stride by the Lord of Oxcommon. Should we not push for peace, rather than fan the flames of future conflict?"

Similarly, Archwizard Xenagos Simon also spoke up in protest. "My liege, do consider that the new Lord of Oxcommon is *not* his father! Lord Andrus is but a boy! After what he experienced during the Battle, it is *highly* improbable he would act in any sort of aggression toward the Crown. Lay aside your reservations and give this new lord a chance."

It was indeed true that during the Battle of the Lakeshore, when Gerric Leon was smuggling Andrus out toward the shores of Lake Moor'lu, the boy was nicked by a stray blade, leaving a regrettable scar upon his noble face. Many claim that the Lord Commander never forgave himself for the incident, for the plot was meant only to draw forth the wrath of Lord Amon, not to bring any actual harm to his son—an innocent boy.

The words of both the Lord Commander and the Archwizard did indeed sway King Jacob's position somewhat. He relented, lessening the tariffs to one-third of their original weight, and amended his law to affect only the trade of Prairieland beef, chicken, and pork. Nonetheless, the king's sanctions did have a crippling effect upon the finances of Oxcommon.

With the sanctions put in place, all positions filled on the council, and the key to the Royal Treasury restored, the time of uneasy peace truly began. The following decades went on like a simmering pot until, all at once, the pot bubbled over, and the frothing would not stop.

One night in 307, King Jacob II awoke in a raging fit. His guards, entering with haste, feared that an enemy had made their way into the king's solar, but it was merely a night terror that had awakened him. A guard with sword in hand—a mistake, as he was soon to learn—

stepped toward the king's bed to investigate the perceived threat. His inquiry was cut short by a swing of Jacob II's bedside sword. The guard died at the break of the rising sun after healers tried all they could to remedy his grisly wounds.[8]

The king refused to leave his chambers for a week, not arising until he had mustered the strength to swallow away his guilt for the accidental killing of his guard and for surviving the Battle of the Lakeshore when his brothers did not. When the king at last emerged, he went straight to the Royal Architect, Lord Taron Rohe, and commanded him to design and construct a grand memorial of stone—a tribute to the king's fallen brethren Grant and Jaron. And so, by the end of 307, construction of the monument began at the foot of Jacob's Hill using stones from the Marble Quarry. While viewing the construction progress, the king remarked, "My brothers are dead, but they will yet live on for generations in stone."

But this did ultimately little to relieve his guilt. His terrors continued on through the nights—though he no longer kept a sword by his bedside in fear of himself.

When the first snows began to fall upon Arcanan that year, so too did Xenagos Simon. The old Archwizard had served the Realm long, having lived to one hundred and thirteen years. His funeral was attended by both Collegiate and Court alike. The Ninth Archwizard was buried in the Royal Cemetery alongside his predecessors, and his eighty-two-year-old son Lucamirus Trinius was named as the Tenth.

In the spring of 308, King Jacob II made a joyous announcement to all the Realm: he was to be married. His queen-to-be was none other than Farah Rhakhamal, a Tungish noble from Biz Shalom. The young maiden of nineteen years impressed the Court and common folk alike when she first addressed the crowds. For the first time, the

---

8   It was noted by the Lord Commander that the dead guard resembled the leader of the notorious Dreadful Dozen, Sir Crugus the Cruel, perhaps explaining the king's strike against him in the dark.

Realm witnessed a Tungish noble speak the common tongue with great ease—shocking even the king, to boot—as though she had spent all her years living in Arcanan. This helped ease the worries of many Nobles and few commonfolk. "This Tung is a master of tongues!" the bards were heard to say.

A Royal Tourney dedicated to Queen Farah—it was called Farah's Tourney, no less—was held during the wedding. Many noble and brave knights found their way to compete in the events, including Sir Jharol Voyant, Sir Luke Hylar, Sir Greyson 'Grey Wolf' Leon, Sir Bobby Felix, and a mystery knight.

Then, while the jousting was in its third round, another contender rode in through the gates unannounced. They were clad in coal black armour bearing a foreign sigil on their chest and shoulders. It was a reddish-gold circlet that appeared to be bleeding. A hefty greatsword sat in a similarly hefty sheath upon the rider's back. Their steed was dark, with a white streak across its face, and it wore black barding and a caparison bearing the same sigil as its rider's armour. The onlookers cheered the newcomer and stood craning their necks, eager to see what feats of valour this new challenger might offer to the festivities. The announcer, noting the sigil, heralded them as the Eclipse Knight.

As fate would have it, the final round of the tourney was between the mystery knight and the Eclipse Knight. It was a spectacle to be sure, but the victor was clear—for when the two clashed together, during the third pass, the mystery knight was knocked off their horse, along with their helm, revealing them to be a woman! Who this woman was, no one could say, but all had witnessed her best some of the king's greatest knights, including the Lord Commander's own son the Grey Wolf—an embarrassment, to be sure.

Her name is known to us now as Madalyn Sweetgrass. In a moment of desperation, she knelt before the king, and requested to join the ranks of his personal knights. Tired and angered, King Jacob II sat next to his bride, lost for words. Lucamirus leaned on his staff and said to Madalyn, "In all my years and many before me, never has a woman held the title of knighthood. While your skill has been noted, we must observe this one truth and honour it: women are to be ladies, maidens, or mothers—not knights, warriors, or wizards. Abandon this folly!"

Madalyn then rode out from the tourney grounds in a fury, leaving the winner of the joust.[9]

King Jacob II rose from his seat and called down to the mystery knight, "Who art thou? And whom do you serve?"

The knight, helm still on, declared, "My name is of no concern to you." He bowed, mounted his dark horse, and promptly left with no reward in hand, for he got what he wanted.

That night, the king lay in bed without a blink of sleep, for he had recognized the Eclipse Knight's voice. It was surely the voice of a knight of the Dreadful Dozen. The knight was not seen again for over two decades—save for in the king's night terrors.

As for the remainder of the Royal Wedding, Keeper Kiaron Tals had sent invitations across the Realm—with the exception of Oxcommon.

However, a week before the wedding, an uninvited guest marched down the King's Road to the White Keep. It was Lord Andrus Oxer and his caravan. When Jacob II learnt of their arrival—and on his front doorstep, no less—he sent the Lord Commander to "shoo them back to their bloody lakes!" or he would send his army "to remove them by force."

Lord Andrus was reported to have spat at Gerric Leon's feet and vehemently remarked, "I'm glad *his majesty* sits comfortably upon that throne. May he remember by what means he has claimed it."

House Oxer bitterly left Arcanan and returned home. The news of how the king spurned the Oxers spread throughout the Realm, and the king was dubbed "the Bitter" thereafter by some.

---

9   It is said that thereafter, she joined the personal guard of the king's cousin Jared, though this may have been a rumour.

Also in attendance at the wedding was Lord Lucifer Voyant, who had brought with him his fair daughter, Elsa. Many admirers claimed it was easy to get lost within her eyes, and that appears to be what happened to the king's cousin Jared.

Archwizard Lucamirus Simon bound Jacob II and Farah together in marriage, and the feast to follow was grand, to say the least. While many claimed during his age that King Jacob II lacked courage, authority, and resilience, none could say he lacked opulence. The Royal Wedding was attended by thousands of Arcanians, as well as the Noble Families of Hylete Square, Feldin, Stathmore, Dunnland, Stone Haven, and Tal Taro, as well as Samiz Bizbee and Biz Shalom of the Tung Empire. The presence of hundreds of Tungish nobility did not go unnoticed by their detractors, and many refused to attend as a result. The ceremonies were not without a few vulgar acts of defiance that were swiftly resolved by the Royal Defender, Gregory Gore. More than one guest in attendance was gelded and thrown in the dungeons of the White Keep that evening, but it did little to dampen the sense of jubilee.

What happened next is a matter of great speculation among those who write the histories, but one such thing is certain: their wedding night was the only verifiable time in which King Jacob II ever took his lawfully wedded wife to bed, for she had realized not even hours into their marriage that the king was in no shape to consummate. His mind was plagued day and night by visions of his brothers' demise. Though it is the duty of all loyal husbands—even kings—to please their wives, Queen Farah of the distinguished Household of Rhakhamal was *not* pleased. Perhaps noble life in Biz Shalom had heightened her expectations, or perhaps, to entertain the more scandalous rumours, some say that she had prior experience from her homeland, and that a renowned bard called Tariq Tevarro had taken her maidenhood in her youth. Perhaps, however, the answer merely lay in the fact with the king's recurring night terrors, and he was simply not as engaged as one ought to be during their Royal Consummation.

Regardless of the true reason, history tells us that afterward, while King Jacob and Queen Farah were married by all legal standing, they were not bound to one another, for the Queen had set her eyes upon another, one who *could* please her—one who had been the fancy of many a Noble Lady in his time: Kiaron Tals. As the bards would sing years later, "the Keeper had used his Keys to enter Queen Farah's heart."

From then on, unbeknownst to anybody—much less King Jacob—the queen shared a bed with the Keeper of the Keys for many years in secret.

A year of jubilee and festivities had finally come to an end, and the following year proved to be one of great rejoicing as well, as the Royal Family grew by a considerable margin. By the spring of 309, Queen Farah was large with child, and by the year's end, King Jacob II was granted a newborn son and heir in Prince Oliver Pike.

And, as if in direct competition, the king's shrewd cousin Jared and his wife Elsa Voyant looked upon the Queen and her "black-haired, sun-kissed Tungish boy" and vowed to have "two pure Pike children for each Tungish mongrel the king's paramour expels from her vile bodice." And so it was that, in the winter of the year 310, Lady Elsa gave birth to twin sons, Jacob—not to honour the king, but rather to evoke the glory of the first Jacob, who had founded the Glorious Realm and the Royal House of Pike that Jared so cherished—and Alexander, after the Old King, not the Explorer who had "forever damned and besmirched the House of Pike with his profaned fornication."

As far as the household of Jared Pike and his wife Elsa were concerned, it was in *direct* response to their twin sons' birth that Queen Farah grew large with child once again. In 311, she birthed a daughter, and her daughter was called Sarah—pronounced like that of her mother's name. Jared and Elsa fumed, and got to work at once in order to "bear more beautiful, pure Pike boys." However tragically, their next two children both perished too early to even be given names.

The first died in the womb, and the second was born, but did not live to see the rising sun. The second was reportedly misshapen and deformed, and some say the babe's fate was wrought by the couple's impatient, jealous hearts. In the words of Archwizard Lucamirus, "Perhaps it was a mercy that the young babe died so young, rather than live as Jared and Elsa's third son."

It was not until the year 314 that Lady Elsa bore another son, who did indeed live to adulthood. He was named Murth, after the third king of the Glorious Realm. The naming was met with murmurs, as many still recalled horror stories of Murth the Menace's Age of Fear. And so it was that Jared and Elsa needed only one more son to fulfill their promise, but fate was not so kind to them. Elsa had become barren following her frequent childbirths and miscarriages. In light of this, Jared and his wife instead vowed to raise their three sons to be "fit for the Arcane Throne" and to "live up to their namesakes."

In regards to princes Jacob and Alexander, this vow was of no concern. But as for the third son, Prince Murth, many brows were furled. As a result, he was watched quite closely at Court, namely by the Lord Commander, to ensure that he did not exhibit tendencies similar to those of Murth the Menace. Gerric Leon was well aware of his own ancestor Geralt's fate during that king's reign. Perhaps it was just superstition, but Lord Gerric was wary that history would repeat itself.

And in the year 315, a new Royal Admiral was in need of choosing. Having served faithfully for twenty-one years, Lord Zachary Dunn at last passed away after many successful raids within the Mouth. Under Lord Zachary's tenure, the Pirates of Paradise Isle had grown craven in avoidance of his wrath, for he was a formidable captain in his prime, and even up to his final days. Wherever his flags flew, pirates quivered and quaked.

Upon his father's death, the new Lord of Dunnland Iain Dunn sailed swiftly for Arcanan with a fleet of five-hundred new Dunnish galleys in tow. As a gift for King Jacob II, he presented the head of the Pirate Dreadlord Two-Eyed Bartibus, a notorious outlaw who had terrorized the Serrated Coast for years, even evading Lord Zachary. The king was duly impressed, and the mantle of Royal Admiral was thereby passed on to Lord Iain.

Two years of mostly uneventful peace transpired in the Glorious Realm. However, beyond the borders of the Realm, in the northern Gornak Ranges, the Three Hundred and Fifty-Third War between the Grey Dwarves and the Mountain Dwarves had commenced. And while the dwarves battled, a new Elven King—Helios Aphelion— was crowned in Celesor. This marked the first time a new Elven King had been chosen in over seven hundred years.

In the year 317, the daughter of the late King Grant, Kamira Pike, came of age. This was brought to the attention of Jacob II by the Lord Commander, who wished for one of his sons to take her hand in marriage. Being a leal servant to King Jacob and his brother Grant I before him, Lord Gerric was granted this boon, and Kamira Pike was wed to Gerric's youngest son Gerard Leon that selfsame year.

Now, Gerard Leon was a proud and ambitious young man, quite unlike his two elder brothers Gerrold and Greyson, the first being both a captain of the Royal Armies and a charming diplomat, and the second being among of the Realm's finest living knights. But all Gerard lacked, he made up for in arrogance and presumption. Yet, alas, Gerrold was already married to a lovely daughter of Lord Francis Felix called Felicia, and the Grey Wolf had taken a daughter of Lord Tiberius Tybolt's to wife. And, even if they were free to wed, both brothers were far older than the eighteen-year-old Kamira Pike, while Gerard was twenty-two—a much more suitable age.

This courting of the Princess Kamira and the Lord Commander's son was indeed ill-fated, but at the time, seemed a wonderfully obvious idea, as it bound the Great House of Leon with the Crown while still keeping them a safe distance away from the throne, as the line of Kamira had little chance of becoming king. Many nobles were conscious of House Leon's prominence at Court, and knew that playing second fiddle to many a king over the decades was ripe fruit for ambition. The Archwizard Lucamirus went so far as to say, "This Lord Commander *truly* reigns over us, for no decision of the king makes it into written law without Lord Gerric's express approval."

When Jacob II heard these words, he threatened to remove the Archwizard's tongue—until he was brought down from his anger by none other than the Lord Commander. Needless to say, the Archwizard's words held true, and all at Court knew it.

Alas, the seeds had been sown, and the Archwizard's warnings— however slightly misplaced—eventually rang true. Two years after the wedding of Princess Kamira and Gerard Leon, a treasonous plot emerged from the dark corridors of the White Keep. Gerard Leon, through deception and lies, had convinced a small portion of the king's men to join his cause, for Gerard saw himself as the next King of the Glorious Realm, and meant to act.

During what later became known as the Night of the Faint Star, men of the king's very own household guard crept into his solar, this time truly with murderous intent. The king would have been slain that night if it weren't for his wife's secret lover, who had spies stationed around the King's Tower on nights when the queen snuck off to be with him. One of these spies had witnessed Gerard and his men sneaking about, their swords drawn, and quickly reported this fact to the Keeper of the Keys and, by extension, the queen.

Lord Kiaron acted immediately. Within moments, the Lord Commander was apprised of the situation and rushed to the aid of his king.

Having been disturbed from his sleep by the sounds of footsteps outside his door, King Jacob II lay still underneath his bed, hiding from the assailants. Bereft of a weapon at his bedside, he would have surely died had Lord Gerric Leon not stormed in just then with a dozen loyal knights—the Grey Wolf among them. Together, they slew Gerard's traitorous men where they stood.

When Lord Gerric and his son grew aware of the instigator's identity, they were utterly distraught. Nonetheless, Gerard was taken into custody, and his new home became the White Keep's dungeons. While Warden Kurtz locked him up deep below, the courts above decided his fate.

Naturally, the king was furious—not to mention still shaken from the attempt on his life—and demanded that Gerard Leon be put to death. He even suggested that his niece Kamira was suspect, as Gerard "may have planted his seeds of treason in *her* mind as well."

It took the entire Glorious Council to talk him down from his fury and convince him not to execute one of own blood, but as for Gerard Leon's fate, not much could be done. It was as clear as the Lake of Ophite that the Lord Commander's son had tried to murder the king and take the throne for himself—though why such a mad notion had taken hold of him, none could say.

When the Warden pried the truth from Gerard, he laughed and declared—with hysteria in his eyes—that "the Age of the Pikes has reached its end," and that "sooner or later, the Star will rise above the Arcane Throne." When these words reached the Royal Ear, not even the words of Lord Commander Gerric could sway him, for the king was convinced that even his Lord Commander was a part of the conspiracy—that he too envied the throne of Arcanan and wanted to claim it for himself. He went so far as to threaten Lord Gerric with the dungeons, and considered replacing him with Kiaron Tals, for he "at least has honour and dignity, unlike your ilk!"

But before the Royal Armies could turn on their Lord Commander and seize him, Lord Gerric spoke. "My liege, I dearly regret what my youngest son has done. He is a fool and a traitor. I denounce him, and swear both on the honour of my House and by the Hand of Gutenberg the Wise that I had no part in his scheme. I have always served you loyally and honestly, as I served your brother. My son must be put to death for his crimes; that I understand. I fear no other fate awaits him now. But let his act of treason die with him, and not put a stain upon the Star of Leon."

The king pondered the Lord Commander's words for a long moment, nodding as he thought. "Let it be done, then. If you took no part in these deeds, as you say, then I say *you* must swing the sword, Lord Commander. Now begone, and let me drink."

The room emptied in silence.

On the following evening, the solemn deed took place. Clad in a black cloak of mourning, his armour bearing a black star rather than the usual silver of his House, Lord Commander Gerric Leon swung the executioner's sword. When it was finished, he simply retired to Pendlebury Manor, and said no more.

From then on, the Lord Commander became known as Gerric the Black Star. "A black star burns cold," so the bards would sing.

Such treasons never bode well for the families of those involved. In a tragic, unexpected turn of events, it so happened that Princess Kamira was large with Gerard's child at the time. Her husband's betrayal and following execution—carried out by his own father, no less—so greatly affected her that the child was lost in the womb. He was to be called Alexander, after his grandfather the Explorer, but never lived to bear the name.

After Gerard Leon, Princess Kamira never married again nor bore more children, and rarely left her chambers. The hall by where the princess lived became known as the Weeping Corridor, as her sobs could be heard echoing through the walls for many years thereafter—mysteriously, even following her death in 339. And thus, the Line of Grant the Just came to an end.

And, in the year 322, the infidelity of the queen finally came to light. One summer night, while Kiaron Tals was abed with Queen Farah in the Keeper's Tower, the old Fool Tickelman heard noises coming from within while he was out on a midnight stroll. Naturally curious, the Fool listened in, and he heard the unmistakable voice of the queen from behind Lord Tals' door. Tickelman immediately reported this information to the Lord Commander, who he believed would know best.

Lord Gerric was troubled—as any would be in this situation—and troubled more so because he did not want to spark the king's ire once again. Regardless, he paid a visit to the king, who had already been awakened by a night terror. This time, the king claimed, he'd dreamt of a dark assassin bearing the mark of a silver star creeping into his bedchamber to slit his throat. Upon the Lord Commander's knock, the king grabbed a poker from his fireplace and held it outward in defence. When Lord Gerric opened the door, the king realized his folly and dropped it. "Lord Commander, why have you bothered me at this hour? I was sleeping," he lied.

Lord Gerric lowered his head and spoke gravely. "My liege, it is a matter pertaining to the queen. She has been found abed with another man."

The king's eyes grew red with rage. "Who is this defiler? I shall have his manhood torn off and fed to the dogs!"

The Lord Commander sighed. "It is Lord Kiaron Tals, my liege. The Keeper of the Keys. Tickelman overheard the queen in his tower during so late an hour."

The king stood up and strode toward the door. Before Lord Gerric could say anything further, King Jacob began to make his way to the Keeper's Tower. The Black Star did not stop him.

However, Lord Kiaron was well aware that he and the queen had been overheard; one of his spies had reported as such. By the time the king and his guards slammed their fists upon the door to his chambers, the Keeper was long gone. The queen, however, had been left behind and forced to hide—though she did not remain hidden for long. One of the king's men pulled her from the closet where she hid amongst Kiaron's robes and brought her before her husband.

"What is the meaning of this?" the king roared. "My Lord Commander says that you did lie with another man! Speak, woman, or I will give you over to Warden Kurtz, so help me Gutenberg!"

The queen stared daggers at the king and did not say a word. King Jacob then ordered Lord Gerric to strike her, an order the Lord Commander refused. One of the king's other men obliged instead. Finally, the queen spoke. "I would rather rot in the dungeons than spend another night abed with you, Your Grace. At least there, the rats would seek my company and my flesh."

The king motioned to send her there, but Lord Gerric intervened. "My liege, your wife is not to blame; rather, the Keeper of the Keys is the one you ought to punish—though it appears he has fled!"

The king then came to his senses. "Alright, alright," he said. "Search the grounds and castle for Kiaron Tals, the bloody bastard who stole my wife! I want him brought before me so I can look upon his face when I order his manhood to be ripped out from between his legs!"

That night, a great search party was held across the White Keep, the Queen's Gardens, and the Nobles' Quarters. Keeper Kiaron Tals was not to be found. Some scholars at the College mused that he had perhaps discovered the hidden passageways Murth I had built beneath the Keep. Others believed that Kiaron had hidden himself among the king's own guard, then smuggled himself out of the city. Either way, the result was the same: Lord Kiaron Tals, Keeper of the Keys since the year 307 and lover to the king's wife for nearly fifteen years, had evaded justice.

Lord Kiaron was not discovered until the year 335, when he was found in a tavern at the Port of the Setting Sun, a homeless drunkard afflicted by numerous infections from years of dockside whoring.[10]

---

10   Some say that this was a lie meant to bring closure to the king after over a decade of searching for Lord Kiaron. Other reports—carefully kept from the king—made mention of a seedy brothel in the Port of the Setting Sun named "The Queenstealer," run by none other than a crime lord calling himself "The Keymaster," but any connection between this crime lord and the missing Keeper of the Keys was never verified.

When King Jacob II learnt of this, he elected to leave the Keeper in his current state, as "death would be a kindness the bastard does not deserve."

As the position of Keeper of the Keys was now empty, a certain Owen Oakwillow—a lowborn squire—found himself elevated to the position the morning after Kiaron fled.

During the early 320s, all children of the Royal Family became old enough to attend Court. This led to many an incident as the Line of Alexander and the Line of Avery attempted in vain to coexist.

Let us focus upon the year 323, at which time Prince Oliver and Princess Sarah were fourteen and twelve years old, while Jacob, Alexander, and Murth were thirteen, thirteen, and nine. The twins Jacob and Alexander were notably cruel to their Royal Cousins during their youths. They would mock the young Prince Oliver and call him "slow," "craven," and "girlish." They pushed him down the stairs of the Keep, slipped manure into his stew, and poured ants into his bedsheets. As for Princess Sarah, they would mock her name, drag her by the hair down the White Keep's halls, and lock her in the corridor with Kasper Rohe's ghost until she screamed and bawled for them to let her out.

But, more insidiously, the young Jacob and Alexander would be overheard referring to the prince and princess as the "Keeper's bastards." That is, of course, when they weren't already referring to them as "Tungish Mutts."

More than once, the twins were taken aside by Lord Gerric Leon at the king's behest and scolded for these words. "Where did you learn such foul language?" the Lord Commander would ask.

The twins would simply smirk smugly and shrug. "It's what they are," they would reply. "We are just stating the truth."

King Jacob II, however, was not fooled—he knew that it was truly the twins' parents behind these conflicts, and wanted to put an end to it. One day that summer, the king summoned his cousin Jared before the Arcane Throne, demanding that he ensure his children behave. "Namely, those twins. They have done naught but torment my children! And that awful thing they imply about my wife the queen—I will not stand for it! One more such word out of their filthy mouths, and I will send Gregory Gore to teach them some manners, mark my words!"

To this, Jared Pike merely feigned ignorance. "My liege, they are just *children*. I cannot control what rumours they hear and spread. Why give their words any credence at all? Unless... there is some truth within them that troubles you?"

At this, the king was furious, and demanded that Jared leave his presence at once. "You may be my blood, Jared, but I do not like what your serpent's tongue implies! Do not think I wouldn't have it torn out for such insolence! Now leave me, and teach your children to behave!"

With that, Jared Pike departed from the Throne Room, but the quarrels continued. The tormenting of Prince Oliver only got more grievous through the years; the worst being in 327, when Alexander snuck a venomous snake from the Tungish dunes of Albariya into the prince's nightgown, claiming that "Oliver's Tungish blood renders him immune to snake bites."

However, once Princess Sarah began to grow into womanhood, Jacob's torment of her slowed to a complete halt. Anyone at Court could begin to see that he had taken a different sort of interest in his cousin, and his cruel words and harsh japes gave way to flowery praise and soft manners when he was in her presence.

One constant throughout this era was the young Murth, third son of Jared and Elsa Pike. Murth never once engaged in such crude behaviour toward his cousins, instead spending much time within the Queen's Gardens or the sanctuary of the West Church. During his rare appearances at Court, he remained mild-mannered, quiet, and courteous. "Very unlike his brothers, and most unlike his namesake," many would say of the young Murth through the years.

As the decade neared its end, and the children came of age, the first arrangement to be made was to find a suitable partner for

Prince Oliver. Following in the footsteps of his father Alexander III and his brother Grant I, the king summoned forth the Great and Noble Houses of the Tung Empire to Arcanan so that the Kingdom of the Glorious Realm and the Empire might further strengthen their bonds. A lavish Royal Ball was held in 328, with members from all Houses of the Realm in attendance—except, once again, the House of Oxer.

The ceremonies were followed by a Royal Tourney in honour of the engagement. This time, no Eclipse Knight made an appearance, as the king had banned any knight from entering the tourney unless he was from a major House and his identity could be verified. Perhaps inspired by the prowess of Madalyn Sweetgrass, many women, even Lord Gerric Leon's own granddaughter Hestia, attempted to enlist in the tourney, but were curtly denied. This sparked a considerable protest among ladies of the Royal Court, to the great surprise of King Jacob. In the Queen's Gardens, a second Tourney was held without the king's authorization, where exclusively women jousted and battled each other bloody. This event became known as The Tournament of the Dresses, or, less commonly, The Queen's Tourney, as Queen Farah herself was said to have been in attendance.

When both Tourneys were all said and done, however, the bride-to-be of Prince Oliver was revealed to be a stunning, dark-haired Tungish Princess named Zahira, the current Emperor's own daughter. They were married five days later in the Throne Room by Archwizard Lucamirus Simon, and their wedding was attended by thousands. This time, Lord Andrus Oxer did not even attempt the journey to Arcanan.

Naturally, as if in response, one of Jared's sons was married weeks later. Alexander had found himself smitten by the daughter of Lord Norton Whit, a comely girl with red hair named Clara. And later that year, she gave him a son. As was by then an established tradition of the Line of Avery, their son was named Jacob after the first Glorious King, but tragically, the young boy perished after a mere three days on this earth. Once again, the words of Lucamirus Simon echoed: that Jared and Elsa's pride and haste had now followed them down a generation. But the Archwizard was careful not to speak such a thing out loud, as Jared and Elsa's presence at Court made many cautious— even Archwizards.

Still, the newly wed Alexander and Clara continued to try for a child, desperate to conceive before Prince Oliver and Princess Zahira. In the last month of 329, they succeeded—this time bearing a son who lived past infancy and much, much longer—and who was *also* named Oliver Pike. Now, it has been long debated as to *why* they named him after their cousin. The most common explanation was merely spite. It was well known that Alexander, son of Jared, loathed his cousin Oliver—he and his twin's many cruelties at Court had more than proved that fact—and so it went without saying that the naming of their son was not meant to honour him, but rather, to provoke. Many believed that Alexander meant for his son Oliver to *replace* the prince, and, even more heinously, to replace him with a *pure-blooded Pike*. The implication was obvious: that the Line of Alexander was no longer of true blood, unlike the Line of Avery.

In the summer of 331, Prince Oliver and Princess Zahira bore a child of their own. He was named Ashar, after a Tungish Emperor of Old, and was a dark-haired, sun-kissed boy with soft, round eyes and a lovely smile. Much unlike the birth of Alexander and Clara's son Oliver, the Glorious Realm celebrated the young Ashar's birth from Westerton to Wolfdale. Still, the event had its detractors, as a movement inspired by Lord Amon Oxer's war was taking form across various cities, towns, and villages of the Realm—but more on that to come later.

And now, we turn our tale to matters of the Faith. As was well known, the Faithful had a conclave of followers who all swore vows of celibacy and service to the West Church in Arcanan. They lived out their days in the plains of the Arcane Province, travelling from village to village and town to town preaching the Good Word of Gutenberg the Wise. For many of the serfs, peasants, and farmers of the Province, Gutenberg was a beacon of hope and stability upon which they could rely, just as their crops relied on fertile soil and the rains above.

Those who would take such vows and join the conclave abandoned their former names and took on new, Holier names according to their Virtue and Purpose. Historically, those who joined the Faith in such a manner were usually of lower birth or lesser prominence, with no great responsibility in this mortal world.

Naturally, it was a great surprise for not only the Royal Family, but the Realm at large, when Murth, son of Jared Pike and nephew to King Jacob II, declared that he was forsaking all titles and claims and joining the West Church as a monk.

When Jared and Elsa learnt of Murth's declaration to the Faith, they immediately moved to recall it. They called forth his brothers Jacob and Alexander, along with twenty of their personal household guard, to bar Murth's room in the White Keep and hold him there under watch until the High Elder could be bargained with, for they held that Murth Pike, son of Jared Pike, was a "Pure Pike" and his blood was not to be "put to waste."

Lady Elsa personally visited the West Church of Gutenberg to discuss the matter with the High Elder, a man of sixty-four simply named Shaikaro'halo'gartoil. He was unmoved by her words, coin, or *other* means of persuasion—he was, after all, a sworn celibate, and beyond such carnal impulses. "His name is now Dorj'heptkii, not Murth. He has sworn his body, mind, soul and all else to Gutenberg, and does not want for anything else in this fragile world."

Elsa Pike was forced to return to the White Keep a failure, and, to make matters worse, during his imprisonment within his castle chambers, Murth had devised a plan to escape. Later, he would say that Gutenberg Himself revealed this plan unto him in a vision. When at last his brothers removed the bars from his door and strode inside, they saw naught but an open window and a string of bedsheets hanging beyond the windowsill. "Murth the Monk," as he came to be known, had escaped more than just the White Keep that day. The next time he was seen, it was in the West Church among the Faithful.

The troubles of Jared and Elsa Pike did not end with Murth's departure to the Faith in 331, for under their very noses, a new, more serious conflict had begun to take shape. Their eldest son Jacob had a fancy for the king's daughter Sarah, and their courtship—though many would call it fornication—became known to her brother Oliver in the following year. While they had been bitter enemies in their youth, Jacob and Sarah found that later in life, as they both grew into adulthood, they were inseparable, despite being cousins. A love affair bloomed betwixt the two of them, and they met secretly across the chambers of the White Keep in the same way Queen Farah and Kiaron Tals had during the years of their affair.

The princess' courtship with Jacob Pike was discovered in 332 by none other than the reclusive Royal Accountant, Clarence Hylar. He was taking inventory in the Royal Archives when he heard "a peculiar noise [he] had not heard before" in the place where the bookshelves were most secluded. His curiosity got the better of him, so he proceeded to navigate the dusty corridors and investigate. What he saw elicited a great gasp of disbelief—and some may say confusion—alerting the young lovers that they were being watched. They attempted to cover their tracks, but as the bards went on to sing, "They were caught in the act, and that was a fact."

The young Sarah and Jacob fled separately to return to their respective chambers. Later that evening, they were each visited by a different member of the Glorious Council: Princess Sarah by the Black Star and Jacob by the Royal Defender, Gregory Gore. The two of them were curtly questioned. While Princess Sarah had held her tongue against the Black Star's gentle questioning, at the first mention by Gregory Gore of Warden Kurtz and his knives, Jacob panicked and "the tea was spilt." Finally, Clarence Hylar's descriptions began to make sense. Jacob Pike was thereby seized and brought directly to the king.

King Jacob II heard the testimonies of Gregory Gore, Gerric Leon, and Clarence Hylar. In an act of desperation, Jacob declared his undying love for the princess before King and Court, revealing to all that they were "deeply in love," and had been since their youths.

At this, the princess simply stared back with cold eyes. Then she spoke. "Father, what my cousin speaks is naught but lies. For years, he has pursued me, and recently, his obsessions have become more aggressive. It is not love that he holds for me, but lust, for he merely wished to know me carnally. What the Royal Accountant saw was my cousin having taken me against my will, for he wanted me, but could not have me—so he forced me instead. Father, please! I ask for you to forgive me, for I did not take part in this willingly. My cousin is a vile, loathsome animal, and deserves to be punished for his crimes."

Upon hearing these words, Jacob fell silent as Kasper Rohe's ghost. Etched upon his face were utter disbelief, betrayal, and despair.

But the king had heard enough. Blustering and furious beyond measure, he demanded that the Black Star bring a deep bottle of Dunnish wine for him to drink. And then he demanded that Jacob Pike be thrown in the dungeons to rot for his "affront to Gutenberg, the Realm, and all that is Holy."

Jacob's twin Alexander, his father Jared, and his mother Elsa all stood up in protest, demanding that the king reconsider, as Jacob was a Pike and member of the Royal Family, after all. Alexander's wife Clara went so far as to fall on her knees before the Arcane Throne and weep for her brother-in-law, begging for him to be freed and instead to punish Sarah, the "Tungish harlot," for her defamatory lies. This, naturally, only fanned the flames of Jacob II's fury, and he called forth Gregory Gore to drag his nephew to the dungeons. He meant for the young Jacob to live out the rest of his days in solitude, never to bear children nor to hold any titles—but to *live*, as he was still blood.

Alas, it was not to be, for at that moment, the king's own son Oliver strode forth and drew his blade. "Father, forgive me for what I must do," he said.

Before the Lord Commander, the Royal Defender, or anyone else could stop him, he struck the chains that bound Jacob Pike's hands, freeing him. Bewildered, Jacob began to stammer his thanks to the cousin with whom he had quarreled with for years, but Oliver did not let him finish. He handed his cousin a sword and demanded that they duel for his sister's Honour before King and Court.

The Black Star stepped forth toward the Arcane Throne and raised his voice in protest, calling for the king to end this madness before it properly started, but the king ignored him. Instead, he got comfortable upon his throne and drank from his goblet.

Jacob Pike, son of Jared Pike and grandson of Avery Pike, was a skilled swordsman who had been trained by the finest men-at-arms in all of Arcanan, but to say the cousins were evenly matched would be a lie. As a Royal Prince, Oliver had trained day and night with the Black Star himself, honing his skills with a sword and preparing himself for years, such that few could rival his abilities. And so, before the Royal Court, their fathers and mothers and rest of their kin, the cousins dueled to the death. By the duel's end, the Royal Carpet gifted to Alexander III by his Imperial Queen Mahya was stained with Jacob Pike's blood.

Jacob Pike's death incited a great schism between the Lines of Alexander and Avery. Jared, Elsa, their son Alexander, his wife Clara, and their young son Oliver promptly vacated the White Keep a week after the funeral of Jacob. They all made their leave from Arcanan, travelling westward to make their permanent home in the Manor of Pike betwixt the lakes Agor and Balor. And, much to Lucamirus' surprise, his younger brother Pylithos Octavius left with them as well.

These dark times would bring the year 332 to a close.

Jared Pike's now-eldest living son, Alexander, gained a daughter, whom he named Sarah, in that summer of 333. When word reached the king's Royal Ear, he had the messenger beaten bloody before drowning his wrath in steep drink. Prince Oliver vowed to his wife

Zahira that when he took the throne, he would disinherit the entire line of Avery Pike from the Royal Succession.

And in that selfsame year, the Royal Accountant Clarence Hylar took a terrible tumble down the Tower of Trust. When his decaying body was discovered by one of Gregory Gore's guardsmen many days later, some rumoured that he had been pushed into such a fate—but by whom or to what end, none could truly say. Despite the fact that all of Avery's Line were now absent from Arcanan, many still suspected that Jared and Elsa Pike had been somehow involved. The title of Royal Accountant was passed on to Clarence's nephew Horace, as, naturally, he had no issue of his own.

It would be prudent henceforth to make mention of the Dune Road, as it became known during this age. The Dune Road was a highway constructed under the Council of King Jacob II in the 320s and 330s to facilitate efficient trade between the Tung Empire and the Glorious Realm. This was done deliberately to circumvent—and in many instances, replace—trade with Oxcommon, another example of Jacob II's spiteful attempts to cripple House Oxer. The Dune Road stretched from Biz Shalom along the southern coast to Holm Tagor, then southward along the Vokmar Pines west of the Takkar Hills. Its final stretch passed through the Arcane Province, stopping in Arcanlodge before connecting with the King's Road in the south.

During the years that the Dune Road was in heavy use—transporting spices, textiles, exotic fruits, gemstones, and gold through the Glorious Realm - three new settlements cropped up along its path. One such settlement was Bronzebourne, founded just south of Holm Tagor at the edge of the Pines. The second settlement cropped up along the road on the western edge of the Takkar Hills, and was called Biz Dabh, or Golden City in Tungish. The third settlement was Silverstone, and was founded a day's journey north of Arcanlodge.

The Dune Road was a very successful venture for the merchants of Arcanlodge and Arcanan, being a direct trade route to the Tung Empire, despite occasional raids in the Gornak Ranges. But soon, many Tung-Junud were tasked by the Emperor to protect the merchants from harm as they passed through the Demesne of the Dwarves.

Over the years, the Dune Road became safer and safer, and its profits were unparalleled by the other trade routes of the Realm. It even rivaled the Fish Road, the route from Feldin to Arcanlodge to Arcanan that was established during the reign of King Tomas I. Naturally, Lord Andrus Oxer was wroth, as his Province's incomes diminished by a factor that had never been seen before, but there were other detractors as well: the Felixes of Feldin decried the competition and longed for the days when Feldin was the Realm's Trade Capital—a title held by Arcanlodge in the 330s. Those who were in opposition to the presence of all things Tungish in the Realm—and their numbers were growing by the thousands each year—also had much to loathe about the Dune Road, as it encouraged the influx of not only Tungish goods and culture, but also the Tungs themselves.

As the years went by, scores of brigands and thieves began to wreak havoc along the southern Dune Road. However, none of these would hold a candle to the actions of a certain grassroots movement. The Sunspots, as they quickly became known, were a Realm-spanning anonymous collective who had but a simple goal to unite their cause: the eradication and removal of all "Tungishfolk" from the Glorious Realm in an effort to return to the days prior to the controversial marriage of King Alexander III.

In the very hot summer of 336, the Royal Architect Taron Rohe was surveying the Dune Road near Silverstone when a band of Sunspots descended on him. His absence was reported to Arcanan by a lone merchant—who, it turns out, was sent by the captors to deliver this message to King Jacob II. The message went as follows: "Unless King Jacob II excises Biz Dabh—the town that ought not to be—removes all Tungish signage and language across the Realm, and removes Prince Oliver Pike from the line of succession, the Royal Architect will be sent back to Arcanan—one piece at a time."

Naturally, the king did not accept any of these demands, much less entertain them. The king instead sent the Black Star to march on Silverstone with a retinue of forty knights to find Lord Taron and bring about his safe return to Arcanan. A fortnight later, Lord Gerric arrived in Silverstone, where he and his men were met with silence from the townspeople.

Following the Sunspots' trail, the Black Star tracked them to the next town, Biz Dabh. It was in flames, with pillars of smoke rising up into the sweltering sun. Lord Gerric and his men rushed in amid the blaze and were accosted by dozens of masked bandits with black suns emblazoned upon their chests. Many of the Black Star's men perished in those burning streets, but the Lord Commander himself emerged unscathed save for the singing of his cloak. At last, he came face to face with the instigator of the plot: a knight clad in coal-black armour with the symbol of a bleeding eclipse upon his shield and breastplate. It was the Eclipse Knight from 308, the Black Star had no doubt.

Lord Gerric and the Eclipse Knight dueled under the fading sun, all while the town of Biz Dabh burnt to ashes around them. The Black Star had seemingly met his match with this nameless knight of unknown origin, and sustained a terrible wound to his thigh when the Eclipse Knight exploited a gap in his platinum armour. He found himself bested, but before the Eclipse Knight could land a killing blow upon him, the house wherein their duel had found them collapsed in a blaze of embers, forming a wall of debris and flame betwixt the two knights.

The Black Star took the chance to retreat, navigating his way through the scorched ruins of the town in search of sanctuary. By chance, he found none other than Lord Taron, left to die in an abandoned hut. Cradling the horribly burnt Royal Architect in his arms, Lord Gerric carried him, leaving the town to smoulder. The Golden City was never rebuilt.

After many trials and tribulations, the Black Star eventually found his way back home to Arcanan. He carefully avoided the Dune Road, as he suspected more Sunspots would be patrolling it in search of him. Lord Taron held onto life, despite his grievous wounds, and when they reached the White Keep, the Court rejoiced that he was alive. Both Lord Gerric and Lord Taron had been thought to be dead for many weeks. In fact, during his absence, the Black Star's own son, Sir Gerrold, had already been named the new Lord Commander, much to the Black Star's surprise. The king sighed and congratulated him on his long service. "You have served faithfully and loyally for many, *many* years, good friend. But alas, as the time comes for all good men, now, that time comes for you as well. Time to hang up your sword, lay down your cloak and armour, and go on to live out the rest of your days wherever you please, whether in a beautiful villa by the Lake of Moor'lu, a mansion in the Port of the Setting Sun, or simply here in Pendlebury Manor."

At this, Lord Gerric was enraged. "My king, I can still serve you as Lord Commander! I am not to sit idly by whilst the Realm lies in peril! My son may serve after me, yes, but not while I still draw breath. My king—I beseech you, please, for the sake of mine honour, do not toss me aside!"

The king heard his words and looked upon him with a forlorn grimace. "Ah, but I am afraid the deed has already been done. Your son, *Lord* Gerrold Leon, has been named Lord Commander a fortnight past, and has already spoken his vows. You are injured, tired, and aged. We both know that your days of valour are long past. It is clear as the rising sun that what you require now is a good long rest. Leave us."

With that, the Black Star threw down his sword at the foot of the Royal Dais and tore his cloak from his shoulders. Without a word, he stormed out from the White Keep, his stride confident and firm.

The Royal Schism and the Rise of the Sunspots

(336—343 AA)

COMPILED FROM THE CHRONICLING WORKS OF
ARCHWIZARD JAREMIUS ONUS SIMON

It was from this point on that the pot could no longer hold back and its contents overflowed, for the unsteady peace that had held since 307 finally reached its end.

While many who study this history point to the following events as the instigator for these years of turmoil, others remain adamant that it was the dismissal of the Black Star that was truly the cause for all this unraveling. For, without Lord Gerric Leon at his side offering him counsel, the king's rulings grew more unruly, and neither the new Lord Commander, Gerrold Leon, nor the rest of the Glorious Council could temper him as Lord Gerric could.

In the winter of the year 336, the Royal Admiral Iain Dunn set sail across the Mouth with the crippled, burnt, and aged Royal Architect Taron Rohe aboard, first to deliver him back to his Noble Family in Stone Haven, and second, to return with a suitable replacement for the title. However, the years since Lord Zachary's death had emboldened the pirates of Paradise Isle. When Lord Iain sailed near, they took the opportunity to strike in vengeance for all his father had wrought.

The naval battle was tragically short. While Lord Iain had brought along a small fleet as a retinue, the pirates were ruthless in their approach. They first crashed their bows into the Royal Fleet, then boarded with cutlasses and axes in hand. They sliced dozens of throats, feeding the corpses of the slain into the sea. The Mouth took on a scarlet hue by the time all was said and done.

The total might of the pirates' fleet then converged on Lord Iain's flagship. Upon boarding the ship, the pirates' leader, Ruger Ratblood, stormed across the deck to find Lord Iain in his cabin protected by a smattering of loyal crewmates. Ratblood cut each of them down in turn and dragged Lord Iain out by his hair. Before a crowd of blood-thirsty onlookers, Ratblood made clear his namesake and ordered one of his men to bring forth a barrelful of mangy deck rats. One by one, he skewered the rats with his sword and opened their bellies over the Royal Admiral's mouth, forcing him to drink. This was Ruger Ratblood's unique form of execution, for all knew that rat's blood carried many diseases and curses.

While Lord Iain sputtered and coughed, he was roughly tied to the centre mast with thick ropes. When Ratblood returned to his own vessel, he ordered his fleet to "Send [Lord Iain] to the depths!" Many flaming bottles were launched from the twenty-plus ships that surrounded Lord Iain's, and the admiral gagged and wheezed as his blood became toxic, all while he watched his galley sink and burn around him.

Unfortunately, Lord Taron Rohe was still abed within the flagship, as he could neither stand nor walk due to his burns. He drowned with the ship.

When word of this savage raid reached the king, he was enraged. Immediately, he ordered for Paradise Isle to be assailed by the entire Royal Fleet—but Archwizard Lucamirus reminded him that they were currently without a Royal Admiral to lead them. Frustrated, Jacob II promptly sent word to Sharktooth Keep and summoned forth the current Lord of Dunnland, Brendan Dunn. And so it was that during the final days of 336, the proud, dark-haired son to the late Lord Iain, thirty years of age, arrived in the Port of Arcanan ready to receive the title of Royal Admiral. The king granted him the reins rather hastily before sending him off with five hundred ships to attack Paradise Isle and deliver the King's Justice unto Ruger Ratblood.

And whilst the Royal Fleet sailed to war, the Sunspots struck again. This time, they set their sights upon the Bridge of Unity, the only bridge joining the Arcane and Hylete provinces to one-another. It was a structure that had stood strong since the reign of Old King Alexander. The Sunspots, led once again by the Eclipse Knight, captured the Bridge in a matter of days by seizure of the town of Alexander. A blockade was established, and trade between Hylete and Arcanan was brought to a standstill.

King Jacob II summoned the council to discuss the matter. The Archwizard urged him to send the Royal Armies at once to recapture the Bridge for the Crown. "Your reign is a far cry from that of your brother's, my liege, if I may be so blunt. The Great Lords see it; the court sees it; even the commonfolk see it. If you let these common brigands hold the most renowned bridge in the Realm hostage any longer, what little respect remains for your rule will surely dwindle, until it is naught but dust in the wind! And, by Gutenberg, you have scant remaining as it is!"

For this statement, and perhaps for a litany of other such comments uttered by the old Archwizard in his time, the king ordered for Lucamirus to be "ushered to his tower" by Lord Gregory Gore, adding that Gore "need not be delicate."

With the Archwizard now absent, the king announced his true plan for the Royal Armies, for he believed he knew where this plot truly had emerged: Oxcommon. At once, he ordered for Lord Commander Gerrold Leon to take four legions of the Royal Armies east to the Prairieland Province to besiege the city of Oxcommon "so that Lord Andrus is made well aware that we see through his schemes." Without question, Lord Gerrold rose from the Council Chambers and mustered the king's men.

When Archwizard Lucamirus learnt of this, he exchanged harsh words with King Jacob II before the throne. "What foolishness is this? Lord Oxer had no part in this, my liege. You are blinded by your hatred for the Line of Amon! While your legions of knights toil and waste in the Prairieland Province, the Bridge of Unity will remain captive! Is nothing to be done about it?"

To this, the king replied, "I *have* done something about it. The Oxers are the true masterminds behind these Sunspots' actions. Once I take Oxcommon for the Crown and place Prince Oliver in charge of the Prairieland Province, as I should have done a long time ago, these attacks will stop—you'll see. Now, Archwizard, I have had about enough of your insolence. Gregory Gore!"

The Royal Defender marched in behind Lucamirus, broke his staff in twain, and proceeded to beat the old man bloody with his gauntlets. Whilst the Archwizard staggered, his body broken in more places than one, he was seized by the Royal Guard and dragged down to the dungeons.

As Arcanan responded to the seizure of the Bridge by sending its armies in the wrong direction, Hylete rose to rectify the crisis herself. Lord Luke Hylar called on the lords of Linden and Fort Unity to muster their bannermen and ride to retake the Bridge from the Sunspots. And so it was that in the spring of 337, these two forces converged upon the western gates of the Bridge from north and south and met their foes in battle, though the Sunspots were more resilient than was expected, being well-armoured, well-armed, and competently commanded by the Eclipse Knight.

Meanwhile, in Oxcommon, Lord Andrus received word from his scouts that the Royal Army was on the march, heading for his city. The Lord of Oxer was beside himself with frustration. Without a moment's delay, he moved to plead innocence to the Great Lords, claiming that he took no part in the Sunspots' schemes. One envoy bearing this message was sent to the Royal Host marching east. However, it is said that when Lord Gerrold read the words, he tore up the letter and replied to the messenger, "It matters not what Lord Andrus claims. His king has declared him a traitor, and the king's word is Law."

The march on Oxcommon continued uninterrupted, and while the Royal Armies marched, Lord Gerrold set loose multitudes of sellswords, brigands, and brutes upon the Prairieland Province, letting them burn, raid, and pillage to their hearts' content.

The Royal Host reached Oxcommon by the summer of 337, and the siege began. Lord Andrus maintained his innocence and pleaded with the king to leave his province alone, but King Jacob II did not waver, for he meant to place his son, Prince Oliver, in charge of Oxcommon by the year's end.

Meanwhile, the battle at the Bridge of Unity was not proceeding in Lord Luke's favour. The hosts summoned by Fort Unity and Linden were depleted by the summer's end, and the Bridge was still held by the Sunspots. Angered, Lord Luke resolved to march on the Bridge himself, commanding his own Host of Hylete Knights to end this conflict once and for all. He left behind his son, Sir Lenn, in charge of Hylete Square during his absence.

Now, in the Mouth, the newly appointed Royal Admiral, Lord Brendan Dunn, was leading the Royal Fleet against the vast pirate fleet that raided the Serrated Coast. Their leader, Ruger Ratblood, had great ambitions, eclipsing that of past pirate lords, who were content with plunder, riches, and glory. He wanted a castle for himself and his men, and land to rule beyond the treacherous waters of the Mouth and desolate isles off the Serrated Coast. Ratblood looked toward Stone Haven, declaring to all his men that the ancestral home of House Rohe "would be [his] lordly seat."

Brendan Dunn's ships stood in their way, and he was a battle-hardened, fierce commander—unlike his father Iain, and more like his grandfather Zachary, whom all the pirates had known to fear.

Many pirates met the Royal Fleet in battle among the stormy seas, and many found themselves in watery graves. For the first time since the beginning of his reign as pirate lord, Ratblood's men began to lose faith. Lord Brendan's fleet crushed them day after day, and it appeared that all the pirates had conquered over the past many years was now slipping into the sea. The worst came when the Royal Fleet surrounded Paradise Isle and bombarded the defensive forces with fire and harpoon, slaughtering pirates by the dozens.

By the summer's end, Lord Brendan Dunn stepped foot on the Isle and hoisted the Royal Banner of House Pike upon their shores.

The Crown's victory over Ratblood's pirates did not last long, but not for the reason one might expect. On a night of celebrations for their victory over Ratblood's pirates, one of Brendan's men gave a toast. "My Lord, you have proven yourself as a fine—no, the *finest* Royal Admiral the Realm has ever seen! For, after a mere summer's worth of conquest, you have claimed this pirates' isle for yourself! And see yet all your ships that still float! Now, *this* is a castle worthy of a true Captain and Lord such as you, my liege!"

To this, Lord Brendan did not raise his own goblet, but smashed it upon the ground, letting the Dunnish wine it held waste upon the stones. "Do you think that, all my life, I have fought and toiled for a *rock*? A nest of scoundrels and whores? No. For centuries, my House has longed for a different prize—one worthy of our ancestor Ethan Dunn, who was called Swordfish."

At this, his men went silent and listened intently to what their Admiral had to say. "To all you brave warriors and friends, I urge you to look *beyond* your standing and recognize that with me as your captain, we may catch bigger fish than this! I have recently come by the news that the seat of my forebears' greatest foes is unguarded and vulnerable to attack. Now, what say you? Is this rock acceptable for you lot, or do you long for something greater? I know where *I* stand."

Lord Brendan Dunn's speech was received with roars of praise. Undoubtedly, many men of the Royal Fleet loyal to the Crown—not merely to their Admiral—were ambivalent about answering this call to action, but still they followed Lord Brendan into battle. And so, in the gloaming of 337's summer, the Royal Fleet abandoned Paradise Isle and sailed west along the southern shores of the Realm, then changed their course due north for Providence Shore.

Now, Lord Brendan was well-aware that many among his men called Hylete Square and the surrounding Vale their home. He feared their loyalties would not last once the fleet looked upon the walls of Hylete Square. Being a shrewd and cautious man, Lord Brendan sent ships ahead of his fleet with crews of men from Hylete—save for their captains. These ships were instructed by the Royal Admiral to "scout ahead for Providence Shore and report back to me what numbers you see." By Lord Brendan's words, they were specifically chosen for this task because they were the most familiar with the territory.

However, once these vessels set sail beyond the reach of the remaining Royal Fleet, their captains veered course and sailed far to the west, away from the shores of Hylete and into open ocean. And one terrible night, before the crew fully realized what was happening, their throats were slit with knives and their hearts pierced through with rapiers. Hundreds of dead men were thrown overboard. It was said that the sharks ate well that night, so it came to be called the Night of the Sharksfeast.

Meanwhile, the bulk of the Royal Fleet sailed for Providence Shore and took it unawares. The garrison stationed there by Lord Luke and overseen by his son Sir Lenn were greeted one ominous night by the sight of hundreds of ships approaching from the west. When Sir Lenn climbed the battlements of Castle Hylar and surveyed the horizon, he saw not the striped banners of Pike upon their vessels, but the crescent moon of Dunn dancing in the moonlight.

At once, Sir Lenn Hylar called forth the garrison to protect the castle and mustered archers to loose flaming arrows upon any men flooding ashore, but alas, Lord Luke had taken the majority of Hylete Square's fighting forces east to retake the Bridge, and so Sir Lenn was left with mere hundreds of able-bodied soldiers to defend their family seat from thousands.

The castle was stormed under the crescent moon. The stables were set ablaze, the fishing villages along the coast raided and pillaged, and Castle Hylar viciously sacked. The men of the castle, lowborn and noble alike, were mercilessly slaughtered, their wives taken by the soldiers of Lord Brendan's fleet as prizes and their children put to the sword. Their blood stained the Checkered Hall.

Sir Lenn watched in horror as the proud halls of his ancestral home were littered with corpses and desecrated by acts of carnal depravity. He led a sortie of loyal household knights and city folk alike to lead a final stand against Lord Brendan's forces without the walls. They fought valiantly, but were killed to the last man. Sir Lenn himself perished upon those sandy shores, having tripped on the body of a fallen knight and impaled his shoulder on a stray spear. He had been on his way to challenge Lord Brendan Dunn personally, but tragically, he never even laid eyes upon the Royal Traitor. Sir Lenn of House Hylar was gone by the time the sun rose.

That morning, the banners of House Hylar were stripped from the castle walls, and the crescent banners of House Dunn adorned them instead.

And, naturally, the Mouth saw itself infested once more. The hour that Lord Brendan and his Royal Fleet set out toward Hylete Square, Ruger Ratblood saw his chance and sent his pirates to recapture their former territory. Emboldened by this swift turn of events, he then rallied his forces and set sail for Stone Haven.

News of Brendan Dunn's betrayal reached the king days after Hylete Square had been taken. At once, Lord Luke forsook the Bridge of Unity to march back westward and liberate his ancestral home. King Jacob II, however, was largely unperturbed but for the fact that his Royal Fleet was now holed up in the west instead of crushing pirates in the Mouth. "What is this new Admiral thinking? His duty was to attack this Ratblood, not claim Hylete Square for himself! He surely must know that he cannot hold it while Lord Luke Hylar commands a Host thousands strong?"

With the Archwizard languishing in the dungeons, the Royal Architect at the bottom of the sea and his replacement yet to be chosen, the Royal Admiral in Hylete Square, and the Lord Commander leading the siege of Oxcommon, the king had scant few Councillors left to provide him counsel. Since the betrayal of Keeper Kiaron over a decade ago, the role of Keeper of the Keys had been occupied by a lowborn squire named Owen Oakwillow, who largely bent to the king's commands. Regretting his decision to imprison Archwizard Lucamirus earlier that year, and desperate for wise counsel, the king sent forth Gregory Gore to retrieve him from Warden Kurtz's grasp.

When the Royal Defender strode down the steps of the White Keep's dungeons, he found himself in quite the predicament. Warden Kurtz had locked him in, and his mute servants had barred all exits. Gregory Gore, as it was widely known, was a fierce servant to King Jacob—but a courageous man he was not. Upon realizing he had stumbled into a trap, he panicked and tried to flee, forgetting the Archwizard, but the dungeons beneath the White Keep are labyrinthian, impossible to navigate without a guide.

Lord Gregory was ambushed in a large chamber housing naught but a vat of sewage. "Warden! Warden! Where are you!" he cried, but he received no answer.

Warden Kurtz then appeared across from him on the other side of the vat, a sickly smile stretching across his sallow face. Gregory Gore remembered his task. "Warden! The king orders you to release the Archwizard, for he requires his counsel!"

The Warden simply waved a hand, and two of his servants appeared behind the Royal Defender. Before Gregory Gore realized what was happening, he was falling face-first into the vat. Now, if the Royal Defender had not been clad in full plate armour, he may have survived—but alas, he perished that day, and Lucamirus remained in the Warden's grasp.

King Jacob II grew afraid when he learnt that his Royal Defender had become swallowed by the dungeons, and he hesitated to send more men down into the Warden's demesne. However, he was approached by none other than Lucamirus' firstborn son, Jaremius Onus Simon. "My king," said the eighty-eight-year-old wizard, "allow me to venture down into the dank depths beneath the Keep and rescue mine own father from the Warden's clutches."

This, the king bade, and so it was that Jaremius Simon, clad in robes the colour of dark jade and holding a porcelain staff ending in a beautiful glowing emerald, descended the steps.

Warden Kurtz, who had served in the White Keep's dungeons since the reign of Grant the Just, was a man of unnatural age—for one not of House Simon—being in his mid-nineties by the year 337. By some dark arts, he was aware that Jaremius Simon was embarking into his demesne, and so he sent forth his mute servants to bar the wizard's passage by invocation of an ancient ward.

The servants at last spoke—for despite their lack of tongues, they could still evoke strange, guttural sounds from deep within their throats—and from the dank waters of the dungeons, shapes began to take form: slimy, serpentine spirits borne from the sewers that resembled the corpses of drowned men. The wizard Jaremius raised his staff and summoned forth a shield of spiked crystals to defend himself from the onslaught of the Warden's creatures. Skin sloughing off their slimy figures, they battered and bashed upon Jaremius' wards, but they could not break them.

Next, the wizard lowered his shield of crystal and sent forth a blaze of searing sunlight from his staff. Even the slime upon the dungeon's walls was vaporized by Jaremius' spell.

Jaremius strode confidently through the dark corridors until he reached the cell where his father was being held. Carrying the old man with him as he went, Jaremius was nearly out from the dungeons when the Warden himself appeared, barring his way. Kurtz brandished his own staff, a peculiar thing crafted of blackened bone with countless unholy symbols inscribed upon its length. Atop the staff sat a misshapen, shrunken head that Jaremius recognized with horror, for it belonged to the former executioner—the warden's own brother, Kraven.

A deadly duel between two wizards, one of the College and one of the Deep, took place within that dungeon.

The Warden acted first, sending forth a tangle of wet hairs soaked in blood upon the wizard and his father. Jaremius brandished his porcelain staff, swinging it above his head to form a circlet of silver runes in the air. When the bloody hairs passed beyond the borders of the circlet, they dissolved into mist, leaving behind a pleasant smell. Frustrated, the Warden summoned yet more hair, but Jaremius grew only more powerful—and well-fragranced—as a result.

When the Warden finally relented, Jaremius smirked and raised his staff once again. The mists that surrounded him all coalesced into one, and before him stood a great boar made of silver glass and covered in glowing runes. The creature charged at the Warden and gored him in the stomach—or so it seemed. For where the Warden formerly stood was instead a writhing mass of maggots in the shape of a man; the Warden had never been there.

Stricken, Jaremius glanced all around for a glimpse of his foe, but it was not until a drop of sludge hit his shoulder that he looked above him. The Warden, gliding down a shaft of slimy stone, pointed his staff toward Jaremius and sent forth an outpouring of steaming bile upon the wizard and his father. In the nick of time, Jaremius raised his staff and formed a glass bowl above his head, collecting the vile liquid within.

Warden Kurtz attempted to slow his fall, but it was in vain, for his fate had already been sealed. He plunged into that bowl of bubbling, boiling bile, and his skin sloughed off his bones.

Triumphant, Jaremius poured the bowl's contents into the drain and strolled off with his father toward the stairs to safety.

But, alas, the battle was not over.

For once the wizard and his father had reached the steps, they heard a noise behind them. The Warden, his skin blistered and his staff destroyed, hobbled forth. He could not speak, for his lips had been sealed together, and he could not see, for his eyes had melted into wax—yet he could still sense the wizard's presence.

Jaremius turned to face the wretched creature and jabbed forth his staff. A bolt of emerald lightning ricocheted off the walls of the dungeon until it struck its target, but what remained of Kurtz appeared unfazed. The Warden somehow laughed hideously and raised his hands.

Jaremius heard at once the rising roar of tortured squeals. He glanced fearfully around him as thousands of mangy rats poured through every orifice of the dank dungeon walls, swarming toward him and his father with a vengeance. With a flick of his staff, the wizard summoned a powerful gale, flinging the multitudes of voracious vermin back through the corridor and onto the disfigured figure of Warden Kurtz.

Jaremius made his leave while the rats had their feast.

However, it was all for naught, for while Lucamirus had been saved in body, his mind had been lost to torture long before his rescue.

When King Jacob II learnt that the old Archwizard was no longer fit to serve, he declared that Jaremius, effective immediately, would assume the title in his stead. And so it came to pass that, in the year 337, Jaremius Onus Simon was appointed as the Eleventh Archwizard of the Glorious Realm.

As his first action as Archwizard, Jaremius recommended to the king that Lord Brendan of House Dunn have "all titles, lands, and claims stripped from him" and be replaced as Royal Admiral by none other than the king's own son Prince Oliver.

King Jacob was intrigued, but reminded the new Archwizard that "[his] son's destiny [was] to be Lord of Oxcommon—and very soon!" But all at Court knew that the Siege of Oxcommon was as of yet unsuccessful, with four legions of the Royal Army still languishing outside the walls.

The king's mind was changed only when his son Oliver himself knelt before the Arcane Throne and requested that he be made Royal Admiral, as the Archwizard intended, but only until the Oxers were deposed, at which time he would take his "rightful" place in Oxcommon. The king agreed, and so in 337—for the first time—a member of the Royal Family and heir to the Arcane Throne was appointed as a Royal Admiral, thereby stripping Brendan Dunn of the title and officially branding him as a traitor.

Naturally, many new appointments to the Glorious Council were now in order. King Jacob II, Archwizard Jaremius, Admiral-Prince Oliver, Royal Accountant Horace Hylar, and Keeper Owen Oakwillow congregated and discussed their options. Given the crises that wracked the Realm—the capture of Hylete Square, the siege at Oxcommon, the occupation of the Bridge of Unity, and the proliferation of Ruger Ratblood's pirate fleet in the Mouth—these appointments required careful examination so as to maximize the Crown's allegiances during these troubled times.

As the king was still furious with the House of Tals for the actions of the former Keeper of the Keys, Lord Kiaron, the title of Royal Defender was offered to an adjacent line of Tals, known as Beauchamp. The offer was swiftly accepted by the Lord of House Beauchamp, who called himself Dillane of the Dawn, and he began to make the journey southwest from Tal Taro to claim his place upon the council. The title of Royal Architect had already been offered to the eldest grandson of the late Lord Taron and Lady Falisha Rohe of Stone Haven, a promising young architect named Armon. However, in the absence of the Royal Fleet, passage across the Mouth was a treacherous endeavor. The task ahead was clear: Prince Oliver, as acting Royal Admiral, was to command a fleet of ships in the Royal Fleet and crush Ratblood's pirates. The only issue remained that the majority of said fleet was still tied up in Hylete Square, occupying Providence Shore. As a result, the king finally resolved to help Lord Luke Hylar retake his family seat, sending Sir Greyson the Grey Wolf of Leon to Hylete Square along with a legion of the Royal Armies. However, due to the Sunspots' hold upon the Bridge of Unity and the Mouth's occupation by the pirates, the only way to reach Lord Luke Hylar's Host was through the treacherous north. And so it was that in the year 337, the Grey Wolf of Leon took a legion of the Royal Armies north along the eastern bank of the Father's River, eventually to venture west through the Wishbone Wood and then south on the other side of the River. In the wake of this considerable thinning of Arcanan's defences, the king commanded the new Defender, Dillane of the Dawn, to put all his resources into recruitment to bolster the City Guard's numbers.

And next, there was a great development in Oxcommon at last. In the early days of 338, the Caged Ox, Lord Andrus Oxer, finally met his end—but not from any of Lord Gerrold's swords. Whilst on a stroll through the snowy battlements, a blade pierced his back. When morning came, Lord Gerrold's men spied the lord dangling from the walls of Oxcommon, a bleeding eclipse carved in his chest.

In short order, the city was seized from within as agents of the Sunspots, led by none other than the Eclipse Knight—who had been inexplicably last spotted on the Bridge of Unity a mere day earlier—captured Horn Hall and the city walls and stowed the late Caged Ox's family and household guard inside the Silo. There was utter chaos behind the walls of Oxcommon, yet the gates remained shut to the Royal Armies. Any hopes of reconciliation between Lord Gerrold and the Oxers were dashed, as the only representatives of the city were now lowborn peasants and nameless knights.

The Lord Commander sent word to Arcanan of what had transpired, inquiring of the king what was to be done. The king's response, sent by Keeper Owen Oakwillow without the Council's intervention, chastised Lord Gerrold. "Failing to capture Oxcommon whilst it is held by a noble lord is one thing—but failure to take it now, while it is garrisoned by vagrants and rabbles, is beyond pathetic. You will take Oxcommon for me now, or I shall find myself a new Lord Commander. And as for this Eclipse Knight, when you do return, be sure it is not without his head."

Whilst Lord Gerrold took these orders to heart, more tidings of war trickled in from the west. The city of Hylete Square, despite being garrisoned by sailors under Brendan Dunn's command, held strong against Lord Luke's forces, for Hylete Square was a formidable keep, established upon a great hill and surrounded by a treacherously wide moat—and evidently not even its own lord could penetrate its defences. From within his camp behind the siege lines, Lord Luke sent his most trusted servant, a certain Sir Jon Rolfe of Jarlsburg, north through the Vale to Westerton to summon the aid of Lord Vincent Wayn and his bannermen. The journey was arduous and long, but Sir Jon persisted through it all—the brigands along the road to Bald Keep, the bitter cold along the northern pass to Lonely Keep, and the barren wastes in the north that marked Westerton's borders. But when he reached Wayn Manor and presented Lord Vincent with the message, the lord's response was one of hesitation. "Why should I forsake the protection of mine own homeland to venture south with all my men? This was Lord Luke's own folly—leaving his castle with such a meager garrison. Why should my people pay the price for his mistakes?"

To this, Sir Jon replied, "Because it your duty! Do you forget the vows you swore to Hylete Square? When the Lord of Hylete calls, you must answer, no matter the cost."

But Lord Vincent was not stirred. "If Lord Luke has failed to keep even his own seat safe, is he truly worthy of my leal service? Perhaps I should swear my allegiance instead to this *new* Lord of Hylete Square. I hear his name is Dunn."

Growing desperate, but unwilling to return to his lord empty-handed, Sir Jon made a bargain. He offered Lord Vincent a deal: that if the Wayns should send south a mighty force of Sentinels to aid Lord Luke in his siege, then Lord Luke's eldest living son and heir would take the hand of one of Lord Vincent's daughters in marriage. This, and a plethora of other conditions, were ironed out over hours spent in Wayn Manor's halls, and finally, by the spring of 338, a great Host of Lord Wayn's formidable Sentinels marched south in armour of black and gold.

Thus, the great Battle of Liberation began.

When the Sentinels of Westerton joined forces with the Hylar Host at Hylete Square, the armies swarmed through the Horsehead Gate, the Gates of Grannd, and the Gate of Aindrea. Many of Brendan Dunn's loyal men died defending them, and the remaining forces in his service retreated back behind Hector's Moat. The hosts of Luke Hylar and Vincent Wayn coalesced upon the Great Bridge of Hylar, but the portcullis was heavily guarded by giant ballistas, and the gates to the inner walls were shut.

However, the sway that Brendan Dunn held upon his men was dwindling. He was, after all, a traitorous ex-Royal Admiral by now, his name besmirched and his titles and holdings stripped from him by the king. Many had begun following him after his conquest of Paradise Isle, when their prospects appeared fortuitous, but by now, faith was scarce. As it appeared more and more likely that the inner walls would not protect them from such a massive host forever, and as it grew evident that their army was not supplied with ample provisions in case of a siege, many elected it was time to forsake this cause and escape with their lives.

Mutiny erupted. The gates were opened from the inside, and the Hosts of Hylar and Wayn flooded within the inner city. Within hours, the castle was reclaimed for Lord Luke, and those who remained in support of Brendan Dunn were put to the sword. However, any who surrendered, denounced Dunn, and swore fealty to Lord Luke Hylar and King Jacob II were spared. After the Battle of Liberation was all said and done, all prisoners were sent north to join the ranks of Lord Wayn's Sentinels—as per his agreement with Sir Jon Rolfe.

As for Brendan Dunn, once it was clear that the battle was lost, he fled the city on a small vessel with neither banners nor crew and set out into the Dorsal Sea to return to Dunnland. But alas, the Dorsal Sea is a fickle creature, and she showed no kindness to the ex-Royal Admiral and Lord of Dunnland. It is said that a great gale gripped Brendan's vessel, and a mountainous wave flooded him over. Brendan Dunn thereby joined those many sailors he had condemned to death but a year prior in a watery grave of his own making.

By the spring's end of 338, all Dunnish banners had been removed from the walls of Hylete Square, and the familiar horsehead of Hylar was once again flown. But alas, the Grey Wolf of Leon and his legion of the Royal Army never reached the Hylete Province. No one knows what happened to the Black Star's second son, along with all those valiant knights of the Crown, so it must suffice to assume that they lost their way whilst traversing the Wishbone Wood.

Next, the combined Hosts of Hylar and Wayn marched east for the Bridge of Unity. The Sentinels proved an unstoppable force against all that the Sunspots could muster, and combined with an uprising of the masses in the town of Alexander, the garrison that had unlawfully held the Bridge for nearly two years finally fell. Those who were not put to the sword were thrown from the Bridge to drown in the raging rapids of the Father's River. Yet among all the dead and living of the Sunspots' forces, the Eclipse Knight was nowhere to be found.

However, during the absence of the Sentinels from Westerton, a great calamity struck. Not much is known of the creatures that lurk in the vast Wishbone Wood north of the Realm, but all who live in Westerton fear them. The Sentinels serve to protect the people from such terrors, but as they were fighting Lord Luke's war in 338, the town was woefully vulnerable. By the time Lord Vincent returned to his family seat, many of his people had died—or worse—and the town was in ruins. The Lord of Westerton's own daughters were missing. The remainder of Lord Vincent's life upon this earth were spent rebuilding his town—and cursing the name of Hylar.

Meanwhile, the Serrated Coast was ablaze. Since Ruger Ratblood regained control of the Mouth in 337, he had taken his fleet of pirates and scoundrels to raid and pillage along the coasts of the Cornerstone Province. Setting out from Paradise Isle, they first ravaged the village of Coastwatch. All of its men were slaughtered and its women enslaved, save for the scant few women who leapt from the high cliffs to break their bodies on the rocks below.

From there, Ratblood took his reavers north and did likewise to Trusk, Khai, Ronar, and Tirnam. By the summer of 338, the entirety of the Serrated Coast was in Ratblood's grasp. Next, he and five hundred men marched from Khai into the mountains; their aim was to capture the town of Crag—the second most populous settlement in the Cornerstone Province—and make it their new home. Of course, this was only meant to be temporary, as Ruger Ratblood's true sights were still set on Stone Haven, and by now, he was frothing at the mouth.

But it was not so easy. For the Lady of Stone Haven was well aware of Ruger Ratblood's ravaging, and while she lamented for all the lives lost along the Cornerstone Province, she knew that the pirate lord aimed to take her ancestral home from her, and acted accordingly. The villages along the way were burned, and Crag was abandoned. When Ratblood and his pirates reached it, they found it empty, its stores cleaned out and its wells poisoned. Lady Falisha stationed two hundred Meshiran along the winding road from Crag to the Marble Quarry to Stone Haven, acting as guerilla fighters to slow the pirates' march with rolling boulders, landslides, and ambushes. The worst encounter came when the pirates were traversing the eastern bend of the road, and a Host of thirty Cahladon Riders barreled down toward them, goring them on the horns of their Rono.

The spirit and resolve of Ratblood's men were as low as an anchor. They were not used to such terrain, and many longed to return to their ships rather than spend a single day further trudging along the Menace's March. The Rohe militants were toying with them, picking them off one by one and leaving the rest to starve or wander aimlessly. Many pirates began to wonder if Ruger Ratblood even knew the way to Stone Haven, or if they were wandering in the wrong direction. Every day, they feared another assault by Meshiran lying in wait along the road or yet another brutal landslide erupting from the mountainside. Mutiny abounded, and Ratblood soon realized that he retained no further control over his men. It was time to leave.

While the last shreds of loyalty among the pirates were devoured by fear, Ratblood decided that he would slip away during the night and make his way back west toward the Serrated Coast. He planned to sail away and lay low in the Charm for a few years. After such a time went by, he would simply gather a new crew, return west, and try again.

Alas, it was not to be.

For when Ruger Ratblood reached the Serrated Coast once again, what he saw was utter devastation. His entire fleet was nothing but charred remains. Occupying the waters of the Mouth was none other than the Royal Fleet, this time under the control of Prince Oliver Pike. And, as for the villages and towns along the coast, as soon as the Royal Fleet had crushed Ratblood's ships, Lady Falisha sent out a hundred Rohe galleys from Franklin's Bay with villagers to repopulate and rebuild, and Meshiran to slay any pirates who remained in occupation. Once the pirates had all perished, the people of Crag returned en masse to continue life as if no time had passed.

Ruger Ratblood made for Coastwatch to try to sneak aboard a ship and flee the Glorious Realm. But fate was not so kind to the scoundrel of scoundrels, for Justice had a say on that day. Whilst crossing the Watcher's Path to reach the docks, a jubilant crowd of villagers alongside a merchant's Rono rushed into the village square, eager to return to their hovels. Perhaps he was simply in the way, but Ratblood was trampled by the crowd while he was sneaking by, and his body was crushed underfoot by both man and beast. It is said that the rats of Coastwatch feasted well that night. And thus, the reign of pirates in the Mouth was ended.

Another winter came and went, and in 339, on the other side of the Realm in Oxcommon, the Sunspots' grasp had begun to falter. Many resented the anarchy that the Sunspots had established over the city and longed for the return of a stable lord to rule over them. And so it was that in the summer of 339, the Lady of Oxcommon, Ariana Oxer, who was sister to the late Lord Andrus, was offered aid from the disgruntled city folk.

Having escaped the Sunspots during the fall of the city one year prior, Ariana had been living among the peasants behind the walls, and was all but unrecognizable as a noble lady—until she was able to slip into more suitable attire once again. Leading a force of emboldened city folk, she rescued her family from the dark solitude of the Silo and brought them back into the light. Together, they wrested control of the city from its squabbling leaders.

When her banners were raised up onto the city walls, asserting that an Oxer ruled the Prairieland Province once again, Lord Gerrold cursed his failure—for the time to take the city and end the siege had slipped him by. The Royal Armies had tried and tried, but despite the many shortcomings of the Sunspots' brief reign over Oxcommon, they still resisted each and every attempt by Lord Gerrold to take the city. And now that the Oxers had regained control, the realization that this siege had been folly finally set in. Lord Gerrold Leon had resolved that he would inform his men that it was time to return home the next morn. However, that night, he was assailed inside his tent by furious mutineers. Hooded men from the Royal Armies' own ranks snuck through the camps and reached the Lord Commander's tent, where he was stabbed repeatedly while abed until dead.

When the morning sun rose above the horizon, and Lord Gerrold was discovered by his men, the siege was declared broken. The four legions of the Royal Army—though much fewer now—began to make their way west to Arcanan with their tails between their legs.

Meanwhile, the Lady of Oxcommon, Ariana Oxer, delivered harsh justice upon those who remained in support of the Sunspots. Her Knights of the Ox strode through the streets, branding any who were suspect with hot irons to the forehead, and publicly hanging any who were formerly a part of the Sunspots' leadership. Those who attempted to rebel against her were seized by her guard and quartered with the masses and Gutenberg bearing witness. Lady Ariana Oxer became known as the Iron Maiden, for she had yet to marry. Though among all of this, the Eclipse Knight escaped justice, having slipped through the Iron Maiden's irons.

And then, in 340, there came a Year of Silence.

While King Jacob II sat uneasily upon the throne, in Arcanlodge, a great plot began to emerge. For the Sunspots had found many sympathetic townspeople within Arcanlodge who looked to the City of Arcanan with disdain for the "exalted" leaders on high. The Sunspots collected many disaffected peasants, farmers, villagers, merchants, and hedge knights to join their cause. Meetings were held at first daily, and then twice daily, and then hourly across every tavern in the town, and by the summer of 341, Arcanlodge was alive with shouts, jeers, and proclamations from corner to corner.

Defender Dillane of the Dawn brought news of this unruly behaviour to his king many a time, but Jacob II treated these tidings with disinterest. "You trouble me with tales of vagrants and rabbles while the Oxers sit comfortably in Horn Hall, lording over us in smug 'victory.' Perhaps it is time to send Lord Commander Grant to Oxcommon with another Royal Host to lay siege to them once again? Perhaps the late Lord Gerrold's son will perform better than his layabout father. What say you?"

The Royal Defender did not reply, for the court had heard nothing but the king's endless complaints about the Oxers of Oxcommon ever since the Royal Armies found their way back to the capital at the end of 339. This, however, did not stop the king from bringing up the matter whenever he could, be it during dinner, court, or evening baths.

Archwizard Jaremius offered up an answer to the king, saying, "My liege, peradventure you are right and these quibbles amount to naught. Then, mayhaps it will all be in order for Lord Grant to march east and trouble Lady Ariana. But if I were so bold to say, your magnificence, first send the Royal Defender and... shall we say, thirty men of the City Watch to Arcanlodge to examine the state of affairs, just for a fortnight? Then, once we are assured that there is nothing to fear across the plains, then we may act upon our *true enemy* to the east. What say you to *that*, my king?"

With that, King Jacob II concurred. With a curt nod and a point of a finger, he sent forth Lord Dillane of the Dawn to ride for Arcanlodge with thirty armoured men. And all at court breathed a sigh of relief—until of course, later that evening, when the king made bitter mention of the Oxers once more during dessert.

When Lord Dillane and his thirty men rode through the gates of Arcanlodge a few days later, they were greeted by none other than an angry, broiling mob of townsfolk who wanted nothing more than to see any Arcanian nobles' heads torn off their shoulders. The sight of the Royal Defender in the town was more than enough to spark their rage, and nearly at once—when word spread through the inns and taverns of the town like wildfire—the peoples congregated, brandishing pitchforks and sharpened sticks and cobblestones and wooden spoons and rotten fruits and sharpened sickles and pots and pans and clotheslines and butter knives and manure.

Lord Dillane of the Dawn, quite frankly, did not come prepared for such an event. First, the peasants tangled up the Royal Defender and his men's horses with clotheslines, toppling the City Guardsmen from their mounts and into the mud and filth that lined the streets. Then, in an uncoordinated mass of battering and bludgeoning, the peasants walloped the Royal Defender and his thirty men with pitchforks, sharpened sticks, cobblestones, wooden spoons, rotten fruits, sickles, pots, pans, butter knives, and manure. Thirty-one men rode in through those gates, and thirty-eight men died. The Royal Defender Dillane of the Dawn was blinded by a stray spoon and fell face-first into the mud and manure, where he drowned.

When the riot had ended, the Defender's head was indeed torn from his shoulders and held high by a certain Ben Boil, who was called as such for a particularly nasty boil on the end of his crooked nose. The guardsmen's bodies were strung up and tied to posts bordering the gates of the town, and the Sunspots called forth the people for a great rally. Present at this meeting were notable townsfolk such as Dillian Wellbucket, Lamp Oil, Lyonel Limpleg, Calvin Coalcheeks, Missy, Joejoe, Ann O'Longhair, Badger, and of course, Ben Boil. The time was nigh; the people would march across the plains to the City of Arcanan, storm the gates, and rush down the King's Road, setting fire to the marketplace and drawing out the City Guard from the White Keep. Without their Royal Defender, the guardsmen would be in disarray, and the people would rush up Jacob's Hill to breach the White Keep and the Nobles' Quarters. There, they would take what was rightfully theirs, though unlawfully kept from them by the hundreds of noblemen and their lady wives for centuries: their homes, their gold, their silverware, and, naturally, their lives.

However, winter's snows came early that year, and the peasants were forced to wait some time before their plans could come into fruition. During those months, the king did find a suitable replacement for Defender Dillane of the Dawn—after his wrath subsided, of course—and the new Defender, a certain Arcanian man named simply Griffin, immediately requested from the king that he be allowed to take two hundred guardsmen this time and punish those townsfolk who had murdered Lord Dillane in the streets. But alas, the winter was a bitter one, and a march was likely to bring devastation and death to any who attempted it. The winds cut like knives, and the gales sapped the breath out of any man who breathed them in. The snows fell long and thick, covering the roads across all of the Arcane Province, and the houses were swallowed up to their roofs. Whilst Lord Griffin did attempt this march, he was forced to retreat mere hours into the trek, for he had already lost twenty of his men to the blizzards.

When this dreadful winter did finally pass, and the spring of 342 came at last, the conflict was reignited once more, for the long months of snow and cold did little to quell the fires burning within the peasants' hearts. But in Arcanan, the courts of the White Keep had long since forgotten the uprisings in Arcanlodge, or at the very least, expected the winter to snuff out any remnants of rebellion that remained.

So, naturally, when ten thousand peasants arrived at the gates of the City of Arcanan in the spring of 342, King Jacob II was beside himself with shock. "What is the meaning of this? What do these rabbles want from us? Has the cold frozen their brains?"

To this, Archwizard Jaremius replied softly, "Too true, my king. These peasants are a loathsome lot. However, that being said, there are a mighty lot of them outside our gates. Shall we perhaps send Lord Griffin out with a legion or two of our City Guard to shoo them away? Or, peradventure that proves a fruitless endeavor, should we call forth Lord Grant and the Royal Armies to run them down?" The king nodded and concurred with a grunt in response. Lord Griffin rode down the King's Road with two hundred of the City Guard behind him, fifty of them mounted, and approached the gates.

By then, the peasants had broken through and swarmed the Kingsroad Marketplace, setting merchants—and their stands—

ablaze, smashing windows with cobblestones from the road, and hurling manure at any who stood in their way. At the head of the mob was none other than the Eclipse Knight, riding tall upon a stallion as black as the midnight sky and holding a greatsword above his head to rally the masses.

When Lord Griffin rode down to meet the mob, the Eclipse Knight rode ahead as if it were a Tourney's Joust. The years, it seemed, had not dampened the Eclipse Knight's prowess, for when Lord Griffin rode by him, his greatsword arced upward with dizzying speed, and the short-lived Royal Defender was thereby cleft in twain. His body fell from his horse in two parts to litter the Marketplace. The peasants swarmed over him and pulled his head from his shoulders, parading it around the city upon the end of a spear to provoke more like-minded townspeople to join their rallying cry. "Kill the King! Kill the King! Cut that Crown from his Fatty Head! Kill the King! Kill the King! Jabber and stab until he's dead!"

The peasants swarmed through the city, and many guardsmen were trampled underfoot. Those who stood their ground did manage to slay a dozen or so peasants with spear or sword, but ten times that number assailed them back, wrenching their weapons from their grasp and proceeding to tear them limb from limb. Those guards who wore rings or other jewelry had it stripped from their cold, dead bodies. Fingers that wore their rings too tightly were bitten off. And when the mob reached the junction where the King's Road split to head southeast toward the College and north toward the White Keep, they stopped to pull down the statues of King Grant the Just and his brother Prince Jaron, smashing them upon the cobblestones and carrying pieces from them to use as further weaponry.

The mob then ascended Jacob's Hill. When news of their violence had reached the king's Royal Ear, he fled to the King's Tower to bar himself within his solar and hide from the masses. Before he resigned to his quarters, the king summoned Lord Grant Leon and ordered him, "Kill them all—every last one of them!"

The Royal Armies descended Jacob's Hill and met the mob en route to the gates of the White Keep. Swords flashed, and hooves stomped, and much blood was spilt, though still the mob carried on, as even knights on horseback proved futile against such multitudes. Spears and pikes and pitchforks, their points smothered in manure, pierced through the armour of the Royal Armies, and rocks and cobblestones and pieces of the king's stone brothers were thrown at the heads of many a noble knight, caving in their helmets and their skulls alike.

The White Keep's gates were breached, and the peasants flooded through the courtyards like a swarm of wild wasps. Any servants tending to the hedges or lawns of the White Keep's courtyards were stabbed through by sharpened sticks or bludgeoned to death with cobblestones. The beautiful stained-glass windows of the White Keep's many halls and towers were smashed through, and much manure was thrown upon the gleaming white walls to stain them. The barracks were swarmed, and many peasants got hold of knights' martial weaponry and armour.

What followed next was nothing short of a massacre.

Whilst the king, the Archwizard, the Lord Commander, and the Royal Warden all vacated the city safely through the castle's hidden tunnels, the rest of the White Keep's occupants were attacked in the halls. None were left standing when the mob had run its course. The Keeper of the Keys, Owen Oakwillow, saw his face smashed in by a formerly white brick from the White Keep's own walls. The Royal Accountant, Horace Hylar, was chased down the west corridor and ambushed in the east. He was hanged by his golden necklace until his face turned black. That necklace, along with all other possessions he held on his person, including his manhood, was claimed by the mob. Thankfully, the Royal Accountant did not have the key to the Royal Treasury on his person at that time, or the Realm may have been in a worse situation than in 307.

The dreadful winter of 341 had left great icebergs in the Mouth, restricting travel by boat, and by this time, the Prince had rid the Mouth of all traces of Ratblood's pirates. All that remained for him was to retrieve Armon Rohe from Stone Haven and return to Arcanan. Thankfully, they had not arrived yet, or they may have suffered the same fate as dear Lord Horace Hylar and Lord Owen Oakwillow.

Queen Farah, however, was not so lucky. It so happened that she and her handmaidens had fled to Eliza's Greenhouse to hide from the masses, but they were soon discovered, nonetheless. What happened next need not be described in any detail, for it was a chilling reminder of the darkness dormant within the hearts of all lowborn men. Suffice to say, the queen and her servants were not spared.

But out of the carnage that ensued upon that day, a certain someone emerged from the Royal Wood—someone who had not been seen by anyone at Court for many a year. It was the former Lord Commander of the Royal Armies, Gerric Leon, known as the Black Star, for he had spied his foe from afar—the knight who rode upon his black stallion at the head of the mob—the Eclipse Knight who had eluded him for years.

Whilst the mob desecrated the halls and corridors of the White Keep, the Black Star rode through the inner courtyard on a pale grey steed, brandishing the ancestral silver longsword of House Leon. A ragged black cloak trailed behind him, and he galloped straight for the Eclipse Knight with the fury of a thousand winds at his back. The Eclipse Knight saw him, however, and with a swing of his greatsword, he blocked the Black Star's initial strike.

And then, a glorious duel took place amidst the sacking of the White Keep: a battle betwixt two nameless knights of a bygone age.

The Eclipse Knight's stallion fell first, for the Black Star was well aware of his foe's skills upon horseback. He struck that midnight horse at the nape of its neck, slicing its head clean off. The steed floundered and collapsed, sending its rider crashing into the trampled flowerbeds. The Black Star swung his sword to try and snag his foe while he struggled to stand, but it proved too difficult a task while ahorse. The Black Star then leapt from his own steed and met his foe upon the ground as an equal.

The Eclipse Knight's greatsword was giant and unwieldy, and while one blow dealt by its hefty blade would surely cleave a man in two, it was slow and cumbersome to swing. Conversely, the Black Star's silver longsword was far swifter, and while the Eclipse Knight dominated while ahorse, the Black Star was second to none in a melee. The sound of steel on steel rang out through both courtyards.

At last, the Eclipse Knight was beaten. His greatsword clattered to the ground, and he was forced back toward the hedges by the Black Star at swordpoint. All the Black Star needed to do was run him through with his silver longsword, but first, he demanded that his foe remove his helm and recall his true name. For the Black Star was certain that this man formerly rode with the Dreadful Dozen of Crugus the Cruel, and was determined to set his curiosity to rest.

The knight removed his helm. To the Black Star's pleasure, he was indeed one of the Dreadful Dozen, though his name has been lost to time and history. But before the Black Star ended this man's life by the blade of his sword, the Eclipse Knight spoke. "But I am not the only one."

The Black Star held his blade.

"Another bested you back in Biz Dabh—clad in the same armour that I wear now. There are *many* of us—many who you and others call Eclipse. And I am not the only one of us who once rode with Sir Crugus the Cruel, either—more than half of the Dozen survived the Battle of the Lakeshore and live on to be a thorn in the side of Grant the Just's ilk. But alas, you will not be alive to bring them down."

For, as the Eclipse Knight finished speaking, the point of a spear protruded from the Black Star's neck. It seems Lyonel Limpleg had hobbled over to the Black Star whilst the Eclipse Knight had distracted him with a monologue. And so the former Lord Commander Gerric

Leon, known to many as the Black Star, perished that day in the 342nd Year After-the-Arrival.

And upon the Arcane Throne, in King Jacob II's absence, sat none other than Joejoe. He muddied the Royal Seat with his soiled trousers, as multitudes of peasants looted the throne room of anything that held any value. And so it was that in the spring of 342, the City of Arcanan was "taken" by the vagrants and rabbles of the Arcane Province.

Meanwhile, the king and the rest of the nobles who had fled the White Keep sought refuge underneath Arcanan, deep within the dark tunnels and basins that snaked below like a rats' nest. Thankfully, there were multiple stores within those tunnels that were stocked full of non-perishable foods: salted meats, pickled fish, dry crackers, dried fruits, barley and rye bread, porridge, as well as wine and mead to drink.

Lord Commander Grant sent guards up above the surface to check if all was clear, but prospects were dim. The peasants had all but captured the city, and all was in disarray. If the king were to show his "Royal Dome" above ground, it would surely be torn from his shoulders and placed upon a spike. This state of refuge was maintained for months following the uprising, and the aging King Jacob II looked worse for wear by the passing weeks.

But then, once time had begun to meld together to the point that night and day held no meaningful difference to those down below, Lord Grant's men returned with good tidings from up above. "The Pikes have returned."

King Jacob was very confused. "But *I* am the Pikes! Whatever do you mean?"

To this, the knights replied, "The *other* Pikes, my liege."

And so it came to pass that in the final days of the 342nd spring, the line of Avery Pike, who had been living in the Manor for the last ten years, returned to the City of Arcanan in a glorious procession. Rows of gleaming knights bearing the Pike crest upon their golden breastplates rode through the city on great warhorses, the footmen of House Voyant and House Oxer following suit, for the brother of Elsa Pike, Earl Voyant—the new Lord of Stathmore since 339—had allied with the Manor, and the Iron Maiden of Oxcommon saw common cause with them as well.

However, the years spent apart had caused Jared Pike to fall into a deep web of plotting and scheming, for he meant to rip the Arcane Throne from his cousin Jacob and seize it for himself in the name of the "true-blooded Pikes." Then, when he eventually passed, his son Alexander would take the throne after him, followed by Alexander's son Oliver. All would be in order, and the Tungs would no longer "sully" the halls and chambers of the hallowed castle of Arcanan with their presence.

But Jared Pike had perished in the year 334, a mere two years after he and his family had vacated Arcanan. He had been fishing out upon the Lake of Balor with his son Alexander and a couple of servants when he came upon a great catch. Reeling back his fishing rod, he pulled and pulled to wrench the stubborn creature from the depths of the sea and bring it into his boat, but it did not come. The rod instead lurched forward, and Jared plunged below the waters, sinking like a stone. Whatever he had nabbed with the hook of his rod had gotten the better of him, and was drowning him in the depths of the lake.

His eldest living son and heir, Alexander Pike, dove in after him in a valiant attempt to rescue his father, but what he saw below the surface was no fish. When he emerged from the waters and crawled, shaken, back into the fishing boat, he hurriedly ordered for the servants to row him back to shore—immediately. Even years later, when probed for further answers in regards to what he saw beneath the lake, he merely froze and shook his head in utter refusal to revisit those memories. Whatever had taken Jared Pike on that shocking day was never seen again nor mentioned by any residents of the Manor, but suffice to say that fishing was conducted primarily in the Lake of Agor from then on instead.

As such, when the combined Host of Pike, Oxer, and Voyant marched into Arcanan in the summer of 342, at the head of their armies was Alexander Pike, now thirty-two years old, alongside his Lady wife Clara Whit, his mother Elsa Voyant, his uncle Earl, and the Iron Maiden of Oxcommon, Ariana Oxer. Alexander Pike and his allies had but one goal: to liberate the city from the loosely organized rabbles that held it, and then—unbeknownst to Jacob II—to rule the Realm themselves.

The deed was done swiftly. The peasants had already grown weary of the White Keep and did not have much desire to rule. "Shepherd" Joejoe—for the peasants who had taken the city were loath to call any among them king—"ruled" over the city upon the Arcane Throne and had assembled a mock council out of the prominent peoples of the uprising. For his "victory" over the former Lord Commander Gerric Leon, Lyonel Limpleg currently resided as Lord Commander, though his army consisted of unwashed townsfolk who had never wielded any weapons besides pitchforks and sharpened sticks. Ben Boil was in charge of the Royal Fleet—though the fleet was currently still with Prince Oliver, so his charge of them would have to wait until the prince returned. The office of Royal Accountant was given to Missy, as she—allegedly—possessed the rare ability amongst them to count past one hundred. Lamp Oil was placed in the office of the Royal Warden, but feared to set foot into the White Keep's dungeons entirely, mentioning a "rank smell" that wafted out from inside those corridors. The Royal Architect was Ann O'Longhair, for it was well-agreed upon by the people that she had lived in the sturdiest hovel back home in Arcanlodge. Calvin Coalcheeks was made Royal Defender, as few liked him much, and that office was always regarded with disdain by the peasants of the Realm. The Royal Executioner was Dillian Wellbucket, the one among them who was best at swinging an axe—he was, after all, the village lumberjack for a time. And, lastly, the title of Archwizard was, naturally, granted unto Badger. None of the peasants could articulate the purpose of the

Keeper of the Keys, and so none was chosen. The office was deemed to be defunct, and a waste of coin, to boot.[11]

But alas, all of these appointments were short-lived, as when Alexander Pike and his army arrived in Arcanan, they made short work of the "garrison" that held the city. Most peasants fled the King's Road when the Pike Knights rode down it, for they no longer were united by the frenzied flame of rebellion that had stirred thousands into action earlier that year. The forces of Alexander Pike were met with little resistance as they marched past the Kingsroad Marketplace and up Jacob's Hill.

When the White Keep's walls were surrounded by hundreds upon hundreds of armoured soldiers, the peasants were caught entirely off guard. The watchers upon the walls called forth the castle's defences, but the "City Guard" under Calvin Coalcheeks fled the scene immediately upon the sight of so many foes. The gates were breached with minimal effort, and Alexander's men flooded the courtyard and stared upon the wreckage that greeted them back: the crushed Royal Hedges, the trampled flowerbeds, and the smashed fountains. The courtyard's lawns were overgrown and ill-tended. The White Keep's walls were smeared with feces and mud, soiling their usually pristine white gleam.

But the bodies were worst. So many bodies. Following the White Keep's sacking, the peasants had not thought to burn or bury the corpses of the dead, and so they laid in a boiling, stinking pile in the middle of the courtyard with black flies buzzing ceaselessly around them and pools of writhing maggots feasting in their rotting flesh. It was a sickening sight to behold, and so Alexander's first order to his men was to "burn the heap, and quickly."

---

11   It is interesting to note that the first women to be on the council made their debut in this peasants' council. However, due to the illegitimacy of the whole ordeal, the first official woman to be on the council would be much, much later.

What followed next was a swift, succinct slaughter. Alexander's most prominent knight, Dame Madalyn Sweetgrass, rode forth on her chestnut mare and cut Calvin Coalcheeks down where he stood. Then, Sir Jharol Voyant—cousin to Lady Elsa—"dueled" Lyonel Limpleg. In a couple of moments, Lyonel was but a stain upon the marble floors of the throne room. The rest of the "council" was dealt with next when Alexander's men stormed the castle and put each of them to the sword.

And the one who sat the throne, Joejoe, was pulled from the seat by his hair and dragged across the Tungish carpet spanning the throne room. Alexander ordered, "Throw him into the pile, so he might join those he has massacred." Naturally, those who studied what transpired learnt that Joejoe gave no such order nor bore any such responsibility for the actions of the masses, but as he had claimed the throne for himself, Alexander foolishly assumed him to be their leader. And so Joejoe was burnt alive amidst the rotting heap of the dead that smouldered under the sweltering summer sun.

With the peasants subdued and the Realm back in the hands of the Pikes, King Jacob II, Archwizard Jaremius Simon, Lord Commander Grant Leon, the Warden, and multitudes of other nobles emerged from the safety of the underrealm. Jacob II thanked his nephew Alexander profusely for the aid that his Host had provided in reclaiming the city. The next many weeks were spent in restoration of the order that had been lost, as well as cleaning Arcanan, the soiled White Keep, and the city at large.

The remainder of King Jacob II's reign was short, for, mere months following the restoration of Arcanan, he tragically and unexpectedly passed away one night within his bedchambers. It was the last day of 342. Accounts of the king's death make mention of the fact that he had "buried himself in his cups," in the days before, and the night of his death in particular was one of heavy drinking. Having been widowed during the Sacking of Arcanan, Jacob II slept alone in those final few months, and so he was not discovered until his Royal Squire, a boy called Uzzi, came to the king's solar to deliver him his morning mead. The boy shrieked louder than the Weeping Corridor upon the sight of the king's corpse. The bells were tolled to announce the news of the king's passing unto the city folk.

After the shock of this incident had subsided, the Archwizard Jaremius Simon performed an autopsy. Outwardly, it appeared to all that the king had simply drunk too much wine the night before and choked upon his own vomit as he slept. But the Archwizard came to a graver conclusion through his analysis: that the king had been administered poisoned wine that night, and that it was not through happenstance that he met his end, but murder.

However, when Jaremius ascended the steps of the White Keep's mortuary to divulge this chilling discovery to Court, he was seized by Royal guards. Before he could even truly grasp what had transpired, he was dragged off to the dungeons, where an unfamiliar Warden, a disfigured man named Toadskin, greeted him with a wide smile and a croak.

And at last, Prince Oliver returned. Sailing at the helm of the Royal Fleet alongside Royal Architect Armon Rohe, Prince Oliver laid anchor in the Port of Arcanan and stepped ashore. He had not yet learnt the news of his father's passing, and was eager to meet with him once again, for it had been many months. The prince was greeted by Lord Earl Voyant at the docks—a man he had neither seen in years nor expected to find in the capital.

Almost immediately upon disembarking their ships, Prince Oliver and Armon Rohe found themselves surrounded by soldiers bearing the sigils of Pike, Voyant, and Oxer. They were promptly escorted to the throne room to "meet [Oliver's] father"—or so they were told by Lord Earl. Instead, they were brought to the foot of the White Keep's steps, then seized by dozens of armoured knights and dragged into the dungeons, where they joined Archwizard Jaremius in captivity.

For upon the Arcane Throne, surrounded by kin and council, was none other than Alexander Pike, called Alexander IV, Saviour of Arcanan, the newly anointed King of the Glorious Realm.

The Second Tungish War: A House Divided

(343 AA)

COMPILED FROM THE CHRONICLING WORKS OF
ARCHWIZARD JAREMIUS ONUS SIMON

In the early days of the year 343, a usurper sat the Arcane Throne. Breaking the natural succession of Jacob II, which by law should have passed to that king's eldest son, Oliver, his nephew Alexander IV was installed as King of the Glorious Realm instead—and bestowed the Crown of Green, no less—following a swift takeover of the White Keep by his mother Elsa and her allies.

As things stood, Prince Oliver, son of King Jacob II, was imprisoned in the White Keep's dungeons along with the Archwizard Jaremius Simon, the Royal Architect-to-be Armon Rohe, and many more loyal to the court of Jacob II. The dungeons were overseen by a vile man known as Toadskin, a bloated man with gnarled, bulbous skin. The man was likely cursed, but no one else would take up the post that had formerly belonged to Warden Kurtz. While Toadskin was no Wizard of the Deep like his predecessor, he was no less of a dreadful man to be in charge of the Royal Dungeons.

But before we delve into that tale, first, it would be prudent to detail the court of Alexander IV and the few laws and reforms his council was able to pass during his short tenure as King of the Glorious Realm.

Naturally, as much of the Council of Jacob II was untrustworthy to the Court of Alexander IV, they were thrown into the dungeons to rot along with their prince. The Lord Commander was missing, the Royal Admiral was Prince Oliver himself, the Archwizard was captured and being tortured along with the Royal Accountant, the Royal Warden's allegiances proved to be quite fickle indeed, and the Royal Executioner's trust was of no great concern.

The Keeper of the Keys, Lupin Hylar, appointed during the Cleaning of the Keep, was originally suspect—until he bowed before King Alexander IV and his mother the Dowager Queen Elsa and pledged his loyalty to them. Lupin claimed that the Hylars of Hylete Square held resentment for Jacob II and his line, for they had abandoned the Hylete Province when their capital was taken by Lord Brendan Dunn—King Jacob II's own Royal Admiral, for that matter—and as such, Lupin Hylar swore fealty to King Alexander IV and his mother and remained on the council as Keeper of the Keys.

The open positions upon the council were thereby filled by the king at the request of his mother Elsa. Lord Earl of the House of Voyant was named Lord Commander of the Royal Armies; Sir Orion Oxer was named Royal Accountant; Garth Voyant, nephew to Lord Earl, was named Royal Architect; Lord Blythe Whit was named as Admiral; and a certain Lord Gohn of the House of Greene, a minor House of the Crown Lands, was named Royal Defender. As for the title of Archwizard, the uncle of Jaremius Simon who had left Arcanan with the new king's family years before, a certain Pylithos Octavius Simon, was the perfect candidate. And lastly, there was a new Royal Executioner appointed as well—a man named Bartolomeu Ze, of which little is known.

In order to quickly establish his reign as rightful in the eyes of the Realm, King Alexander IV ordered for lineages to be printed detailing his descent from King Samuel I, and in particular drawing attention to the fact that King Jacob II and Queen Farah had no trueborn heirs, proving Prince Oliver as a false claimant to the throne. The idea that the prince and his sister Sarah were bastard-born children of Kiaron Tals was to be made public knowledge. Copies of this "corrected" lineage were posted all throughout the City of Arcanan in districts poor and wealthy, and scrolls containing their message were sent out by courier to all the Provinces of the Realm, as well as to each of the Great Lords. If Alexander IV were to remain in power, he wanted to go about it legitimately so as to not incite mass rebellion and be cursed as a usurper.

However, one major problem remained: Grant Leon, Lord Commander to Jacob II, was still at large and unaccounted for. Once he was captured, then the king could rest easy—but until then, he slept with one eye open and his guard close at hand.

And in the dungeons beneath the White Keep, Prince Oliver and his other close allies, Jaremius Simon and Armon Rohe, were rats in a cage. The warden, Toadskin, routinely visited them on Dowager Queen Elsa's orders to question them about Grant Leon. "Where is he hiding? What is he planning? Who is with him?" But neither Oliver nor his companions were any the wiser as to the Lord Commander's whereabouts or plans.

When questioning alone proved fruitless, the warden began to utilize more harrowing methods in order to glean the truth. This new warden possessed an extensive collection of skinning knives. While he was forbidden to cause bodily harm or mutilation to Prince Oliver— too valuable a hostage in one piece—there were no such restrictions placed upon Armon Rohe and Jaremius Simon. The young architect had two fingers and a thumb flayed clean before he relented and cried "Stone Haven!"

Intrigued, the warden left Armon to whimper and moan in excruciating pain while he informed the king and his mother about this new lead. Scouts were sent to Stone Haven on short notice to spy upon Lady Falisha Rohe and confirm the truth of her son's words. A fortnight later, the spies returned to regrettably inform the king and his mother that the Lady of Stone Haven was indeed not, as far as they could tell, harbouring the former Lord Commander in her capital.

That dreadful night, Warden Toadskin returned to the prisoners with his knives once again. With Armon Rohe brought to the verge of madness, Jaremius Simon spoke up and rescued him from such a fate. "Warden! It is clear that the man knows naught further about the Lord Commander in question. End this needless cruelty!"

Warden Toadskin turned instead to the Archwizard. While Jaremius knew no more than the Architect, he endured the pain dealt to him all the same.

The torture continued unceasingly for hours beyond counting. In his old age, it is a wonder that Jaremius survived. The warden took out his right eye before finally relenting. But still, neither the king nor his mother were any more aware of Grant Leon's whereabouts.

On one dark, moonless night, seven ships sailed in secret through the Mouth and docked along the edge of Arcanan's port. A small band of cloaked figures stole ashore and snuck through the Queen's Gardens to reach the walls of the White Keep. Armed with sufficient materials to scale the walls, they slipped inside the castle and made their way into the dungeons, slitting the throats of any guardsmen who stood watch. Among these cloaked men was none other than Grant Leon, former Lord Commander during the reign of Jacob II, friend to Prince Oliver Pike, and grandson of the Black Star.

Before Warden Toadskin had any clue what was happening inside his demesne, a knife was held to his throat. Grant Leon whispered quietly in his deformed ear. "Where are you keeping them? Where is the prince and his council?"

The Warden proceeded to shriek as if he had seen a ghost, alerting his gaolers. To silence him, Grant Leon spilled his blood with the end of his knife, and Warden Toadskin croaked.

The ex-Commander and his men were now alone, down in the depths of the White Keep's dungeons—or so they thought.

The gaolers had arrived.

Out from the darkness, the men who had stormed the dungeons with Grant Leon were assailed by strange creatures that scuttled on all fours, their eyes sunken in and their skin grey and wrinkled like spoiled fruit. Grant Leon watched in horror as the creatures leapt up from the dank dungeon ground and clawed off his men's faces. Naught but the bloody sinews remained when the creatures had their fill. Grant Leon tried to run, but every corridor had one of these "gaolers" at its end. Where they came from, he did not know—nor do we today—but the Scholars of the College believe that they may have been experiments left behind by Warden Kurtz and merely inherited by Toadskin. But some secrets are best left undisturbed.

Grant Leon had but one hope: to reach Jaremius Simon.

The former Commander found himself at Prince Oliver's cell after all his men had already perished. Using the dead Warden's keys to open the barred doors, he let out the prince, the Architect-to-be, and the Archwizard from their confinement, but as he did so, the scratching sounds of scuttling limbs grew louder behind him. "Quickly! Jaremius, I require your aid!"

The Archwizard was forlorn. "They took my staff, good Lord Grant. There is little I can do without it."

At this, Grant Leon smiled and lifted up a polished metal wand. "Will this do?"

It did indeed suffice. With a flick of his wrist, Jaremius sent forth a great gust of wind to banish the mass of gaolers from their midst. But alas, while some did fall, others took their place. One simple evocation from Jaremius' new wand was scant enough to combat such a force.

And so, the party chose what option remained to them. They ran.

The prince, the Archwizard, the Lord Commander, and the Architect-to-be all scrambled to find the stairs leading out. But it was all a ruse. The gaolers, monstrous as they might have been, were nothing if not tricksy. They purposefully chased the prince and his party toward the corridor containing the large vat of sewage—the very same one that Gregory Gore had sunken into in years prior. Thinking on his feet, Jaremius Simon cast a spell that allowed himself and the others to float above the vat and safely cross to the other side. Chasing after them at full force, the gaolers attempted to slow their sprint, but it was in vain. They tumbled headfirst into the sewage, slipping until several were submerged in the sludge.

It was then that Jaremius stood at the edge of the vat. With a jab of his wand, the liquid beneath him began to bubble and pop. The temperature rose and rose, and the gaolers within were boiled like prawns in a pot. Their haggard skin sloughed off their bones and further muddied the waters with murky flesh, blood, and liquified entrails. The prince and his companions were quick to cover their noses, as the air surrounding them quickly became rank with an ungodly odour.

With their foes vanquished, the prince and his allies finally found sanctuary. They fled the dungeons and snuck out into the greater Keep. Before the Castle and Court could be alerted to the fact that a gaolbreak had taken place, Grant Leon guided Prince Oliver, Jaremius Simon, and Armon Rohe to his ships. As he had returned without his men, he bade Jaremius sink the other ships such that no trace of their venture remained.

The four of them thereby sailed away victorious to Stone Haven, where Grant Leon's ally, Lady Falisha Rohe, awaited their return. For, when the Dowager Queen Elsa sent her spies to Stone Haven, the Lady Rohe had been careful to satisfy their inquiries whilst also keeping Grant Leon—who was indeed present—out of sight. During his brief time in the Cornerstone Province, Grant Leon had posed as one of Lady Falisha's wine boys, and bowed modestly and low when serving Queen Elsa's spies a lovely Tungish Red—for few nobles lend a second glance to a lowly servant.

Once Grant Leon had returned to Stone Haven with Jaremius, Armon Rohe, and his king, Oliver Pike, in tow, he was smuggled in through the sea-tunnels underneath the ancient city and brought into the castle by Lady Falisha herself. They reconvened later that evening in Castle Dina behind closed doors to discuss matters of state. Oliver's beloved Zahira and his sister Sarah were overjoyed that he was alive and unharmed, though Lady Falisha was wrought with fury upon the sight of her son Armon's wounds, and all were forlorn to see what had become of Jaremius, what with his eye being taken. Soon, affixed to his eye socket was a glorious ruby, courtesy of Lady Falisha, which he wore with pride; the loss of his eye was, after all, a brave sacrifice made for the rightful king.

Among trusted allies in Castle Dina, the council of King Oliver I plotted to retake Arcanan from the usurper Alexander IV and his mother. They had a fleet of battle-hardened Rohe warships that had for years been used against the pirates of the Mouth. Since the destruction of such foes, the fleet had been itching for a fight, and many of the captains of said fleet would have taken any excuse for bloodshed. This was the perfect opportunity to give them what they desired: a war. Also on their side were many knights of the Royal Armies formerly led by Grant Leon—loyal soldiers committed to the restoration of the True Line of House Pike.

However, unbeknownst to the Council of Oliver I, Elsa still had spies incumbent within Stone Haven. When the Rohe fleet set sail in the summer of 343, these informants sent word immediately to Arcanan.

King Alexander IV grew weary. "How do we mean to resist a naval invasion? With the Dunns remaining distant as they are, we have no substantial fleet to defend the city! Archers alone will not suffice."

To this, his Royal Admiral Blythe Whit responded, "There are numerous light towers along the coast of the Port, my liege. Perhaps if we douse the lower lights, the enemy fleet will go to ruin upon the rocks? We might lessen their numbers by doing so."

The king was pleased, and sent Lord Gohn Greene and his City Guard to carry out this task. Gohn Greene bade the portmen understand why the Port would need to be shrouded in darkness for the time being. Lord Blythe got to work assembling what remained of the Royal Fleet in the Port to defend the city against the Rohes.

Three days later, under cover of night, the fleet of Lady Falisha Rohe, with Grant Leon and Oliver Pike along, appeared on the horizon of the Mouth's murky black waters. With the lights doused, the waters were treacherous and unfathomable, and before any of the Rohe ships could land upon the shores, dozens had found themselves shipwrecked by jutting black spines that were hidden from sight just underneath the rippling waves.

Seeing this as a dire situation, King Oliver called for the fleet to hold their advance until the coast could be seen. Stranded miles from the shores of the Port, the fleet awaited a rekindling of the lower lights. Toward this task, Oliver sent none other than his leal Archwizard, Jaremius Onus Simon.

Armed with a new staff acquired in Stone Haven, Jaremius opened a portal upon the deck of his king's galley and stepped through, appearing behind the lines of archers Gohn Greene had stationed on the shores of Arcanan. The Archwizard surreptitiously made his way to the first of four light towers. Scrambling up its shoddy stone steps, he snuck his way to the top and rekindled the light. Immediately, the City Guard grew aware of what was happening, and Lord Greene sent forth a half-score of soldiers to investigate, but when they arrived, they not only found the place abandoned, but also some sort of magickal ward around the light, rendering it impervious to any forces set against it.

Meanwhile, Jaremius was off to the remainder of the light towers. The second and third light towers were of no issue to him, but when he came across the fourth and final one, he found it already occupied. A mysterious, robed figure stood in the shadows, seemingly goading him to come forth and attempt to light the flame. Jaremius called out into the night, "Who art thou? Peradventure, a challenger? A thorn to my task? Do not be foolhardy! Step aside and no harm shall come to thee!"

But alas, step aside the figure did not. Jaremius was forced to press on, readying himself for battle. When the gap was closed between the two, he could see that it was none other than his own uncle, Pylithos Octavius Simon. "Nuncle! We need not do this! Thou art a Simon, as am I. We are kin, not bitter enemies!"

To this, Pylithos did respond, "Hmm, mayhaps we are of the same blood, but while I have no future under King Jacob's heir, there is much promise under Alexander. At last, my talents have been recognized, and the title of Archwizard has been bestowed upon me!"

Jaremius furled his brow. "Nuncle, the reason thou hast not been rewarded for thy endeavours into the Arcane as I have been lies with your ambition and disbandment of tradition. Thy Arcane practices are Occult in nature and deed! If thou wouldst lay down these dark excursions and abide by the code that our House has followed for centuries, mayhaps thou wouldst curry the favour of the Rightful King Oliver I! Be not a fool—see reason and stand down!"

But alas, the opposing Archwizard was not swayed. "Nay, nephew. Stand down I shall not. For if you are defeated, then none shall remain to challenge me for the title of Archwizard. My brother Lucamirus never appreciated the knowledge that I brought forth to our family, never understood its significance in the annals of our research. But as Archwizard, I will ensure that my work will not go without praise—regardless of what cowardly mages such as yourself believe of its nature. With *both* eyes, perhaps you would come to see this most clearly."

Recognizing that there was no hope of any further negotiation, Jaremius sent forth a volley of Arcane arrows at his uncle Pylithos, sparking a deadly duel between wizards that would decide the fate of this battle—and the resulting king in Arcanan to follow.

Acting in quick defence, Pylithos conjured a shield of pure Arcane energy that caught the arrows. Tossing them aside like sticks, he then flicked his wrist towards his nephew and sent a stream of green flame out from his ruby-tipped staff. This was a poor choice of spell. The moment the flames licked near the robes of Jaremius, a gust gathered the green blaze into the air, dispelling it, and from the smoke, Jaremius sent forth a plume of darkness that enveloped the other mage, making his eyes water and sting. Angered, Pylithos raised his voice, and a deep rumbling took hold of the ground underfoot. Jaremius lost his footing and tumbled, nearly dropping his staff.

When the smoke cleared, Pylithos glanced around and could not spy his foe, for Jaremius had rolled away and out of sight. "Come forth, you coward! If rights were decided by might and fortitude rather than birth, you would have been a page, and *I* would have been Archwizard! You hide, whilst I stand tall!"

But Jaremius was no coward. Emerging behind Pylithos, he raised his staff and summoned forth a crack of lightning from the blustering black clouds above like a javelin thrown. The bolt crashed upon Pylithos and burnt him where he stood. His staff crumbled into ash and his robes caught flame. Falling from his feet, Pylithos shrieked, cursing Jaremius and his entire line.

Jaremius Onus Simon stepped forth and looked his uncle in the eye-sockets—for he no longer had eyes. "Nuncle, thou hath overreached thy hand. Peradventure thou were a more studied mage, mayhaps thou could have bested me. It is as you said: rights are decided by might, and not by blood. But alas, I have both." And with that, Pylithos Octavius Simon perished.

When Jaremius lit the final beacon to guide his king's fleet safely into the Bay of Arcanan, the assault proceeded as planned. Legions of Pike and Rohe forces loyal to Oliver I flooded the shores east of the City and beyond, pouring onto Jacob's Hill and climbing it to the White Keep. Short work was made of the haphazard garrison installed by King Alexander IV, and the Keep was taken by morning's sunrise.

Among the fallen was the Royal Admiral on the side of Alexander IV, Lord Blythe Whit, who reportedly attempted to flee the scene once the Rohe fleet landed their ships. Having little honest naval experience, and less in combat against armed and armoured foes, the Lord of Whit made his best attempt to hide within the Mudpits and lie low until the battle was over, but he did not even get that far, for when he fled into Arcanan's inner city, he was accosted by a score of bitter townsfolk who, it turned out, hated him and his false king. Lord Whit—or "Lord Whitless," as he was called by the townsfolk who assailed him—was robbed of all he carried on him, which included his armour, his clothes, his sword—a family heirloom of House Whit called the Rosethorn—his coinpurse holding upward of two hundred golden crowns, and even his false hair. He was left in the gutters of the Mudpits so thoroughly steeped in city slop that he was not found until the next morning. Unfortunately, by that time, he was long dead, having drowned facedown in the roadside sewage.

Also among the fallen was the Royal Defender on the side of Alexander IV, Gohn Greene. He had valiantly—though perhaps foolishly—led the City Guard against Oliver I's Host, but the Meshiran of the Cornerstone Province were a much stronger force to be reckoned with. The ragtag group of conscripted townsfolk and Greene knights who served in Arcanan's City guard were either slaughtered like chickens before a Royal Wedding, or fled like a flock of seagulls when a rock is thrown their way. It was a dreadfully lopsided battle.

By ill luck, Gohn Greene found himself in a one-on-one duel with the Lord Commander Grant Leon himself. It is said that when Gohn Greene's corpse was found upon the steps leading to the White

Keep's entrance gates the next morning, it was barely recognizable. His blood had steeped so deeply into his gambeson that he "looked more like a Browne than a Greene."

And so it was that after a decisive storming of the city and the following battle, in one night, Oliver I and Grant Leon retook Arcanan for their cause and ousted the usurper. As for that king, once the White Keep began to fall, he, his kin, and his Court were swiftly ushered into the tunnels beneath the castle by the Keeper of the Keys Lupin Hylar. On discreet ships waiting in a smuggler's cove north of the Port, the king, his mother, and all the rest found their way west to the Manor of Pike under cover of night. Lupin himself—an enigmatic man, never quite on one side or the other—elected to stay behind.

When Oliver I and Lord Grant ascended Jacob's Hill and reached the White Keep, Lupin Hylar was present to open the gates and let them through. It is said that Lord Grant desired immediately to cut him down, stating, "I do not trust this man any more than I would a poisoner-turned-winemaker." However, Oliver I elected to show him mercy as long as he bent the knee. Lupin Hylar obliged, and thus kept his position as Keeper of the Keys, even as the rest of Alexander IV's council changed around him like winter into spring.

And so, in the year 343 AA, not eight months since Elsa Pike and her kingly son had usurped the throne from him, Oliver Pike was officially crowned King Oliver—first of his name—and Jaremius Simon placed the Crown of Blue upon his head.

At the tail end of the Royal Coronation, a man cloaked in the yellow of the Brotherhood of Gutenberg slowly walked towards the dais unannounced. Reaching forth his hand, he placed it over the king's heart. Dorj'heptkii blessed his cousin that day with words none heard save for the new king himself.

When asked, the king's reply was unchanging: "They were the words of an old friend and the Blessing of the Daisy."

The Second Tungish War: The Zehiram

(343—350 AA)

COMPILED FROM THE CHRONICLING WORKS OF
ARCHWIZARD JAREMIUS ONUS SIMON

The new king Oliver I got to ruling, along with his own council consisting of Lord Commander Grant Leon, Archwizard Jaremius Simon, Royal Admiral Calvin Dunn, Royal Defender Marvin Lister—a man often called Manticore—Royal Architect Armon Rohe, and Keeper of the Keys Lupin Hylar.

The position of Royal Accountant was offered to Lady Falisha Rohe by King Oliver, but she refused it, saying instead, "My duty and my heart lies within Stone Haven, and so there I must remain—as my mother and my mother's mother before her." And so, she departed a mere fortnight later to return home and rule over the Cornerstone Province—but a staunch ally of Oliver I did House Rohe remain until the end, when his reign inevitably crumbled asunder.

And so, the title of Royal Accountant went instead to one of House Leon, a brother of Lord Grant named Rolph who was keen with calculations and a fine conversationalist—a rare trait, to be sure, for a holder of that title. The title of Royal Warden was granted unto a man by the name of Vandergriff, and the title of Executioner remained with Bartolomeu Ze.

And while Arcanan was reformed at the top, in the Manor of Pike, the former council found refuge to plot their revenge and lick their wounds. However, their ability to retaliate would not ripen for many years to come. The losses they suffered had dealt a brutal blow to their power and influence across the Glorious Realm, so many of their allies were reluctant to "back the wrong horse," as the bards were oft heard to say.

As one of his first actions as king, Oliver I Pike established a clandestine conclave of informants who would report on the engagements of his potential and real enemies in Court and abroad the Glorious Realm. They were a carefully chosen and exceedingly adept selection of spies, charlatans, burglars, and smugglers who were offered vast riches and guaranteed prestige for themselves and their lines—if they accepted the fact that they would, by nature of their role in the service of the Crown, be nameless and bereft of any titles or recognition for their work. The exact number is not known—nor will it ever be truly known, by design—but estimates now believe that upward of fifty members were chosen and enlisted into this private service. They became known as the Zehiram, meaning *corner-shadows* in the Tungish tongue, and the order would come to serve the sitting king in Arcanan for many generations to follow. This was an act that, at the time, seemed necessary and obvious—but down the line would bring both benefits and detriments that could never have been foreseen.

Over the course of the next many years, the king summoned many prominent nobles and bloodlines from the Tung Empire back to the White Keep, and Arcanan at large, to undo the "great mistake" of his father Jacob II in caving to Amon Oxer's demands during the First Tungish War. And so, throughout the years 344 and 345, many a Tung trickled down from the northern deserts of the Empire and into the Glorious Realm to look upon its rolling green hills, golden fields, and glimmering lakes. To follow came a grand flourishing of culture within the Realm, as Tungish influences from both near and far shaped and reshaped art, music, fashion, language, and thought over the following years. The king even went so far as to decree that all his councillors were to train in the Tungish language and become fluent—or at least give it their best attempt—so as to further establish the Glorious Realm and Tung Empire as "Sibling States."

One particular bard, a man named Bahrzen, brought with him a song that still lingers in the ears of men to this day. Sung in his native language, *"Yeu Farhaem e Kalfer"* tells a humbling tale from the view of a fig tree named Kalfer. In a poetic form, the story relates how Kalfer grew from seed to tree, and that he saw time pass from year to year as though it were but a day. Then, on a night stolen by thieves and bandits, the orchard Kalfer called home for all his life was burnt down to the roots, leaving nothing standing but Kalfer himself. Alone, with the lord of the orchard away, this fig tree lamented the embers of his fallen family and friends. Then, after much lamentation, he turned to anger toward the gods for taking his family and friends away from him. Wishing for death to take him too, he waited patiently for the gods to punish him for his foolish outrage, but no such destruction befell him. Kalfer, alone still, watched as the sun rose upon the land once more.

While few people of Arcanan would have understood the words of *"Yeu Farhaem e Kalfer,"* the tune was taken by an Arcanian bard, and the nursery rhyme *"The Walls of the Slanted House"* became commonplace throughout the Realm.

But amid this golden age of Tungish re-acceptance and prosperity in the South came the resurgence of an old foe for the king to contend with. After many years festering in the deepest bowels and abscesses of the Realm, the movement known during the age of Jacob II as the Sunspots once again reared its ugly head.

It began with a speech in a seedy tavern of the Port of the Setting Sun, a putrid place called the Queenstealer Inn. It was the coldest day in the winter of late 345, and so many bodies were crowded so tightly in the Queenstealer that it was difficult to breathe. A certain wine merchant named Delbus of Briggs, proudly bearing the Iron Brand upon his forehead courtesy of Lady Ariana Oxer, proclaimed that "the time of the Sunspots' return [was] long nigh! This Tungish pretender, Oliver I, must be ousted, else the entire Glorious Realm will become a mere colony!"

From that day forward, the movement had been rekindled, and like an infection that ran untreated, the rot began to spread across the Provinces of the Glorious Realm until all was consumed in rancid hate. The Dune Road, which had been tread heavily as of late, was bombarded by bandits and vagrants from south to north, robbing caravans bearing Tungish textiles, fruits, and spices, harassing travellers heading north to the Empire or south *from* the Empire, and even going so far as to murder merchants who only spoke Tungish and leave their tongues nailed to posts. Tungish men across the entire Realm were spat on, mocked, or even attacked unprovoked. Tungish women were humiliated, stripped of their foreign headdresses and garb—or, worse, kidnapped, only to re-emerge later in the seediest brothels the Realm had to offer.

It was a travesty, and truly a dark time for the Realm. Oliver I heard of these crimes, and yet did nothing to temper the influx of new Tungish peoples into his Glorious Realm, nor passed any policies or decrees that restricted the emergent influence of Tungish culture. And as such, the trials continued.

By 346, the Sunspots had begun an organized effort to tear up the Dune Road entirely, invading towns and villages en route and destroying trading posts built along it. One particularly infamous Sunspot known as Tod Tonguetickled reportedly wore nothing but a cloak adorned exclusively with tongues he had ripped from the mouths of Tungish folk ignorant of the Common Tongue. He proudly paraded along the Dune Road with an entourage of hundreds, who followed him chanting, "Long Live Oliver Tung," and "Gutenberg Bless King

Mutt." Any travellers that came their way—Tungish or not—were interrogated and often robbed for all they were worth, left naked and battered along the road in the wake of the shambling throng.

Many tales were spun by Sunspots present in Arcanan, Arcanlodge, Feldin, Oxcommon, Wolfdale, and naturally the Port of the Setting Sun, detailing the lengthy and nefarious ways by which King Oliver I meant to sell off the entire Realm to the Tung Emperor—whom few, if any, among those at these rallies could name—province by province, starting first with the Prairieland as punishment for Amon Oxer's rebellion during the reign of his uncle Grant I. If the king got his way, they said, every man in the Glorious Realm would be assigned a Tungish wife and ordered to father "mutt" children until the entire population of the Glorious Realm was indistinguishable from the peoples of the Empire to the north. They also claimed that the king meant for all other languages to be banned from speech and the Tungish tongue to be the only spoken language allowed upon the entire continent, punishable by—ironically—loss of tongue.

Public opinion had greatly turned on the king. While many still remained tolerant of the new influx of Tungish folk from the north, praising the many enrichments they provided the Realm, popular perception of the king in the Glorious Realm as a whole was greatly muddied and overall poor.

The tales spun by the Sunspots' staunchest supporters quickly evolved into conspiracies bordering on insanity. One such claim, at its peak believed by thousands of people across the entire Realm, was known as the Proliferation of Sand. This assertion claimed that the more Tungish people residing south of the Empire, the further the desert would spread, encroaching upon the glorious green pastures of the Realm until naught but desolate dunes remained. And sure enough, tales of sightings of desert sands south of the Empire began to trickle from tavern to tavern and ear to ear. Reports claimed that the Tungish desert had begun to "sprout" even as far south as Feldin!

However, this brought forth a time of great change amid the turmoil of this age, as more people travelled to see with their own eyes these sightings of desert "growth" in the Arcane Province. They did indeed see such things, though not in the manner they were expecting. For various Sunspots—or peoples sympathetic to their cause—were seen with barrels of sand collected from the dunes of the Borderland Hills, scattering it en masse across the fertile lands of the Vale of Feldin and the Vale of Arcanlodge. When word of this inevitably spread to the selfsame taverns in which this tale was being shared, the legitimacy of the Sunspots' preachings were largely called into question. The bounds of reason could only be stretched so far, it seemed, and a tipping point was reached at which popular opinion of the Sunspots and their movement began to dwindle rapidly.

It was at this point in time that King Oliver I decided to finally act. He called forth the Glorious Council and announced, "In a fortnight's time, the Sunspots will be no more."

Many on his council were confused by this claim. Calvin Dunn replied as such. "My Liege, whatever do you mean? These rabble-rousers have a hold upon multitudes, their rhetoric worming its way into the ears of impressionable minds who know naught but hate."

Archwizard Jaremius reminded the king that, "The Sunspots have existed for decades—emergent since the time of your own uncle Grant I. Mayhaps even before then! To suggest that they will be vanquished within a fortnight, my king... even as hyperbole, ye surely do not mean this?"

But the Lord Commander Grant and the Keeper Lupin remained silently in support of their king—though for different reasons, there is no doubt—and Oliver I himself responded in turn. "You all forget that the Crown wields a *new* power—a power that cuts sharper than any sword."

And by that, all in the council knew of what their king spoke, and there were no further questions on that day.

Within a fortnight, all the prominent speakers and leaders of the Sunspots—no matter which corner of the Realm they occupied—found themselves dead as dinner, just as the king had prescribed. Delbus of Briggs was on the chamberpot, no less, when he was intruded upon by his privy maid—or, at least, someone who *looked* like her. Whilst he stood to clean himself, he was attacked from behind, his branded head forcibly plunged inside his—full—chamberpot. A barrel of his wine was delivered to the Council of King Oliver I to announce that the deed was done, and the members of the council all drank to his death.

As for Tod Tonguetickle, he was strolling along the remains of the Dune Road near Bronzebourne when his retainer turned on him. He was dragged from the road and out of sight of his loyal, though dwindling throng, where he was held down and forced to drink a tankard of sand. By the time the sands had settled, his belly in death was dry as the dunes he so feared in life. His prized Cloak of Tung Tongues—for that is what he called it—was laid before King Oliver I, and it was revealed that many of these "tongues" were mere strips of leather and bark. And the members of the council all drank to his death.

The Sunspots were not finished yet, however. Their retaliation came swiftly and surely. Alladim Biz-Rahim, a Tungish official on his way south from Tung Tameel upon the Dune Road, found himself and his retinue accosted north of Arcanlodge by a score of bandits bearing the Iron Brand. His retinue was slain to the last man and left to rot upon the road. Biz-Rahim himself was taken to the town of Remmenstone, where he was bound, gagged, and beaten senseless.

Word travelled inevitably thereafter to Arcanan, reaching the royal ear of Oliver I and his council. The king discussed this matter with his advisors. The Lord Commander and Archwizard were both in agreement: these Sunspots needed to be put in their place, and the Realm needed to see once and for all that there was no place for prejudice against the Tungish people. Justice would have to be swift and harsh. Jaremius Simon himself offered to venture forth to Remmenstone with a small band of loyal mages of the College. "My liege, send me, and if it be so that the Sunspots consider such a folly again, they shall ponder what the Archwizard hath delivered upon them and give pause."

Lord Grant also volunteered to venture out with a small band of loyal knights. "I have always served you faithfully, my king. Send me, and I will retrieve our Tungish brother and bring him safely back to you, sparing no Sunspots amid the task."

The rest of the council was not so inclined to engage as the Lord Commander and Archwizard. Calvin Dunn mentioned that to risk a member of the Glorious Council in sending them to retrieve one Tungish official was exactly the sort of outcome the Sunspots hoped for, as they wished to weaken Arcanan in any way they could. "I say leave them, and do not negotiate with these rabble-rousers, who wish only to incite terror across this Glorious Realm."

To this, the king replied, "So you would let Alladim Biz-Rahim die, then? Does his life mean nothing to you?"

The Royal Admiral had no response. Rolph Leon, the Royal Accountant, then spoke up. "My king, what our Admiral says rings true. Someone as prestigious in title as the Lord Commander of your Royal Armies, or the Archwizard of the College of Sorcery, ought not to risk their life for a foreign emissary, no matter how hefty their coin purse or noble their blood."

The Royal Defender, Marvin Lister, raised the point that, "A band of mercenaries could solve this matter." For he had many a contact across the Realm, namely near Tal Taro, where bands of sellswords could be hired for coin.

While the members of the council all wagged their tongues, the Keeper of the Keys held his own in silence. The king heard all of these points and more, but his mind had already been made up minutes before. "Lord Grant, you will go." For the king did concur with his good friend Grant Leon's sentiments most: that to rescue Biz-Rahim and bring him to Arcanan unscathed was the highest priority. Plus, he knew that the Sunspots had played a part in the death of Grant's grandfather, the Black Star.

And so it was that in the autumn of 346 that Lord Commander Grant Leon set out from Arcanan with thirteen knights. A cold winter's chill was upon them—an omen of great dread, some might say. They reached Remmenstone one week from when they left and found the place beset by a terrible silence. Homes were boarded up, streets were emptied, and chimneys breathed no smoke. Spies leered in every corner; eyes peered out every window. Grant marshalled his knights to search every nook and cranny of the village until they found where the Sunspots had made their nest.

The problem was, as Grant discovered too late, that the entire village had already succumbed to the Sunspots' control. Some knights of Grant's retinue were cornered in the alleyways and knocked off their mounts, crashing to the ground, where they were bludgeoned to death with clubs, boards, and blunt spears. The rest were lured into dark lodgings and never seen again.

Eventually, Grant Leon was alone in his pursuit of Alladim Biz-Rahim, and hope was dwindling like the summer's warmth. As night was falling, the Lord Commander was riding down the main road when he was greeted by a foe upon the dimming horizon. His enemy was atop a black stallion, clad in blackened armour with signs of much wear and weathering. Upon his breast was the golden symbol of a bleeding eclipse. Lord Grant had found himself face-to-face with a great enemy—perhaps the very same who had battled his grandfather the Black Star.

"Who goes there? I am Lord Commander Grant Leon of the Royal Armies, second in command of the Glorious Realm and stalwart sword of Oliver I! I have come for the Sunspots, for they have captured someone of great importance to our king! Do you stand in my way, Eclipse Knight, or do you yield?"

The black knight did not speak, but spurred his steed forward. His shadow lengthening in the wake of the descending sun, he rode to meet Lord Grant. Approaching close, he lifted the black visor of his helm and showed the young Lord Commander a grizzled, scarred visage. "You may know me, or you may not. But I was there, four years ago, in the Courtyard of the White Keep. It is for me that you have *truly* come, is it not?"

None truly know if Lord Grant did expect to find the Eclipse Knight in Remmenstone that day. He unsheathed the silver sword of House Leon and held it out before him. "I knew that one day we would meet. As all rivers lead to the sea, so are our paths fated to cross. I have not ever forgotten the day my grandfather passed, and when you are dead, I shall not forget this day either."

Their blades clashed; the silver sword of Leon upon the black greatsword carried by the Eclipse Knight. As the coming of night cloaked their duel in dark shrouds, they battled tirelessly upon their horses, making passes until the other fell or broke. But they appeared evenly matched, even with the Eclipse Knight nearing his later sixties by all accounts. However, Lord Grant Leon had vengeance in his heart, a fire that could only be quenched by the Eclipse Knight's death.

Night had come by the time Lord Grant's horse had been slain—its head cleaved from its body by the Eclipse Knight's giant greatsword—but there was no moon, for fate truly has her jests. That night was the very night of a lunar eclipse, one that blanketed Remmenstone and the ensuing duel in utter blackness.

It was in this dark that Lord Grant Leon cut the hind legs of his foe's mount. The black stallion crumpled, sending its rider into the dirt. Bereft of his helm, the Eclipse Knight lay motionless, but awake. Grant approached him, silver sword at the ready, but realized that his foe could not move, save for his head. "Well, alas, it appears you have won!" said the Eclipse Knight with scorn remaining in his haggard voice. "All you needs do is kill an unarmed, immobile, defenceless old man, and your vengeance will be at an end! Or will it?

For even though I will have died, your grandfather remains buried in the Cemetery of Arcanan still, and my death shall not him resurrect. So come now, kill me, and live the rest of your life knowing you never killed us all."

This gave Grant pause. "What do you mean? Still more of you yet remain?"

The Eclipse Knight laughed mockingly, blood trickling down his chin. "Indeed there are. And perhaps I am not the one who slayed your grandfather. Alas, you shall never know, for I will die with the truth."

And with that, Grant Leon stabbed him through the eclipse on his chest. Provoked to anger, he ended his foe, but the lingering thought that the Black Star's *true* killer still remained would eventually drive him mad.

Silver rays of the moon then revealed Remmenstone in the night.

Alladim Biz-Rahim was recovered that next morning and brought back to Arcanan by Lord Grant alone, and the Sunspots passed into history. For that was, as all came to understand, their final act of desperation, thereby thwarted by the king.

And thus, a new year began as a dreadful winter dug its icy claws into the Realm. It was known as the Winter of Woe, and while the people of the Realm grappled with all it wrought, all other conflicts slowed to a halt.

The bitter cold afflicted much of the Glorious Realm to hideous results. In Hylete, the peasants of the Vale lost their fields to frost, and thousands starved from Narfolk to Fort Hylar. Even the Lord of Hylete Square, Errol Hylar, lost two sons and a daughter to disease, famine, and the Dark Wind that year—a time of great mourning for all in the West. In the Arcane Province, Arcanlodge found itself in great turmoil, as townsfolk grew so hungry that they ate all the horses in the stables and even began to turn on their own lords for sustenance. The situation in Arcanan fared no better, for many peasants within the city and without were so bereft of food they began stripping the trees of the Royal Wood for bark. A band of peasants even attempted to storm the White Keep and raid its larders, convinced that the king and his court were feasting upon lavish stores of food. Royal Defender Martin Lister and his City Guard thwarted the attempt, and all involved were hanged, and the townsfolk congregated underneath the gallows to nibble at their lifeless toes for sustenance. Despite the imaginations of starved Arcanians, Oliver I and his court were no less hungry than their subjects.

The Winter of Woe was an uncaring, hateful crone, and she spurned all, regardless of toil or titles. Many minds were turned to the ages of Samuel I and Jared II and the Great Famine that scourged during their reigns, and all prayed that it would not linger as it had in those times.

And, in the Manor of Pike, the Winter of Woe struck as well. In a cruel twist of fate, it took the life of the short-lived King of the Glorious Realm, Alexander IV Pike, who fell gravely ill with a raging fever and died a quarter-moon later in his bed. His mother Elsa sat by him through it all. She wept bitter tears when he passed, and did not leave her chambers for weeks. Not even her granddaughter Sarah, now thirteen, could reach her during those dark times.

The Winter of Woe claimed lives like a specter, entering peoples' homes and leaving with the spirits of loved ones in its cold hands, disregarding any carved daisies upon the doors. But while death endured throughout the Realm at large, many schemes began to take form within the frozen walls of both the White Keep and the Manor of Pike.

In the years since Oliver I had taken the throne, many Tungish officials such as Alladim Biz-Rahim had begun to occupy the courts and chambers of the White Keep, and grudges had begun to grow, for the Tungish nobility present in the capital never quite saw eye-to-eye with the established courtesans who had come before. While in policy, the Court of Oliver I preached acceptance of Tungish folk and culture, in practice, they still held many prejudices and resentments close to heart.

And these resentments were not only between those who were Tungish and those who were not, but also between old rivals as well. For one must not forget that both a Hylar and a Dunn sat upon Oliver I's council, what with Lupin Hylar as Keeper of the Keys and Calvin Dunn as Admiral. Calvin's enmity towards his fellow councilman was as plain as the crescent moon upon his doublet, though Lupin Hylar remained an amicable—if slightly ingratiating—councillor all the same. But throughout 347, any of Oliver I's Court sharing a resentment for Tungs, or others they considered undesirable, found others of like mind in the silent halls and darkened corridors of the White Keep. Alliances were being forged.

And in the Manor, the death of Alexander IV brought forth many questions among the remnant supporters of his Claim. When Elsa emerged at last from her grieving, she summoned her banners to the Manor and—according to all who claim to have heard it—made an empowering speech. Lords and their vassals from Marston, Terren, Landron, Greene, and Tenn all swore fealty that day to King Oliver II, the firstborn son of Alexander IV and a young man of seventeen. Their campaign against Oliver I, it seemed, had been rekindled as the snows of the Winter of Woe began to melt.

As the year 348 arrived at last, sentiment toward the Tungish people had begun to wane, as the Winter of Woe had put a damper on Oliver I's campaign for greater acceptance. To be quite frank, people had far more pressing matters on their minds—matters of life and death—and could not much be troubled with the king's priorities of the previous few years.

And things took a turn for the worst when a beloved Arcanian merchant was slain in the spring of 348 within the Kingsroad Marketplace. A certain Yollo Grange was a smuggler-turned-salesman who was famed for bringing in shipments of rye bread and golden apples from the Port of the Setting Sun to Arcanan during the Winter of Woe's great famine. Instead of being chastised for this criminal act, the king saw reason and commended Yollo for his actions, granting him a ship from the Royal Fleet to further encourage his ventures. When the famine relented, and the colds retreated back from whence they came, Yollo had found himself as an established merchant. Though it is said that he continued to smuggle on the side—it had become something of a habit despite turning legitimate—he had become the centre of admiration by many Arcanians.

And so, it was no small thing when Yollo was stabbed to death by a disgruntled buyer over a disagreement on the price of his apples. The fact that his killer was Tungish only fanned the flames of prejudice.

Despite many accounts suggesting that Yollo Grange drew a knife first and attempted to slice the man's hand—whilst he shouted slurs the man's way, some claim as well—the vast majority of Arcanians were content to brand this Tungishman the villain in their minds, and so a wave of anti-Tungish sentiment began to take root within the capital. This deeply saddened the king, who had done much throughout his tenure to try to preach acceptance among the people of the Realm. It seemed Oliver I had waged war against the Sunspots and their rhetoric for years, only for his efforts to be overturned by a marketplace squabble.

Angry riots and uprisings took shape within the city that summer, and the Dregs and the Gutters became littered with the corpses of Martin Lister's guardsmen who tried to quell them. One such riot found its origins within the southern Windmaker's Inn, during which its instigator, a fierce young woman named Windy, claimed that "perhaps the Sunspots knew a thing or two." Scores of angered peasants poured out from the tavern and into South Arcanan, where a slightly wealthier class of Arcanians lived in two-storied homes, in comparison to the exclusively single-storied dumps occupied within the Dregs, Gutters, and Mudpits.

Martin Lister was dispatched by the king to quell this massive revolt and journeyed to South Arcanan with a score of City Guardsmen, many on horseback. However, he and his men were not so lucky. The peasants overwhelmed them, stabbing the legs of their horses until they collapsed, then tearing off the armour and helmets of the guards before caving in their skulls with bricks and large rocks.

Martin Lister, however, was not known as the Manticore for nothing. His weapon of choice was a triple flail, which he brandished around him while he rode down dozens of peasants with his chestnut stallion. Any who approached him with pitchforks or sharpened sticks had their heads burst like thrown tomatoes when his flail swung their way. The corpses of a hundred Arcanian townspeoples littered the streets of South Arcanan by the time the Royal Defender decided to return to the White Keep, but his brutality only summoned forth further retaliation.

Disappointed by his careless actions toward the less-fortunate, none other than the Brotherhood of Gutenberg had arrived at the scene. They did scold the Royal Defender and did chastise him for his "frankly unpleasant and rather Unholy actions. Gutenberg forbid this awful scene!"

But the Manticore's flail knew not friend from foe once it had begun to taste blood, and so unfortunately, many a holy man was slain upon that Unholy day, though, thankfully, a certain Dorj'heptkii was not present, for he was deep in prayer at the time.

The actions of the Defender only further fanned the flames of enmity, and now, the peoples' resentment turned toward the king as well. The riots did not stop, and while the Manticore was verbally reprimanded for his senseless killing of twenty-three Brothers of Gutenberg, he was also sent out many more times as the fires of revolt sprouted in every corner of the city. By then, the West Church of Gutenberg itself had joined the side of the people, and even the High Elder preached that Oliver I was "a heretic, with no regard or respect for human life. By Gutenberg! A spiller of Holy Blood!"

And, while Arcanan was aflame with angry demonstrations against the king, the Manor saw its time to strike. Elsa and her loyal banners set out from the Crown Lands and marched east, taking the south bend beneath the Borderland Hills before turning north to Arcanan. She had five thousand in her Host, with one-fifth of them mounted knights, and all of them staunchly in support of her grandson Oliver II. She had sent many a letter to the Iron Maiden of Oxcommon, securing the support of the Prairielands as well.

As the summer's sun blazed hot above the plains of the Arcane Province, the Pikes of the Manor reached the King's Road. But while Oliver II wanted to storm the city and claim his throne then and there, his grandmother spoke words of caution. "My sweet, sweet grandson, the crown will be yours in time. But we still do not have the bulk of our Host yet, as our agreement with the East was to reconvene in Arcanlodge and march as one. Listen to your grandmother, Oliver. You will get the throne you deserve—that you will—but we need to consolidate our armies first."

And so, the Manor's Host continued their march until they reached the town of Arcanlodge. Expecting resistance, they were pleasantly surprised when the guard let them through the gates with no issue, and many even bent the knee for Oliver II as he rode past on his grey mount.

While stationed in Arcanlodge, Elsa Pike received a courier with more great news: Lord Timothy Felix of Feldin had declared himself for Oliver II's cause. Lord Timothy expressed resentment toward the line of Jacob II for the creation of the Dune Road, which had reduced Feldin from the trading capital it once was.[12] Elsa was pleased, for it appeared that her line could see itself at last upon the Arcane Throne that it "by rights" deserved.

Naturally, by early 349, when word of the Manor's Host in Arcanlodge found itself at Oliver I's royal ear, he summoned his

---

12   In reality, Feldin was still a major hub of trade and commerce, but
      when they fell from the number one spot to the number two spot, the
      discrepancy in profits stung their pride.

council to discuss their options. "Send the Lord Commander," suggested Admiral Calvin Dunn, "just as was done in 346 when Alladam Biz-Rahim was taken captive in Remmenstone."

To this, the king was ambivalent. He called on the Keeper of the Keys for information regarding Oliver II's allies. "Disconcerting news, to be sure," replied the Keeper. "My informants intercepted a message on its way from Feldin that contained sympathies for Lady Elsa's campaign and scorn for our rule, Your Grace. If Feldin has joined them, then their Host may grow significantly in the weeks to follow—that is, if we do not act soon. And there is also the matter of Oxcommon, my liege—for we all know the Iron Maiden, as she is called, was a staunch supporter of the Line of Avery and is like to support them in this campaign as well. There have been sightings of soldiers bearing the Oxer banners as far west as Cornerton, my liege."

Upon hearing this news, the king resolved to send the Royal Armies after all. He commanded Lord Grant to take a legion of knights to surround Arcanlodge and another to storm it seeking Elsa Pike and her grandson. "For if we cut off the two heads of the snake, then the troublesome ilk of my uncle Jared will finally be at an end."

And so, Lord Grant Leon set out with two legions of the Royal Armies at his back to smash the Manor's Host before their allies of Feldin and Oxcommon could join them.

While Grant Leon led the assault on Arcanlodge, a tragic thing came to pass within the walls of the White Keep, for, like a concealed blade beneath the sleeve, by the time the deadly plot struck, it was far too late for anything to be done about it.

Calvin Dunn, now long-time Royal Admiral to King Oliver I, turned on his king and council. With a band of loyal captains, he surrounded Oliver I in the Weeping Corridor and ordered his men to pierce the king with their swords until dead. It is said that the last words spoken by Calvin Dunn to his dying king were "Forgive me, my king, for I had no choice."

Thereafter, Calvin Dunn swiftly commanded his men to smuggle the body to the docks in a covered wagon, and once out of sight, dump it into the white waters of the Mouth. The Crown of Blue was taken off Oliver I by Calvin himself.

Once the deed was done, and the king's body had been disposed of, the Royal Admiral and his captains sought to seize control over the White Keep. The plan was to barricade the portcullis that looked down Jacob's Hill and fortify the Keep with a strong garrison such that when the Lord Commander inevitably got word of Oliver I's untimely death, he—and what remained of his two legions—could not thwart them.

But they had underestimated one key factor: the loyalty of the king's new secret power.

The hidden conclave of spies and assassins known as the Zehiram descended on Calvin Dunn and his men, and one by one whilst they stood at their posts, their throats were slit and their bodies left in pools of their own blood. The Royal Admiral was last to die—perhaps a purposeful action by the Zehiram, though we will never truly know. While on his way to the front gates of the White Keep, he passed through the inner courtyard, saw his men slumped dead where they formerly stood, and began to panic. He had drawn his own shortsword when suddenly, a bolt protruded out the front of his neck. He fell to the ground upon the trimmed green grass, dropped his sword, and lingered in this mortal world just long enough for the Zehiram to circle around him, all clad in black masks that revealed naught but their beady, judgemental eyes. One stooped down to take the Crown of Blue before they all left him to choke on his own blood.

On the following day, news of the king's death finally reached the ear of Lord Grant Leon, who in haste abandoned his attack on Arcanlodge and rode for the White Keep. The two legions he had taken with him were still largely intact, and so he left one behind to maintain the perimeter around the town and bar anyone from exiting the premises. With his other legion in tow, he returned to Arcanan and rode up the King's Road like a vengeful thunderstorm. When he found the ragtag garrison of Calvin Dunn already dead, he was beside himself with puzzlement. At that moment, the Keeper of the Keys Lupin Hylar came out to greet him.

"What a terrible thing that has happened," he said in a mournful tone. "The king has perished, and his body is nowhere to be found. At the very least, his secret power has recovered the Crown of Blue so that it might be passed on to his son and rightful heir, the boy Ashar." He presented the Crown of Blue to the Lord Commander, and a single tear rolled down the Keeper's cheek. It is said that the Lord Commander gruffly snatched the crown from Lupin's hands—for he never trusted the man, and least of all in that moment—and stormed inside the White Keep to set the Realm in order.

Sitting upon the Arcane Throne as Steward of the Realm, Grant Leon deliberated on what to do next. Following Calvin Dunn's betrayal, suffice to say he did not trust the Council—save for Jaremius Simon, of whom he was a long-time friend. "Wise Archwizard, what would you have me do in such dark times? We have enemies within and without, in Arcanlodge and on the march, and also in the very halls of this keep. I need guidance, I need strength, and most of all, I wish the king were still alive." And then he wept.

Jaremius Simon was slow to reply, for it was wise to choose his next words carefully. "My lord, it is a loss hard to bear, but do not burden thy mind and heart with guilt or shame. You did as thy king commanded always. Take courage and strength in that truth. Now, in these dark times, I suggest that first we crown Prince Ashar, so that there remains a king in Arcanan. If anything, it will help strengthen our True Claim against the foes who currently linger in Arcanlodge, so close to our city."

This, the Steward and Archwizard did agree upon. On the very next morn, Prince Ashar Pike was given a hasty coronation in the Throne Room of the White Keep, wherein he sat upon the Arcane Throne, and Jaremius bestowed upon him the Crown of Blue. He was named Ashar I Pike, King of the Glorious Realm, though scant few were in attendance. Notwithstanding Ashar's coronation, he was confronted by Grant Leon and asked to withhold his right to rule for the time being, as, in Grant's terms, "To change the acting commander during wartime would bring instability and potential ruin to our—at present—tenuous hold upon the Realm. Surely you understand?" The young king did indeed, and granted Grant leave to continue ruling in his stead as Steward of Arcanan.

Next, the Council and Court were thereby questioned one after another by the Steward and Archwizard in an attempt to determine who might be an enemy and co-conspirator with Calvin Dunn. Martin Lister, Lupin Hylar, Vandergriff, Bartolomeu Ze, and even the Steward's own nephew Rolph were all heavily scrutinized. All had credible alibis, and moreover were positively morose at the prospect of Oliver I's death. Bartolomeu Ze in particular had been overtaken so strongly by a fit of sobbing that he could barely answer their questions, but when all was said and done, nobody on the Council appeared to share any of Calvin Dunn's guilt. Keeper Lupin was questioned most heavily by Grant Leon, but the possibility that he was a con-spirator dwindled dramatically once the facts were all laid out. Most convincing of the arguments for his innocence was the reminder that the Hylars and Dunns were bitter enemies of one another, and had been for generations, and so to unite together to commit an act of regicide was not only inconceivable, but laughable. With a grumble, the Steward ceased his questioning and reinvited the entire Council back to Court.

While the Court was reeling from its inquisition, dishearten-ing news spilled forth, this time from without the capital rather than within, for the legion left behind in Arcanlodge by Grant Leon had fallen. The Iron Maiden had combined forces with that of Timothy Felix, and a massive army was now incumbent inside the town. Estimates reported to the Steward and the Council that the Great Host of the enemy was perhaps eleven thousand strong. Alarmed, the Steward sent forth Jaremius to recruit any abled mages from the College to stand upon the walls of the city and bombard their enemies with magick upon their approach. He also sent forth Martin Lister to gather every member of the City Guard and station them along the King's Road to block the proliferation of enemy forces in the direction of Jacob's Hill. As for the remainder of the Royal Armies, Grant Leon decided to bring them all atop Jacob's Hill in defence of the White Keep, as he viewed the protection of the new king to be of paramount importance. The fate of their rule stood then on a sword's edge, for if King Ashar were to perish, the entire line of Alexander III would be extinguished.

The march upon Arcanan did not come immediately, for the Great Host in Arcanlodge did find itself in quite some disarray. The terms demanded of Elsa Pike by the Iron Maiden of Oxcommon and Lord Timothy Felix of Feldin were quite at odds with one another—and negotiations took weeks to conclude. During that time, the stores of Arcanlodge were thoroughly depleted by the massive Host stationed there, and so supply lines running from Oxcommon to Feldin to Arcanlodge needed to be established to sustain their combined forces. This led to further infighting, as the lords of Feldin and Oxcommon bickered amongst each other as to who would supply the bulk of the food and supplies, and within whose land the supply lines would run, and so on.

Lady Elsa ended the squabbles once and for all as the new year snuck up on them all one day. "For too long have we let our enemies in Arcanan prepare themselves to thwart our noble cause! Lady Oxer, by all accounts, you have been my most loyal supporter all these years; I will grant you any request you wish if you lay at rest this fruitless bickering with the Felixes! And Lord Timothy, I understand that you wish to be upon my grandson's council—that boon I grant you, but you must first find common ground with the Lady of Oxcommon!"

At this, the Iron Maiden and Lord of Feldin both saw reason and resolved their negotiations, though not entirely amicably. The Iron

Maiden then named her one request: that her grandniece Martha would be wed to King Oliver II once the Arcane Throne was seized and the city was won. To this, Lady Elsa agreed—though it must be noted that she did not inform her grandson of this pact, fearing he would make a scene and reject it altogether. "Better he learns of his duty once there is a crown upon his head and a throne beneath his arse," she was heard to say by one of her handmaidens.

As the winter snows of 350 first blew in, the Great Host did at last march upon Arcanan, but the Steward and Council had prepared their defences well. Hundreds of mages trained specifically in the Art of Evocation stood upon the walls of the city. Formerly, that particular school was seen as Occult, but the taboo had been lifted in a twelve-to-one vote of the Collegiate in 204 AA, during which time the Archwizard was Quintus Quintus. Those in favour argued that the College ought to recognize that some forms of the Arcane considered forbidden could be used "with caution, and by a trained mind." All agreed that such a power would be invaluable in defence of the king's True Claim.

Martin Lister, however, had experienced great difficulty recruiting more men to the City Guard. Since his rampant killing of those twenty-three Brothers of Gutenberg, the entire Faith had branded him an Enemy of God—and the Faith held considerable sway over the people of Arcanan during those times. And so, the Royal Defender looked instead to Tal Taro. In support of King Ashar I came the Bloody Carvers, the Spiked Shields, and the Scorpions, each boasting a force two thousand strong. However, their prices were steep, especially those of the Scorpions, who viewed themselves as superior to even the Meshiran of Rohe. The Steward found that soon after their hiring, the Royal Treasury ran dry. As for the Royal Army, Grant Leon had them all stationed upon Jacob's Hill—all three thousand of them—where they remained until the day the Great Host arrived. In fact, there were so many knights upon that hill during those weeks, many who occupied the Nobles' Quarters felt dearly threatened, and whispers of enmity were oft heard by soldiers patrolling the streets.

When the attack finally came, the battle was equally as glorious and hideous as the Realm had anticipated. The Great Host stormed the front gates of the city while terrible fire and smoke covered their forces courtesy of Jaremius and his army of war mages. In a wondrous display of magickal prowess, his mages opened up sinkholes in the ground surrounding the city and engulfed hundreds of the Great Host's forces, closing them back up when the deed was done.

But alas, the gates could not hold forever, and eventually, they were breached. Once inside, the Great Host had to contend with the Manticore's hired sellswords and the City Guard, who put up a considerable fight. The entire King's Road was abandoned save for the soldiers who stood to confront the enemy forces, and any houses, stands, or lodgings that remained along the road were utterly smashed by the time the fighting ceased. Many houses in Tomas' Square and the Dregs were burnt to ash amid the carnage. While the Bloody Carvers, Spiked Shields, and Scorpions fought valiantly for the first few hours, once the tides of battle were clearly not in their favour, they fled for the Port. As he ran, tail between his legs, to the docks in the hope that a vessel of the Royal Fleet would ship him off to safety, the leader of the Scorpions was overheard by some in the City Guard muttering, "No gold is worth this!"

But the biggest blow to the Steward's defence came not from the Great Host nor the cowardice of sellswords, but from the people of the city itself. For the resentment for Oliver I, the great migration of so many Tungish peoples during his reign, and the brutal quelling of uprisings and riots that took place in 349 still lingered in the hearts and minds of many Arcanians. The West Church of Gutenberg did much to remind them that the source of their troubles lay with those in the White Keep—namely the "Corrupted Court of Oliver I." And, despite that king's death, the same "rot" that afflicted him was still present in the current leadership; many hated Grant Leon by 350, seeing him as a blind follower of Oliver I's ways at best, and a bitter heathen at worst, and their thoughts on Martin Lister go without saying. Suffice to say, when the Great Host barged through Arcanan's gates, many in the city saw Elsa and her grandson as their saviours. There was a great uprising against the Steward, who was seen as a pretender, and King Ashar I, who was seen as a Tung.

Spurred forward by the Faith, the Brotherhood of Gutenberg anointed Holy Maces with the blessings of Gutenberg and gave them to the people of Arcanan, who promptly joined in the Great Host's cause. They beat the City Guard to a pulp, ambushing them at every street corner. At last, after hundreds had died on both sides, the Manticore found himself surrounded near the Windmaker's Inn. Swinging his triple flail to-and-fro, and caving in a great many skulls in the process, he tried to carve himself a path of escape back to Jacob's Hill, where the Royal Armies stood in last defence of King Ashar.

But his retreat was thwarted by none other than Dorj'heptkii.

Before the raucous townspeople, the knights of the Great Host, and the City Guard, Dorj'heptkii denounced Martin Lister as the Demon Manticore, and in the same breath, denounced the line of Alexander III. "Mine nephew Oliver II is the True King of this land; for Gutenberg Himself has granted him this Holy Blessing."

And with that, the humble Dorj'heptkii called upon a power most Divine. Of all the strange events that occurred during the Second Tungish War, what happened next may be the strangest. For, in an instant, after Dorj'heptkii had muttered to himself and outstretched his hand, the stallion beneath the Manticore buckled and collapsed to the ground, dead. The Royal Defender tumbled into the crowds and was torn apart.

The next site of conflict was, naturally, upon Jacob's Hill. Nine thousand strong remained of the Great Host, and the Hill had fallen under dire siege. The Steward commanded his Royal Armies with stalwart bravery, and along with the higher ground and fortifications they possessed, they effectively slew hundreds of the Great Host's forces, but they still found themselves overwhelmed. The Great Host flooded the gates of the White Keep's outer courtyard and surrounded the castle.

The battle was won—but for one final task. The young king, Ashar I, needed to be captured. Lady Elsa was adamant that he be taken alive so that he could formally abdicate the throne and proclaim his cousin Oliver II as the rightful king.

Alas, it was not to be. For there were other plots at work within the White Keep—plots that had been planted years ago which finally bore their rotten fruit.

When Elsa Pike, Oliver II, Lady Ariana Oxer, and Lord Timothy Tals stepped foot inside the White Keep, the news reached them that the king was already dead. Stricken by this news, Lady Elsa demanded to know who was responsible—and was greeted by the very man. As it turned out, the Keeper of the Keys, Lupin Hylar, had remained loyal to their cause all along. After escorting Elsa Pike, Alexander IV, and the rest of their court out of Arcanan when the city was stormed years ago, he had remained behind and gained the trust of Oliver I—though never quite Grant Leon, not that it mattered in the end. For assurance, he had blackmailed Calvin Dunn with the knowledge that Calvin was not a trueborn son of Brendan Dunn, but a bastard who had lied his way onto the Glorious Council.

And now, Lupin's plots had finally come to fruition, and the rightful king—Oliver II—would be crowned King of the Glorious Realm. For his leal service, all Lupin asked was that he remain as Keeper of the Keys during the "long and fortuitous reign of Oliver II to come." Lady Elsa and her court were astonished by this revelation, and did not entirely know what to do with it. Lupin then explained why he'd had King Ashar murdered. "With the young king dead, the entire line of Alexander III is vanquished, leaving no further rivals to your grandson's rule. It was a dreadful decision to make, to be sure, but a necessary one. Now, Oliver II may reign for years upon years unchallenged, and the True Line of Avery shall prevail."

It was at that moment when Oliver II himself spoke up. "But, grandmother," he said, "our army was eleven-thousand strong. Did we even need this old fool? If he betrayed one king, why not another? I say we slit his throat."

Elsa hushed him and replied, "Lupin Hylar is a great ally to your cause, my sweet grandson, and you should not insult him so. We may have had the strength to assail the city without him, yes, but his deception of our enemies proved to be quite necessary as well." For a great many things were beginning to make sense within her mind—the sending of Grant Leon to Arcanlodge, the resulting death of Oliver I, the change in perception of his rule by the people of Arcanan, the fact that sellswords were in the city's employ, and other machinations that Elsa did not feel the need to explain to her grandson. The king relented, to the great relief of Lupin Hylar.

But there was another matter on the minds of those present—a question spoken by the Iron Maiden this time. "What of the Steward of Arcanan, Grant Leon? Is he dead or is he fled?"

To this, the Keeper responded, "Neither, my Lady. One of my men, Bartolomeu Ze, has him captured in the King's Tower, where the body of King Ashar lies cold."

This was, in fact, true. Up in the highest room of the King's Tower, in the King's Solar, the young king Ashar I still lay in a bath filled with red, where one of Lupin Hylar's conspirators—a handmaiden—had slit his throat while tending to his bathing. It was rumoured that she had serviced the young Ashar I in more ways than one when gaining his trust, so that during the battle she would be given the chance to kill him for "the Good of the Realm"—and a hefty coin purse.

Mere strides from the king's bath, the Steward of Arcanan was held under Bartolomeu Ze's axe, where he remained until Lady Elsa and a retainer of Pike Knights arrived at the scene.

Horrified by the young king's wrinkling corpse, she ordered for it to be taken away—and for the handmaid who had killed him to be silenced. As for Grant Leon, she had him brought to the dungeons of the White Keep, where he would remain in darkness until the day came when he would renounce his allegiance to the line of Alexander III and proclaim that Oliver II was the rightful King of the Glorious Realm. And so it was that the Steward of Arcanan was Steward no longer, and instead became a prisoner of Lady Elsa Pike and her grandson, Oliver II.

Oliver II was thereby crowned King of the Glorious Realm in the spring of 350 AA in a lavish, grand coronation funded by Oxcommon, though the crown was bestowed not by Jaremius Onus Simon, for he was still in hiding following the Battle of Arcanan earlier that year. Instead, a new Archwizard was chosen—a certain Lamentius Septimus Simon, the eldest living son of Pylithos Octavius. And the only Royal Crown that remained in the White Keep happened to be the Crown of Yellow, inlaid with topaz gems of various shapes and sizes, for the Crown of Blue, along with all the others save the Crown of Yellow, were smuggled out from Arcanan during the battle by none other than Rolph Leon, who managed to escape by boat with the fleeing sellswords and find refuge in the Port of the Setting Sun.[13]

And so it was that the Second Tungish War had reached its end, and the Royal Schism was resolved at last with the Line of Alexander extinguished and the Line of Avery victorious. But on the horizon, a third, most dreadful war was nigh.

---

13   While Rolph Leon by all accounts had fled to the Port of the Setting Sun with the intent of selling the Royal Crowns and living the rest of his days in gratuitous wealth, perhaps he had a change of heart, for the Royal Crowns were recovered at the sunset of the reign of Oliver II. But that is a tale to be expanded on later.

The Last Tungish War

(350—353 AA)

COMPILED FROM THE CHRONICLING WORKS OF ARCHWIZARDS JAREMIUS ONUS SIMON AND LAMENTIUS SEPTIMUS SIMON

The day King Oliver Pike, the Second of His Name first sat the Arcane Throne in the 350th Year After-the-Arrival marked the start of a dark era for the Glorious Realm, and one that would not end until Oliver and all his ilk were deposed from rule. But alas, that day would not come for many a year, and the age following his ascension would be wrought with terror and turmoil.

The issue of the missing Crowns did not go unpunished by the new king. When it was brought to his attention by his Archwizard, Lamentius Simon, Oliver II was said to have ordered Warden Vandergriff to "pry the Crowns' whereabouts from anyone who served my mutt uncle." This, the Warden did carry out—some sources claim reluctantly, as Vandergriff did serve the previous king and court faithfully, and was close with many of its lords and ladies. Others maintain that Vandergriff loathed Oliver I and his court of "lackwits and Tungs" more—though these sources were dubious—and are now believed to have been Lady Elsa's spokespeople. Regardless of the

Warden's personal feelings on the matter, Sir Garth Leon—brother to Rolph Leon—Lady Tahmina Biz-Qadri, Lord Stoker Minster, Sir Ethan Trinket, Lady Clair Copperfield, and even Lord Armon Rohe were tortured in the depths of the White Keep's dungeons.

Quite infamously, the Lady Tahmina, who was niece to the current Tung Emperor, not that it mattered much to the king, was given over to the Choking Pear, a device that need not be embellished upon any further in this history except to say that such methods of torture ought never to be utilized by anyone. The Accountant's brother Garth was subjected to the Iron Chair, which did not kill, but bore numerous holes into his body while he could not move. What killed him eventually were the maggots that festered and feasted upon his flesh. Sir Ethan Trinket, Lord Minster, and Lady Copperfield were simply fed to rats.

But the worst came for the Royal Architect, Armon Rohe, who had already suffered much in these dungeons at the behest of Oliver II's father Alexander IV. Sadly, his body gave out when he was subjected to Vandergriff's knee-splitters, and he perished that year in 350. His bones were shipped to Stone Haven, which did little to ease the pain of his people and soothe the hatred that House Rohe held for the Line of Avery.

None of these individuals who were put under the Warden's questioning did reveal where the Crowns were taken, however, for none knew. But Oliver II was ill-inclined toward mercy, and so these nobles remained in the dungeons, though they no longer had to bear torture save for living with the knowledge that they would likely never see the light of day again. Other matters were seen to by the king as well, of course, though the torture of his enemies was doubtless his first priority.

While Oliver II eagerly pestered the Warden for updates on the victims below in the dungeons, his grandmother Elsa got to rule. Assembling the Glorious Council of Oliver II—if it can truly be called Glorious—the following nobles of the Realm were summoned:

Lord Earl Voyant, grandfather to the king, naturally resumed his post as Lord Commander as if no time had passed since the reign of Alexander IV. Lord Timothy Felix, who had contributed a great number to Oliver II's Great Host during the Second Tungish War, was named as Royal Defender. The Archwizard was the aforementioned Lamentius Simon. As the Rohes were in great opposition to Oliver II, the title of Royal Architect went to Lord Goseph Greene, who was famed for some remarkable renovations of Castle Greene back home. The title of Royal Accountant was granted to Sir Clement Oxer, nephew to the Iron Maiden, who, herself, elected to return to Oxcommon following the war. The Royal Admiral was named to be Lord Killian Dunn, who swore fealty to the new king almost immediately following his Royal Coronation. The titles of Warden and Executioner remained with Vandergriff and Bartolomeu Ze respectively, and the title of Keeper of the Keys tentatively remained with Lupin Hylar as well.

The first order of business was the marriage of Oliver II. The king required a suitable spouse so as to "mend the seams that had been tugged at during the Royal Schism and torn during the Second Tungish War"—eloquent words spoken by the Archwizard. The eighteen-year-old Alyssa Leon was posed as an option by Lord Earl, but Lady Elsa thought it would be "ill-advised at worst, and difficult at best." After all, Alyssa's twin brother Samwell, uncle Garth, and father Lord Grant were currently prisoners of the Crown. Not to mention, her other uncle Rolph was believed to have stolen the Royal Crowns. It was a messy situation, to say the least.

Lord Killian Dunn offered the hand of his own daughter Kelta, though the offer was deemed too presumptuous and quickly dismissed by the rest of the council. Lord Timothy posited that they wed Oliver II to Lord Errol Hylar's last remaining daughter, Elanor. This was considered greatly, as the Hylars would be invaluable allies during the years to come, and none suspected that the Lord of Felix's suggestion may have been planted a few days earlier by the Keeper of the Keys.

However, all discussions were silenced when Lady Elsa reminded them that the king's hand had already been offered to the Iron Maiden's grandniece Martha Oxer during the war. Lord Greene balked at this, stating, "The Oxers are already our allies. What would that match gain us? The approval of a wrinkled old maid?"

All present at the council could wholeheartedly agree that the Lord of Greene had overstepped the line of proper courtesy for his remarks about the beloved Iron Maiden; as the bards like to say, "He failed to read the room." The Lady Elsa's mind was made up at that moment, some believe, because afterwards, she dismissed the council and declared that the match between Martha Oxer and Oliver II was final.

The last item discussed during these council meetings held by Lady Elsa was what to do with the captive Lord Commander, Grant Leon. He was a storied and well-beloved knight, and the grandson of the Black Star, a name that had already passed into legend in the minds of the common folk. To take his head would be widely unpopular and forever put a stain upon Oliver II's reign. The council agreed upon his exile, as it seemed the safer option.

"Send him to the Charm," said Lupin Hylar. "Or perhaps the Uncharted North. Better he be slaying Mammuts with that silver sword than directing it toward one of us."

When—a fortnight later—the king himself caught wind of the fact that not only was his grandmother holding council sessions without him present, but also that matters such as his own Royal Wedding were being discussed, he was wroth. Witnesses claim that he slapped his grandmother across the face with such force that she fell and broke a rib. The king then summoned the Glorious Council immediately—though not to discuss matters of the Realm, but rather to dictate them.

Once all were present in the Tower of Trust for a meeting, they were surprised not to see Lady Elsa present at all—but rather, her grandson. It was a short session, by all accounts. By the end, all councillors present were reeling with shock, but too stricken to balk. King Oliver II announced that all of their talk about suitors was "wasted breath"—and that their breath ought not to be something they take for granted—for he was to marry the Princess Sarah, his own sister! In fact, he went on, he had already deflowered her in the King's Tower. In his mind, she was the most beautiful woman alive, and better yet— in honour of all he had been taught in his youth by his grandmother— her bearing his children would best keep the Pike Line pure.

But the king was not finished yet. Next, he announced, "All this deliberation on what to do with a known traitor to the Crown is drivel at worst and treasonous at best!" For he intended to have Lord Grant Leon executed, and that was the end of it. Many Lords of the Council tried to protest once this was said, Lupin Hylar among them, but their protests fell on deaf ears. The king even gave the Keeper of the Keys a malicious smile and said, "You had best keep your tongue tucked behind your teeth, Keeper. For you might be tried next."

By the time Lady Elsa had learnt of her grandson's impromptu meeting—for she was abed recovering from her fall—it was far too late. Helped by four of her handmaidens to walk out from her chambers and into the Inner Courtyard, she nearly fainted once she saw Lord Grant Leon being brought out toward the block. It was pouring heavily that day, as if the skies were dark with rage toward the act of injustice being dealt. But save the former Lord Commander the clouds could not—not for all the bitterness of their rains.

For his last words, Lord Grant requested that he be buried beside his grandfather, the Black Star, who enviably died in battle with one of his greatest foes rather than being "beheaded by a coward's blade."

Furious, Oliver II demanded that Bartolomeu swing the sword. When the deed was done, Lord Grant's body was instead dumped into the Mouth in the same manner as his king, Oliver I.

Oliver II was wed a fortnight afterwards, and his betrothed sister Sarah was made Queen of the Glorious Realm. It is said that she appeared smitten by her brother on their wedding day, and when it came time to seal their bond with a kiss, she leapt toward him lustily. Just as on Lord Grant's execution, it was raining heavily that day, and so the ceremony was conducted inside the Throne Room, followed by a lavish feast in the Great Hall. The wedding was attended by thousands, as was expected of every noble of every House of the Glorious Realm to do—though there were some notable absences, such as the Leons, the Rohes, and most concerningly, the Oxers, for it appeared that the Iron Maiden did not take kindly to being spurned.

During the ceremony and afterwards, there were a great deal of mutterings among the guests, and the word "abomination" was loose upon their lips—for many recalled stories of the reign of David I, who himself was borne of incest, and who heralded one of the worst ages the Glorious Realm had seen in its past. However, as time would prove, many of these guests might have tightened their tongues if they had known what could result from the wrong person catching their words, as the king had many eyes and ears among the ceremonies— and one in particular that proved to be most dangerous.

To further celebrate his union with his sister-wife Sarah Pike, the king hosted the first of many Royal Orgies to come during his reign. He ordered for one of the manors to be repurposed into a pleasure house. This manor was home to Lord Minster, who was languishing in the dungeons under Warden Vandergriff's knives. The king callously declared, "Lord Minster will nary be requiring his holdings any further, for he has a new dwelling much better suited to his lordship." Then, he decreed that any citizens of Arcanan who brought forth their unspoiled, maiden daughters to "Chastity Manor" would be paid a golden crown and given "the blessing of a king's seed"—a chance for their daughters to bear one of the king's bastards.

In an unfortunately dreary portrait of the nature of men's hearts when offered the notion of coin—or the "honour" of having the offspring of a king's loins for a grandchild—the Crown had to begin turning people away by the fifth day following the king's decree, as lining the King's Road all the way up Jacob's Hill were hundreds of impoverished townspeople willing to offer up their daughters for a golden crown. The Royal Accountant, Clement Oxer, had to inform the king that by his calculations, the Crown could not afford to pay such a high price to all these fathers, given the high turnout. The king instead lowered the price to three silvers, but this amendment to his decree did little to slim the crowd, though now, the cost could be afforded.

What followed after need not be given the courtesy of a detailed description, but suffice to say the king deflowered many a maiden that week. Those chosen by the king were washed and bathed by the king's own handmaidens, dressed in fine silks, and brought to Chastity Manor, where the king and his friends at court indulged in all their vices. Lords Timothy Felix and Goseph Green were among those lords present, and even the Archwizard Lamentius was said to have joined the "festivities of the flesh." As for the king's new wife, Queen Sarah, she was known to have condoned these events, and even joined in herself from time to time, according to some. But to call into question the queen's virtue in such a way was a sure-fire way to lose one's tongue, so of this matter, few words were spoken or shared.

What came next was a further undoing of Lady Elsa's hold over the king's new rule. The Glorious Council was summoned following the last of the celebratory Royal Orgies that month—though none, except the Keeper of the Keys, surely, expected the nature of this meeting to be their own review. The king expressed discontent with his grandmother's choices of "cretins and ingratiators" upon the council. Moreover, many of them had revealed themselves—in more ways than one—at Chastity Manor.

Expecting to be dismissed, Lord Timothy Felix and Lord Goseph Greene sank to their knees and groveled before the king for mercy— but it was not them whom the king was displeased with, for he took their presence at his festivities to be a display of loyalty toward his reign—but could not say the same about those absent. Lord Earl Voyant he did not question, for he was of blood with the king; nor did he call into question Archwizard Lamentius, lending further credence to the rumours that the old wizard had frequented Chastity Manor.

But he looked to Clement Oxer and Lupin Hylar. Taken by insult, the Royal Accountant indignantly sputtered and stammered, trying to defend his right to sit the Glorious Council with platitudes and veiled threats invoking the power of his House. The king then questioned why Oxer's own kin had not been present for his Royal Wedding, and why the Accountant himself had attempted to "sabotage the festivities." To this, Clement Oxer had little response, for all knew that the king had greatly upset the Lady of Oxcommon by spurning her grandniece, Martha.

But the king was not interested in excuses, nor really any defence from Lord Clement, for his mind had already been decided. The title of Royal Accountant was thereby passed to one of the king's friends at court, Salem Finch, who had helped finance matters at Chastity Manor, unbeknownst to Clement Oxer.

And next, the king turned to Lupin Hylar, whom he had distrusted ever since arriving in the White Keep at the end of the Second Tungish War. But the Keeper of the Keys was nothing if not prepared for anything, and he was well aware of the king's intentions that day. Bowing graciously and humbly before his liege, he made clear that he understood the king's "misgivings," and that he had been hard at work as Keeper of the Keys the past few weeks gathering valuable information for Oliver II to use against his enemies "current or future; it matters little, for an enemy is an enemy, and they must be dealt with all the same."

The Keeper of the Keys' words intrigued the king, and so he bade him continue. Lupin Hylar then went on to provide a detailed list of every wedding guest who had been overheard making mention of King David I or, worse, muttering the word "abomination" among hushed tones. Nobles even as prominent as those of House Whit were among those listed.

The king was rather impressed, and so forwent his earlier decision to have Lupin Hylar sent to Warden Vandergriff, and instead opted to keep him close by, retaining his position on the Glorious Council as Keeper of the Keys. "I can use a man like you," the king was heard to say. "You possess talents that I value greatly, even though to trust you would be more foolish than to show a pickpocket my coin purse."

To this, the Keeper replied, "Naturally, Your Grace. I would not expect you to trust me. But I promise you, I will not fail you."

And he was true to those words. Later that night, the Keeper of the Keys led Oliver II to his tower, the Keeper's Tower, for he had a thing of wonderful importance to show. Oliver II was not fully convinced by Lupin Hylar's claims—for it was absurd for the Keeper to have heard and recorded every wedding guest who spoke slander. "What man has twenty ears and eyes?"

But alas, it was true. Oliver II—let alone most people of the Realm—knew nothing of the band of secret informants King Oliver I had formed in his day. Nor was it revealed until this time that if the king should fall and none be left alive to fill his seat, the Keeper of the Keys would take charge of the Zehiram until a suitable replacement was found and appointed. This measure was in hopes of keeping the Glorious Realm safe from any successful usurper deemed ill-fit to rule the Realm. The Keeper, as Oliver I had said in secret before, would "have final say as to if the Realm *keeps* its new ruler or *removes* its new ruler." All that power now laid in Lupin Hylar's hands. "At a word, my king, their loyalty shall turn to thee."

Even though this was promised, Lupin still had demands that the king was obliged to follow—or the Zehiram would not be his. He treaded carefully, for he understood that he could very well have found himself deposed by the end of the hour.

What were these demands? None know with certainty, for it was left behind those doors in the shrouded candlelight. Some assume that something as simple as coin was demanded, with rumours claiming it to be as much as thirty thousand golden crowns. While some whisperings of the servants and jesters in the White Keep claimed Lupin had a night with Oliver II, in the king's very own bedchambers, no less, many accounts claim that it was at the king's command and not Lupin's, so their exchange may have been unrelated to this transfer of power. Needless to say, King Oliver II remained the ruler of the Glorious Realm—and for a long time at that—so it can be safely stated that he obliged the Keeper's requests. Oliver II did use the Zehiram quite often to upturn any inconvenience that was placed before him and his rule.

In fact, almost immediately after learning of and gaining the Zehiram for himself, Oliver II devised a way to begin his "cleansing of the city." While the streets still festered with thieves, undesirables, and filth, Tungish nobility and members of the Royal Family continued life comfortably in their mansions given to them so many decades prior.

On a midsummer's morn, an hour before the sun's arrival, smoke rose from the Nobles' Quarters. Nine mansions, some dating back to 110, went ablaze with roaring flames. These nine mansions, naturally, were the homes of all Tungish nobility and royalty in Arcanan, and before the sun could see it done, nine great piles of ash and stone remained.

For some, a tragedy had taken place, and thoughts of arson were raised under hushed tones. Sadly, for the majority of Arcanians, it was a day of jubilee and celebration. "Their bodies lay as glass," King Oliver II began, "and their scent and stain have joined with the flame. The flames took them; let it take them all!"

That massacre ordered by Oliver II was known as the Morning Rinse—and executed by the Zehiram, no less.

To solidify the king's delight, a Royal Feast for all nobles in and around Arcanan to attend was held a week later in the White Keep. Naturally, they discussed what had transpired in the Nobles' Quarters, with some speaking of the great blessing it had been and a few speaking of it as a tragedy. When a noble spoke ill of that fiery event in the dining hall, that noble's name was added to the Royal List, written in ink by Lupin Hylar's hand. In short, those particular nobles were never seen or heard of again, but became well acquainted with Warden Vandergriff.

And now, we turn our tale over to the West Church of Gutenberg, which in the year 350 was undergoing a crisis of faith—a schism that split the clergy down the middle. There were many who dissented against Oliver II now that he had shown his true colours, saying that he was "a godless man," what with his Royal Orgies and worse, his incestuous marriage. Outspoken Brothers and Sisters of Gutenberg condemned these actions, grappling with the fact that they had so believed Oliver II to be "Gutenberg's chosen" during the Second Tungish War.

However, there were those who remained faithful despite these new tidings, and maintained that Oliver II was an "anointed, blessed monarch" who was simply enacting "Gutenberg's Will" upon the Realm. The most fervent of these was Dorj'heptkii, who adamantly preached the virtue and piety of Oliver II *and* the queen, and would not hear any contradictions. The matter of this particular Brother's heritage was raised as an issue by others of the Faith, but Dorj'heptkii dismissed them outright, claiming, "That name means naught to me, for when I became Dorj'heptkii, 'Murth Pike' perished. No, I do not support our king because he was once my kin; I support him now because he is *righteous*. To question his reign is to question Gutenberg's own Plan for this Realm! And to question our Gracious God is to commit the highest of treasons!"

Meanwhile, following the tragic fire in the Nobles' Quarters, Oliver II got straight to work with his Council, stripping the Realm of any vestiges of Tungish influence. The Tungish tongue was thereby banned from speech and script across the Glorious Realm. Tungish music, folktales, fabrics, linens, foods, and even phrases were prohibited upon punishment of fine or flogging. However, it is worth mentioning that slanderous names for Tungish people or their culture were still allowed—and even encouraged—by Oliver II and his government. In two short years, by the end of 351, Oliver II had nearly undone all of Grant I, Jacob II, and even Oliver I's legacies, all but removing any traces of "Tungish-ness" from the land.

But, as the bards are wont to sing, "What one reaps is what one sows." And the time for sowing was long nigh for Oliver the Spurner. The Tungish Emperor, Rahim Biz-Qadri, had learnt of the imprisonment of his daughter Tahmina, and also of the fire that had mysteriously scorched all of his friends, extended family, and political allies residing in Arcanan. The nearly eighty-year-long friendship between the Glorious Realm and Tung Empire had literally, one might say, gone up in flames.

And, to Emperor Rahim, this meant war.

By the summer of 351, Samiz Bizbee had mustered an army of battle-ready Tung-Junud warriors from the far reaches of the Empire: Alrahmah, spear-knights from the Lorath Hills, joined forces with Alqahmahr, moon-sons from Biz Shalom, and Muharibh Dahr, armoured sentinels from Tung Tameel as well. Under the command of Junud-Jiniral Akil Althæbinh—General Snake-eater—from Samiz Bizbee, an army upwards of forty thousand was assembled, poised to set sail southward across the Pocket.

News of this great muster reached King Oliver II's royal ear not a day too late. Lupin Hylar's informants had spied the sails of warships in the Baharon Sea and the Pocket, transporting warriors from Biz Shalom to Samiz Bizbee, and quickly understood what was happening. The Rygars were informed as well, and Lord Raymond Rygar prepared the Port of Rygar for a potential northern invasion. A thousand Phoenix Knights were created by the Rygarian Pyromancers, and a legion of Warflames—war-pyromancers—were marched to the coast to defend the Rygar Province.

By the king's decree, the Rygars were to be the "first line of defence" for the Glorious Realm, and that to "spare all Glorious Peoples from being butchered, burnt, and defiled" by the Tungish "savages," they must stop Jiniral Akil's forces at the Rygarian Peninsula and prevent their marching further south into the Arcane Province and beyond. To ensure Lord Raymond's loyalty—as, naturally, it was subject to doubt, given the history between the Crown and the Phoenix—Oliver II declared that a Rygar would be named to the Glorious Council if the Tungs were successfully repelled.

Satisfied with this call to aid, and confident that Lord Raymond would answer to the Crown and protect the Realm, Oliver II sat back on the Arcane Throne and waited for the invaders to be crushed.

By the autumn of 351, scores of massive Tungish warships, their black-and-gold sails bearing the sapphire-eyed sphinx of the Empire, crossed the Pocket to land at the Port of Rygar. In what was called the Battle of the Bloody Bay, thousands of Tung-Junud spilled into the bay, cutting down Warflames and Fyreborne knights in the Port and clearing a path for the rest of their Host.

The Phoenix Knights, however, proved to be a more trouble-some opponent to the armies of Jiniral Akil—for when his Alrahmah stuck them with their barbed spears; when the Alqahmahr decapitated them with their scimitars; when the Muharibh Dahr crushed them with their hammers, the Phoenix Knights simply rose again, eyes blazing like fiery red furnaces and grey dead hands grasping their greatswords.

But despite all this, the Tung-Junud broke through the Rygarian defences, raided the Darkstone, Glass, and Redfyre districts, marched through Redmayne's Wall, and braved the Scorchlands to leave the Rygars' territory and reach the golden vales of the Arcane Province.

This was the tale that reached Oliver II and his council in Arcanan. However, as scholars from the College have uncovered in years past, this was far from the truth.

When Lord Raymond read the king's offer, it is said that he "laughed long and heartily" before tossing it to the flames. For the Tungish Emperor and the Lord of Rygar were fast friends, and had been for years. In fact, the history of the Houses of Biz-Qadri and

Rygar had been irrevocably linked since Raymond's ancestor Lord Redfyre had first allied himself with the Tung Empire for trade and commerce at the dawn of the Glorious Realm. Perhaps if Oliver II had cared more to research the possible ties between the Rygar Province and Samiz Bizbee, he would have smelled this treachery from miles away, but alas, the king was quick to act and slow to ponder.

The Battle of the Bloody Bay was, by all accounts, a sham. There was no blood spilt in that bay, nor a battle to be held. The Rygars were well aware of the Emperor's intent to invade the Realm, and Lord Raymond was obliged to let them. For generations, the Rygars had been spurned by House Pike and the rest of the Realm; in fact, ever since Lord Redfyre's secession from the rule of Arcanan in 50 AA, the Rygars had been villainized and detested by the south. Even when the Rygars made an attempt to mend their differences diplomatically with the marriage of Lord Rand Rygar to Princess Jenna Pike during the reign of Alexander I—from the Rygarian perspective at least—the fallout was a brash reminder of the hostility their House still faced.

So, when the Tung Emperor decided to invade the Realm in 350, the Rygars felt no sympathy for the Crown. Jiniral Akil was welcomed with open arms into the Port of Rygar, allowed to dock his fleet of ships in the harbour, and the Tung-Junud were escorted through Lord Raymond's lands, offered spiced wine, blackened meats, and cinderweed to smoke, and lodged in fine camps with silken beds. Those in command of the Tung-Junud legions were draped in robes of Amber, denoting that they were Friends of Fyre, and their warriors were given searing oils and darkglass weaponry to aid them in their conquest of vengeance. Then, they were led through Redmayne's Wall in an orderly procession and guided by the Parched through the deadly Scorchlands so that the terrain would not thin their numbers.

The Tung-Junud then advanced upon Tal Taro.

Now, the people of Tal Taro were, by the year 351 AA, no strangers to invasion. They had seen their city sacked, scorched, assailed, and divided by war and strife countless times, such that the very culture of the place had developed a sort of mad stoicism, maintaining that "our city may burn again, but tears will not rebuild our homes, only hard work shall." The city had become heavily segregated into peoples based on their heritages and origins, as well as by their allegiances and faiths. There were the Alder Guardians: those who worshiped the Great Alderhand tree of stone that looms over the city's central district. There were the Solaram: Paladins of an ancient Holy Order in service to their goddess, Eglaine the Innocent. There were the Rygarin, a faction of Rygar sympathizers who were devoted to turning Tal Taro over to vassaldom of Lord Raymond and House Rygar. And, to a lesser extent, there were the Angaeli, an order of Elden Elves who had emigrated to Tal Taro and brought their strange fey customs with them; there were the Limbs of the Lake, followers of the Lake-Goddess Moorema, who is heavily worshiped by druids around the Lake of Moor'lu, and even by Feldin-folk; and there were the Grime of Gron, a militantly anti-Rygar faction that congregated primarily in the seedy underbelly of the city.

Further details aside, these factions could never agree with one another, so when the time of invasion was nigh, suffice to say that Tal Taro fell swiftly. By the end of the year 351, Lord Tylar Tals was captured by Jiniral Akil and tossed into a pit of vipers, where he slowly died from poison over four long days. Tal Taro had become the new military hub of the Tung-Junud, and from there, their supply lines would stretch across the Arcane Province to the south to strengthen and bolster the invading Host.

And in Arcanan, the new year of 352 saw the old Dowager Queen Elsa attempt to wrest power from her grandson once again. Increasingly concerned with the king's volatility, as well as his unrestrained hatred for all things Tungish, Elsa and her brother the Lord Commander Earl forged a pact to reign in Oliver II's excesses and restore a semblance of order to the Glorious Realm. On a cold winter's day, she assembled a loyal order of personal Voyant sentries called the Starsworn and marched up the steps of the throne room to confront her "misguided grandson." The king was amused by this, it is said, and allowed his grandmother to shout demands for the greater part of an hour. But when she was done—or, perhaps, when the king had heard enough—he nodded to the Keeper of the Keys.

With a simple gesture, Lupin Hylar ordered the Zehiram to dispose of the Dowager Queen's men. Their starry cloaks were steeped in dark blood by the end, with the fletchings of arrows protruding out their armoured bodies. The Lady Elsa herself was captured and taken to her chambers, where she was put under house-arrest. There she sat, terrified, praying to Gutenberg for her grandson's heart to soften and mercy to grace his lips.

It was not until the next morning that the king arrived, dressed in plain clothes and bereft of his crown. "Grandmother, forgive me, for I have been dishonest," he began—so says Lord Goseph Greene, who was standing vigil by Lady Elsa's door. "If there was any confusion as to my feelings toward you, I apologize."

At that, Lady Elsa breathed a sigh of deep relief.

But then, the king kept speaking. "I have known since before I took to the Arcane Throne that you have sought to undermine me and direct my council as you see fit. You wish to be Queen of the Glorious Realm in all but name, and you wish that I had married some Oxer wench rather than my own beautiful sister. You wish that I had not been so harsh toward our enemies, and not dismissed your lackeys from my court. Alas, grandmother, here you are now, powerless, and kept alive only by mine own courtesies. But as of yesterday, I now see that it was not enough. You still vie for my crown, and still wish to control me like you did my father. For this—I say with deep regret—I cannot stand."

The king then called for Lord Goseph Greene and ordered him to fling Lady Elsa from her solar's window. The Royal Architect carried out the king's command without question. And so it was that in the year 352, the Lady Elsa Pike, formerly of House Voyant, husband to Jared, son of Avery, mother to Alexander IV, and grandmother to Oliver II, was defenestrated from the King's Tower of the White Keep.

And, to the north, the Tung-Junud advanced upon Feldin.

Upon hearing this news, Lord Timothy Felix asked the king for leave to return to Feldin and lead the defence of his Ancestral Seat against the invading Tungs. King Oliver II was not inclined to grant his Defender this "privilege," for, in the king's words, "You have duties *here*, good Lord Timothy. Do you mean to forsake them?"

At this, the Royal Defender grew quite wroth. "I will not abandon my kin and subjects in the east!" Lord Timothy declared. "If I must choose between my seat on your Council or the safeguarding of my own people, then I choose the latter. Good day, my liege." And with that, he removed the Defender's pin and left it on the king's desk.

Oliver II was called the Spurner, though it was not often that the king himself was spurned. This set the king into a terrible mood—one that was not quenched until he spent three days and four nights in Chastity Manor indulging in carnal delights. It is said that he let out his rage upon the Ladies of the Manor, and many returned home to their fathers with bleeding gashes upon their backs and blackened eyes. For the first time in his reign, the king began to cultivate a reputation that was violent as well as lecherous.

And, as for the matter of Royal Defender, the king led an inquiry into the state of politics in Feldin with the aid of Keeper Lupin and the Zehiram. Out of five major Houses and thirty-seven minor Houses that served as vassals or subjects to House Felix, the most hated and derided were the Kites. Their banners were a plain green and blue chequy pattern with no other remarkable qualities—reflective of their relative prestige as a House. To enact a sort of petty revenge upon the Lord of Feldin, King Oliver II chose Sir Pippin Kite, called Pippin the Pauper, to serve as Royal Defender of the Glorious Realm in Lord Timothy Felix's stead. The Kites had never expected to gain such a prestigious appointment—and nor should they have—and so when Sir Pippin rode to Arcanan on his mule, he was quite shocked to see that his choosing was, indeed, for real and not a jest, as his good lady wife Wanda did assert.

But Oliver II's problems at Court were not over yet. After the burial of his dear grandmother Elsa the Dowager Queen, the king did not evade questioning by his Lord Commander and his great uncle, Lord Earl Voyant, for Lord Earl did strongly believe that the king had a hand in his own grandmother's demise; in fact, he was sure of it. Knowing that such a matter could not be brought to the king directly, he instead met with potential allies within the Court at various places around the city. The Windmaker's Inn was a common spot, what with its usual din of drunkards and off-key bards. The College of Sorcery's campus was another such location wherein the Lord Commander would hold meetings—but when he caught wind of the Keeper's intention to follow his whereabouts with the Zehiram, he instead moved his meetings to the region of the city where the light rarely touched: the north.

There, many crime lords and bandits squatted in abandoned shops and houses, plotting their next schemes, as did the Lord Commander when he arrived in the Kneebreaker's Pub. Meeting with various nobles from King Oliver II's court, including—according to some sources—Killian Dunn and Clement Oxer, they discussed a plan to convince the Court, the College, and the Church of the truth behind Elsa's death. They all named more potential allies within the Court who could band together to prosecute the king for his crimes and convince others that they had been committed.

They next went forth to the College of Sorcery and revealed the plot to the Collegiate—barring Archwizard Lamentius, who Lord Earl knew was the king's creature. Many wizards of the Collegiate heard their tale and believed it, with all who were privy to the words promising to keep their lips sealed before the Archwizard and anyone else who was not already in the know.

And lastly, they paid a visit to the Church of Gutenberg, well aware that many in the Faith had their doubts about the king's

Holiness—the High Elder among them. However, when Lord Earl and his allies passed beyond the threshold of the Church, there was a *new* High Elder among them.[14] Shaikaro'halo'gartoil had passed away at last, and in his place, the penitent Dorj'heptkii was named as his successor.

When the new High Elder learnt of the Lord Commander's reason for visiting, he ordered the Faith to bar the exits to the Church. With Gutenberg as witness, High Elder Dorj'heptkii declared Lord Earl Voyant, Lord Killian Dunn, Sir Clement Oxer, and the others present "blasphemers and traitors." The Royal Defender—the newly appointed Pippin Kite—was thereby summoned, along with the City Guard, and the Lord Commander and his companions were seized and apprehended. They soon found themselves in the White Keep's Throne Room, brought before the steps of the Arcane Throne upon which Oliver II sat in judgement.

"You meant to overthrow me and supplant my reign with that of House Voyant's, my uncle Murth the Monk does tell me," said the king. "This is a treasonous act, and all laws and precedents demand that I sentence you all to death for such a crime. But I have chosen on this day to be merciful. We have a war to fight; the Tungs are at our doorstep." For Feldin had fallen under siege a day prior to these events.

"Therefore, I sentence you, Lord Earl Voyant, to exile from Arcanan until the Tungish Dogs are defeated and pushed back to their Empire of Sand." The king then turned to the others present. "However, for Lord Killian Dunn, I am disappointed by this act. At present, I do not require the Royal Fleet, nor *you* for that matter. To honour my good uncle Murth the Monk, who informed me of your

---

14   This was, at some point, an inevitability; for in the year 352, the High
      Elder Shaikaro'halo'gartoil was eighty-five years old. Few men other
      than those of House Simon lived beyond such an age, but for him to
      pass with such poor timing as this was quite unfortunate indeed.

treason, I hereby sentence you to a life of penitence. You shall give up your lands, your titles, and your name, and shall be reborn anew under the light of Gutenberg."

The king was reading off a piece of parchment supplied to him by his uncle Dorj'heptkii during this time. It is said that Lord Killian fell prostrate before the throne and pleaded for death rather than such a fate, but his request was denied by Oliver II.[15] And so it was that Lord Killian Dunn was a Royal Admiral no more—neither was he a lord, nor a Dunn for that matter. From then on, he became known as Lobath'kar'soo, and he served the Church of Gutenberg for the rest of his life of one year and a day. Taking his place as Royal Admiral was his younger brother Drayton Dunn, who had been eager to supplant his elder brother as Lord of Dunnland and Royal Admiral for many years, and finally had his wish granted by the king.

And lastly, the king dealt with Clement Oxer and the rest of the traitors present. Suffice to say, they all hanged.

The next day, Lord Commander Earl Voyant left Arcanan to ride for Feldin with five legions of the Royal Armies. He was not meant to return—nor did he.

The siege of Feldin raged on for the greater part of a year. Jiniral Akil and his Tung-Junud were fearsome warriors, and they tore through two legions of the Royal Armies over the course of 352. Reinforcements were needed, and so Lord Commander Earl Voyant called to Oxcommon for aid, but the Oxers did not answer. It was well known by this point that the Iron Maiden of House Oxer held Oliver II and his reign in deep contempt, what with the reneging of his agreement to wed her grandniece Martha and the more recent execution of her nephew Clement for supposed treason. The Iron

---

15   It should be noted that it was not the shedding of lands, titles, or his Dunnish name that were of primary concern to Lord Killian, but rather the Vow of Celibacy all Brothers of Gutenberg were expected to swear.

Maiden had an iron resolve and would not support the king's defence of Feldin. "Let the city burn," she was heard to say by the Court of Oxcommon, "and let Arcanan follow, for all I care."

Despite all Oliver II had done to antagonize the Oxers of Oxcommon during his reign thus far, it is said that he was "shocked beyond reprieve" when he learnt of the Iron Maiden's refusal to aid. "Who does this wrinkled wench think she is?" said the king. "There ought to be a *Lord* of Oxcommon by now, not this loathsome hag."

And then, the king had an idea. He sent for Keeper Lupin Hylar. "My loyal Keeper of the Keys, this Iron Maiden has been a thorn in my toe for long enough. Why has not her nephew Sir Orion called for a change in leadership? Surely he has the birthright to inherit the Prairieland Province, as his father Andrus died years ago?"

Lupin Hylar was well appraised. "My liege, while it is true that Sir Orion is entitled to such a right, he has chosen a life of knighthood instead. He, and many others of that province, it is known, believe the Iron Maiden to be a very capable leader, and few wish to see her reign ended."

At this, the king was quite frustrated. "Is there any way we might convince Sir Orion to... perhaps... embrace his birthright?"

The Keeper sighed. "Alas not, for when you spurned the hand of his daughter Martha, his support for his aunt increased tenfold. He would not be so inclined to side with us on this matter, I am afraid. But... there is another yet." The king was intrigued. "The third son of Andrus Oxer, Abus. He long has desired the throne of Oxcommon, or so I'm told. While his brother is content to remain a sir, I do believe Abus would be quite accepting of *lord*."

This pleased Oliver II. "Send forth the Zehiram at once, and make it so."

While the Zehiram got to work, the new High Elder had been at work in his sanctuary, praying and fasting and meditating for great lengths of time in solitude. Then, without consulting the other members of the Brotherhood, Dorj'heptkii called for a Gathering of the Faithful. There, under the light of the noon sun, he declared these words to the masses: "The Words of the great and ever-watching Gutenberg have come to both mine mind and mine soul. There are great things to be had, for wonderful are the things I know now because of Gutenburg's Grace. And through that Grace, and through much fasting and praying and supplication to the highest order, the desires and needs of our god have been manifested to me. I, Dorj'heptkii, High Elder of the Church of Gutenberg in Arcanan, do declare happy tidings to you all, for a new truth and order shall be proclaimed by mine holy lips on this spot at the coming of the year's end—it being the three-hundredth and fifty-second year After-the-Arrival. Let Gutenberg see you to your rest." With that, the High Elder turned on the spot and walked back to his sanctuary, avoiding any and all members of the Brotherhood.

And in the autumn of that year, whilst the king plotted to overthrow the Iron Maiden and the Tung-Junud clashed with the Royal Armies at Feldin, a new threat emerged on the horizon. The former Archwizard Jaremius Onus Simon returned at last—and he was not alone. Marching on Arcanan armed with sword and staff, Jaremius and five hundred mages of the College and beyond meant to strike back against King Oliver II and depose him from rule. They held banners among their Host bearing the red eight-sided ruby of House Simon, the bejeweled blue banners of the College of Sorcery, and the quartered banners of Oliver I.[16]

When the Royal Defender Pippin Kite spied this Host marching on Arcanan's west gates, he immediately sent a messenger up Jacob's Hill to inform the king. Reportedly, the king's response to Lord

---

16 The standard used by Oliver I and his son Ashar I was the following: two parts the standard of the Tung Empire and two parts the modified Pike standard—the Crown of Blue overlaid upon black and purple vertical stripes.

Pippin was, "Well, you know what to do. You are the Royal Defender, are you not? Defend!"

However, Lord Pippin lacked both the confidence and the experience to repel such a force. Knowing that the king would be of no further assistance, he sent another messenger, this time to the College of Sorcery, where Archwizard Lamentius and his Collegiate resided. When the Archwizard received the Royal Defender's message, it is said he stroked his great white beard and pondered. "What might Jaremius' aim be, I wonder? The kings whose standard he waves both lie dead and buried, and the College is mine to control." But, coming to a sudden revelation, perhaps, he stood up and sent the messenger back to the walls. "Tell the Royal Defender that the Collegiate and all the students of third-year or older will be brought to the city's defence." The messenger swiftly returned to Lord Pippin, just as the western gates were brought down by a great barrage of winds.

But alas, once Jaremius and his army passed the threshold of the city, they came face to face with Lamentius and his own army of mages. The two Archwizards—one former and one current—hailed each other. "Cousin," said Lamentius with a great smile and opened arms, "you have come home at last! Have you come to bend the knee to the rightful king? Or perhaps for another purpose?"

Jaremius stood tall and proud, and responded, "Thou knowest very well for what purpose I have ventured here with mine throng of five hundred mages, dear cousin. The Age of the Pikes has ended, though thy king be too blind to see it. The Sun of his Royal Line has set! The Royal Family is that of the Empire, now. The Emperor of Tung has every right to invade these lands and place his own son upon the Arcane Throne, for his kin and the line of Alexander III were bound by marriage many times over the generations. But I have not only come for this purpose, cousin. No, I also mean to retake that which is mine right: the College that with your very presence you defile. Now, step aside, and surrender this city."

Naturally, the Archwizard Lamentius did not surrender. The battle that took place between the mage armies was a sight to behold. Thousands of spectral arrows rained down terror upon each side. Fires wreathed and slithered around the marketplace, devouring all they touched in a blaze. The ground opened up betwixt the armies and swallowed many in a deep crevasse. The very weather in Arcanan was changed; a great storm raged above, with lightning and thunder called down by the mages to strike and deafen their foes.

Many mages died that day, young and old. Of the students that Lamentius had conscripted to aid the defence of the city and King Oliver II, over two-thirds perished by the spells of Jaremius and his forces. Neither could the City Guard of Pippin Kite repel them, as sword and spear were poor matches for staff and spell. Lord Pippin himself stayed behind and merely watched the battle unfold from the safety of a watchtower.

Lamentius' forces routed up Jacob's Hill. Jaremius and the two-hundred mages that remained to fight for his cause pursued their foes all the way to the gates of the White Keep, but it was there where they fell victim to Lamentius' contingency plan. While they readied their spells to crush Lamentius and his remaining supporters once and for all, storm the White Keep, and depose Oliver II from rule, they became aware of a great stirring from within the Royal Wood. Holding their position, they bore witness to the march of the trees, for the Archwizard had arranged for the Collegiate to cast a powerful enchantment upon the Royal Wood, causing the hundreds of old oaks within to *come alive*. The trees lumbered forward, and neither spell nor sword could damage them. The only answer was to set them all ablaze, but Jaremius was hesitant to burn the ancestral wood of Arcanan.

His hesitation meant his defeat. His army of mages was scattered and put to rout, and while Jaremius himself attempted to regain control of his forces, the deed was already done. Lamentius Septimus Simon stepped forth, and from his staff, he cast a spell to bind Jaremius where he stood. Unable to move a muscle, Jaremius could not even curse his cousin's name.

And so it was that by the end of the Great Storm of 352, Jaremius Onus Simon was taken as prisoner to King Oliver II, his fate to be left in that king's hands.

As the first snows of 352 began to fall, Lupin Hylar reached Oxcommon and rode into Horn Hall. His only retinue was a smattering of unarmed servants carrying the king's banners. The Iron Maiden begrudgingly let the Keeper of the Keys remain as a guest, but she made it immediately clear that his welcome would not last. Lupin bowed low before the Lady of Oxcommon and explained that he was there strictly for the King's Business, and would not remain overlong.

Lady Ariana was already aware of his aims. "If you mean to barter with me for my support at Feldin, you are sadly mistaken. I do not mean to sacrifice my men for your Spurner King. He has been the bane of House Oxer ever since he sat his spoiled rump upon that throne!"

The Keeper merely smiled politely. "Naturally, my lady. I have come as an envoy to offer the king's sincere apologies for the way he has treated your House. The death of Sir Clement was… regrettable, but alas, he was a traitor, after all. But the king's reneging on his planned engagement with the fair lady Martha is inexcusable, and he does apologize most sincerely. Now, if you will grant me leave, it has been a long journey, and I would much like to rest my weary bones." The Iron Maiden waved him away, visibly irritated by his presence.

And that night, the servants paid a visit to her nephew, Abus Oxer. The third son of the late Lord Andrus was asleep in his chambers when several dark figures surrounded his bed. Before he could alert the guards, Lupin Hylar emerged through the doorway and calmed him. "Ah, Abus, I have heard so much about you. The king knows of your valour, your acumen, and your… ambition. In fact, he has great plans for you. This is the reason I have come to your home. It is the king's will that you achieve your deepest ambition; all it will take is for you to convince your aunt of something for me. Can you accomplish this small task? If so, the lordship of Oxcommon and all the Prairieland Province will be yours."

Abus was perplexed. "But... how can that be so? My aunt Ariana is in charge of these lands; she has been for years! And even if she weren't, the succession would pass to my elder brother Orion, not to me. How might the king bypass the laws and conventions of succession to make *me* lord?"

Lupin stifled a laugh. "Abus, Oliver is the *king*. The one who he *decides* shall be lord shall be lord. The power of lords and ladies—even as one as storied as the Iron Maiden—is nothing before the power of kings. Do this: tell your aunt that you do not trust me, and that you wish to speak with her alone, somewhere secluded—the best place will be up to your discretion, as you know these grounds better than I or my servants—in regards to what shall be done with me. Then, all you need do is tell me the where and when, and the deed shall be done."

Abus' eyes widened. "You mean... you mean to *murder* her! But she is an old woman! Is this truly the king's will?"

Lupin replied, "The king divulged to me alone that he has grown weary with the Lady of Oxcommon and is in need of one perhaps more *loyal* to the Crown. The Realm is at war, and division amongst the Great Houses and the Crown only aids our enemies in their conquest of our lands. If you are lord, you shall owe the king a debt of service and gratitude. I presume you understand my meaning?"

Abus Oxer did.

The next morning, the people of Oxcommon awoke to the ringing of bells. Tragically, the Iron Maiden of Oxer, Lady Ariana, had passed away at the ripe old age of seventy-two. The people were told that she had been on an early morning stroll through the Water Gardens when she collapsed, clutching her heart. However, as this was not seen by any of her household guard, nor any servants of Horn Hall, this tale was doubtful to many. Yet still, the announcement was made by none other than the new Lord of the Prairielands, Abus Oxer, and his word was backed by the Keeper of the Keys—implying the king's support—so any who doubted the veracity of this claim wisely held their tongue. That is, any other than Sir Orion Oxer.

Sir Orion was off in Wolfdale, about to join a Hunt, when he heard the news of his beloved aunt's passing. He rode for Oxcommon so rigorously that his horse buckled and collapsed by the time he arrived. There was a vicious downpour of rain that day when he strode angrily into Horn Hall to set eyes upon his brother, who had usurped his throne. "What is this farce?" he shouted with a bull's fury in his eyes. "I leave for a mere fortnight, only to learn that our Lady has died, and you, the *youngest* son of our father, has taken up her throne? What of birthright? What of succession? What of *law*?"

Keeper Lupin, who sat beside Lord Abus surrounded by a dozen disguised Zehiram, replied, "Sir Orion, what you see before you now is the king's will. Oliver II himself has instructed me that he has chosen your brother Abus to rule the Prairielands. Now, bend the knee to your new Lord, and let this matter be put to rest."

Sir Orion instead spat upon the ground. "I will do no such thing. How convenient for the king to have chosen my brother as the successor and for you to have arrived in this city mere days before the Lady Ariana met her end. What was the tale I heard—she passed of an ailing heart? I knew my aunt well, and she was still spry and good of health, despite her age. No such ailments plagued her. I see through your schemes, Keeper. And I will not bend the knee."

Lord Abus then stood up indignantly from his throne. "Watch your tongue, brother, for the words you speak could be seen as High Treason! I may be your kin, but I am also now your lord, and above all, I have the King's Royal Blessing! Please, I implore you, bend the knee and speak no further of these mistruths."

Sir Orion instead unsheathed his blade. "Step down from that throne, brother. It does not belong to you. The Spurner King has meddled in the affairs of our House long enough. He will not overturn the natural order to suit his aims—not as long as I live!"

But alas, Sir Orion did not live much longer, as it were. For the second he stepped a foot toward Lord Abus, the Zehiram fell upon him with their concealed knives. Abus Oxer watched as his brother Orion was stabbed seventy-two times.

After Orion's body was dragged across the polished marble floors of Horn Hall and out of sight, Keeper Lupin turned to Lord Abus with a forlorn look. "Alas, my lord, there was nothing else that could be done. For he was a traitor."

In the following weeks, there was a great muster in the Prairielands. A Host of seventeen hundred was assembled in Oxcommon, bringing knights and men-at-arms from Wolfdale, Stockworth, Farcross, Hornsby, Aurochs, Argost, and Fort Gryphon. Staying true to his word, Lord Abus Oxer sent forth this army to march north and aid Lord Earl Voyant and Lord Timothy Felix in their defence of Feldin.

Meanwhile, the former Archwizard Jaremius Simon was languishing in the dungeons of the White Keep. Warden Vandergriff, it is said, was a unique sort of warden in the way that he had become quite averse to torture, and saw the dungeons better utilized as a means of isolation from the outside world. This view was, however, not shared by Lamentius Simon. The Archwizard demanded no less than retribution for the death of his father Pylithos, whom Jaremius had killed back during the Storming of Arcanan in 343. Eager to see his cousin punished corporally, he requested to the king that Warden Vandergriff be dismissed, and that instead, Jaremius be imprisoned under the College of Sorcery's jurisdiction.

The king swiftly denied this motion. "You wish to sidestep the Crown's own laws for the sake of petty revenge? You presume too much, Archwizard. For simply asking such a thing, I hereby declare that you shall never see your cousin again, and will be given no further updates on his condition. Now, begone!"

Angered by this rejection, Archwizard Lamentius returned to the College, where he remained for months, though he did not give up on his revenge. For the Archwizard, during his long life, had delved deep into research bordering on Occult... and now, an opportunity had arisen to put some of his theory into practice. In particular, Lamentius held an interest in the School of Enchantment, a school wherein many of its spells are of dubious moral character if wielded with intent to manipulate. And so Lamentius worked on a complicated incantation that, when spoken, would place a victim under his complete control.

And while Lamentius pored over old manuscripts and scrolls in the depths of the College, the year's end arrived at last. True to his word, the High Elder of the Church of Gutenberg, Dorj'heptkii, emerged from solitude to speak once again before the masses of Arcanan. The Time of Revelation had come. Standing on a white dais wreathed by daisies, he held his Holy Scepter high above his head and spake thusly:

"My loyal flock, your time of patience shall now be rewarded, for the Great Truth spoken in mine ear earlier this year shall now be revealed unto you all! Our god, Gutenberg, in His wise judgment, has spoken. Yes, he has spoken to me! It is His wish that a new Order be founded here in the City of Arcanan, and that it be named the Order of Holy Clerics of the White Daisy! It shall be known as an anointed band of men and women alike, who shall heal the sick and infirm within this city and without, in Gutenberg's name and honour, and as well defend the lives of all people Holy and Faithful. Unto each who devotes their life to this new Order, a Holy Mace shall be bestowed, and they shall be clad in mail of chain and Holy Robes that announce their allegiance to all who lay eyes upon them. This is the will of our god, and this is the action that our Church, under my supervision, will see realized upon this new year's beginning. Thank you all, and let Gutenberg see you to your rest!"

The Holy Clerics of the White Daisy did indeed form over the coming months, with nearly seven hundred Faithful from Arcanan alone pledging their lives to the Church. Each and every man or woman was thereby anointed by the High Elder, and, true to his word, granted mace and cloak. This did not concern Oliver II, however, as he was well aware that as long as his uncle remained as High Elder, this Order would be the Crown's to command, and as for the day that Dorj'heptkii might perish, the king had plans as well—discussed prudently with the Keeper of the Keys, who had become his most valuable ally in the years past.

And at last, in the early months of 353, the Great Host of the Prairielands reached Feldin. A truly legendary battle was waged beyond the walls of Feldin between the fearless Tung-Junud and the combined hosts of Felix, Oxer, and the Royal Armies. It became known as the Battle for the Sun, for it was believed that the fate of the Glorious Realm hung in the balance; if the defending armies should lose, the Tung Empire would be freed to march upon Arcanan and install an Imperial monarch upon the throne.

The Tung-Junud had long besieged Feldin, and if not for the arrival of Lord Abus' host, they likely would have taken the Lakelands by winter's end. Jiniral Akil's forces still numbered over thirty thousand strong, with reinforcements ready in Tal Taro to march for aid if the need arose, however, the combined hosts of House Felix, House Oxer, and the Crown were now twenty-two thousand. Though the numbers alone did not make the difference, the freshness of the Prairieland Host did; for the Tungish armies had long been at war, and many of their soldiers had become weary.

The battle was decisive; Lord Abus' Host smashed the Tungish forces, and in turn, reignited the will to fight in the Hosts of Felix and the Crown. However, Lord Earl Voyant did not survive the battle, though whether he was slain by the sword of his foes or the blade of one of the king's loyal agents, none can truly say.

Over half of Jiniral Akil's forces were slain, muddying the Vale of Feldin from Feldenville to Felixton with blood and corpses. The Tungish invaders were sent into rout, and fled north to return to

Tal Taro and recuperate with their reinforcements. There, Jiniral Akil meant to rest his army until winter's end, resupply his Host, and strategize a second invasion of Feldin, this time applying all the experience he had gained in the Lakelands.

Alas, it was not to be.

Tal Taro is a fickle place, having seen so much war and strife since its founding. Being so prone to infighting as it was known to be, the incumbent Tungish army that ruled the city during the Empire's conquest of the Glorious Realm did not fear uprising, for whenever one faction attempted such an endeavor, another one rose up in sabotage. And thus the cycle continued until the winter of 353.

The Rygarin Taroans, ever loyal to their northern neighbours, had found common ground with the followers of Eglaine the Innocent. Their leader, a man named Thomas Marcus, had courted the High Priestess of the Solaram, a woman called Elwen Pureflame. Through their bond of marriage and their unity of purpose in the "scouring of Tungishfolk from these sacred lands," an alliance was forged, powerful enough to rise up against their common foe: the Eye of Eazimun.

Now, the Eye were a faction that had adopted the faith of the Tung Empire: belief in the Wahid-Eazimun. Bearing banners of blue and gold displaying the bejeweled eyes of a Tungish sphynx, they were the primary upholders of the city's occupation, and for months, they had thwarted any acts of resistance. Their defence ended at last with the Rygarin-Solaram pact, known as the Pact of Purification or the Pact of the Purifying Flame.

Together, the Rygarin and the Solaram destroyed the Eye of Eazimun, brutally disposing of its members and supporters—no matter how devout—and littering the streets with their corpses. Entrails, sewn together at the ends, were placed in long lines of weeping gore that marked the city's centre with a vast sixteen-pointed star—the Symbol of Eglaine. With the occupiers' supporters slain, they found themselves exposed for attack, as the Eye of Eazimun's continued presence had rendered them complacent. Short work was made of the Tungish garrison, and the reach of Eglaine's star grew longer.

So, when the routing forces of Jiniral Akil's Host reached the supposed safety of Tal Taro, they were greeted by a very different outcome indeed. The city was ruled by Thomas Marcus, who had self-styled himself Purified Phoenix-Lord Thomas Marcus, and his Lady was Elwen, called Pureflame. At their beck and call were thousands of Tal Taroans united under their banners, a phoenix inlaid upon a sixteen-pointed star.

Unable to rest his army in Tal Taro, Jiniral Akil was forced to rout further north, but to the north lay the Scorchlands, which were untraversable unless by the guidance of the Parched. The Tungish forces scattered, and hundreds were picked off by the Great Host of the Crown that pursued them.

The Tungish Invasion of the Glorious Realm, alternatively known to history as the Third Tungish War, had come to an end, with King Oliver II victorious.[17]

And in Arcanan, the Archwizard's incantation had succeeded. Warden Vandergriff had fallen under Lamentius' complete and utter control. From behind the safety of the College of Sorcery's warded walls, Lamentius directed the Warden like a living puppet, torturing and maiming Jaremius for weeks. Soon enough, the king caught wind of the warden's inexplicable change in disposition, and he ventured

---

17   While the vast majority of Jiniral Akil's army had broken ranks and scattered about the lands of the Lakeland Province and Tal Taro, with many among them succumbing to lives of brigandry and banditry, a great number of commanders, highborn knights, and generals who served in the invading armies were smuggled by the Parched across the Scorchlands, following secret orders of Lord Raymond Rygar. Lord Raymond meant for them to reach the Port of Rygar, sail across the Pocket, and return home to the Tung Empire. It is believed that the Lord of Rygar's intent was to remain in good graces with the Emperor of Tung, despite the failure of their invasion of the south. This secret refuge plot was not revealed to history until the reign of Gerric I.

into the dungeons with Lord Goseph Greene and Lord Pippin Kite to investigate.

What the king saw in Jaremius' cell turned his stomach. The Warden had gone utterly mad. As the former Archwizard had clearly been dead for days by that point already—his heart torn from his chest, his bowels spilled upon the dank dungeon ground, and his face so horrifically carved that the king and his councillors did not recognize him—at least, until Lord Goseph spied a ruby in one of the eye sockets—the Warden had taken instead to dissecting his own living body. By the time the king had arrived, Vandergriff had already bored several holes into his stomach and groin and was muttering nonsensically, as well as smearing his own blood and feces upon the walls in strange patterns.

When Oliver II was finished vomiting, he ordered the Royal Defender to "put the Warden out of his misery," and returned upstairs with Lord Goseph.

Regrettably, Lord Pippin did not survive.

Following his victory in the Third Tungish War, King Oliver II did, as one might expect by now, celebrate with a fortnight of Royal Orgies. Among those present at Chastity Manor were the Royal Admiral Drayton Dunn, the Royal Architect Goseph Greene, the Royal Accountant Salem Finch, the new Royal Defender Orson Oxer, firstborn of Lord Abus, and the Archwizard Lamentius Simon. If the king thought to connect Lamentius to what transpired in the dungeons, he was not eager to broach the subject. The king was so elated by his victory that he opened up applications to Chastity Manor to women that had already been deflowered, deciding that "wenches with perhaps a bit of *experience* should be welcome to join in the festivities." For the king had reportedly grown bored of maidens.

When the revelries had ended, the king decided to choose a new Lord Commander in the wake of Lord Earl's "most tragic" passing. Returning to the old precedent, he restored the House of Leon to a place of prominence within the Glorious Realm. "The Tungish Wars have ended," the king reasoned, "so the time of enmity ought to pass between the Great Houses of Pike and Leon."

And so, in the spring of 353, Lord Samwell Leon, son of Grant, was named Lord Commander of the Royal Armies. However, this was done under the condition that House Leon swear unwavering fealty to King Oliver II and his line from then on and evermore. This, Lord Samwell Leon did swear when he bent the knee before the Arcane Throne.

Thus began a long era of peacetime... and gluttony.

The Great Gluttony: The Bloated Reign of Oliver II

(353—384 AA)

*COMPILED FROM THE CHRONICLING WORKS OF
ARCHWIZARD LAMENTIUS SEPTIMUS SIMON*

The long reign of King Oliver II Pike was, by all accounts, a certain sort of nightmare that would not end. Oliver II was not as much a tyrant as Murth the Menace, not as ineffectual as Samuel I, nor was he as hated as David the Abomination, but scholars regard him as one of the Realm's worst kings just the same. The distaste for Oliver II largely concerned his moral character as a monarch—or, rather, his lack thereof. As the Third Tungish War did reveal, Oliver II was brash, vindictive, and cruel, and it was impossible to temper his gluttonous appetites for coin, flesh, and power. And being the most powerful man in the Glorious Realm for many decades, he could indulge without limits, much to the woe of the Realm and its peoples. The "festivities" he debuted in the early days of his rule were merely the tip of the iceberg, for as his reign went on, his appetites grew more insatiable and grandiose in scale. His council, meanwhile, became populated solely by the king's cowardly lackeys and corrupt friends, none of whom were wont to question him or rein in his indulgences.

Oliver II's Royal Accountant, Salem Finch, was a man of whom little was known at the time of his appointment; few scholars at the College were aware that the name Finch could trace its origins to both Pike and Rygar blood, and they did not divulge this fact to anyone, much less the court. To the king, Salem Finch was a capable and subservient accountant who funded any and all of Oliver II's extravagances and festivities without compromise. As such, throughout the years 353 to 384, there was a Royal Tourney held bi-monthly in Arcanan, and with additional dates for the king's birthday, the queen's birthday, the king and queen's anniversary, the anniversary of Oliver II's coronation, the anniversary of the king's victory in the Third Tungish War, and later the birthdays of his three sons.

The Crown quickly fell into debt, a matter that was resolved— or, perhaps, a better word would be *forestalled*—in 359 when Salem Finch gave up the Crackstones, islands southeast of the Prairieland Province, to the Stronghold Bank in exchange for two-and-a-half million golden crowns. Another loan was taken out in 375 when the last of the sum was finally spent, and this time, Paradise Isle was sold to the bank in exchange for six million crowns. This finally equipped the Crown with enough funds to carry on with its lavish lifestyle for many more years—though, regrettably, the funds ran dry by the twilight of Oliver II's reign, reintroducing the issue of the Royal Treasury for that king's successor to contend with.

Among the other expenses of Oliver II's gluttonous reign were, naturally, the Royal Orgies, which by the year 355 were being held weekly in Chastity Manor—endlessly renovated to house more guests.[18] Following a precedent that began in the Third Tungish War,

---

18   In fact, by the year 359, the rate of the Royal Orgies had increased to twice weekly; thrice weekly by 368, and four times weekly by 376. In part due to the copious amounts of wine and the eight-course meals that were served to all the invited guests, the costs associated with the Royal Orgies eventually eclipsed the expense of the Royal Tourneys by the year 380.

any members of the court who wished to gain the king's favour could do so by joining his festivities. There was nothing that pleased Oliver II more than the sight of his fellow courtiers partaking at Chastity Manor; it is said that he did not trust anyone until he saw them there. "I wish to see them as they *truly* are," the king was oft heard to say.

With the influx of more courtiers in the mid-350s, the initial practice of paying the fathers of common-born Arcanians for their daughters' presence at Chastity Manor ceased. The mere idea of seeing a common-born woman bereft of her clothes, much less bedding one, was repulsive to many in the White Keep's court, and so eventually, the king conceded to their wishes to restrict the attendees to nobility only. This was met with great uproar from the people of Arcanan, as these festivities had by then served as a steady source of income for many mothers and fathers, but nonetheless, the Royal Orgies became a restricted event.

However, as nobles were loath to give up their own daughters for these festivities—their virtue was worth far too much unspoiled— instead, the king and his Royal Accountant turned to the Port of the Setting Sun, Stathmore, and across the Dorsal Sea to the Spice Lands, where it was known that the most well-trained, skilled, and beautiful women lived; this change inevitably caused the expense of the Royal Orgies to increase tenfold as a result.

During these festivities, it was common for the nobles present to compete with one another; if they could "make the rounds," as it was called, in a single night, then they would be permitted to bed Queen Sarah herself. The Queen was often present at these events, though she reserved herself for only a select few men and women. The king was well aware of her presence at Chastity Manor, and in fact, encouraged it. Mere years into Oliver II's reign, the queen's former scandalous nature as the king's sister-wife grew far eclipsed by her later status as the Harlot Queen of Chastity Manor. And through all this, the Church of Gutenberg remained silent, for the High Elder Dorj'heptkii remained adamant that the king was Gutenberg's chosen.

Salem Finch remained as Royal Accountant until the final years of Oliver II's reign. When it was finally discovered in 383 that he had been embezzling funds from the Royal Treasury for decades in order to finance the Rygars' innovations—both militant and magickal—he was executed for treason that selfsame year. The thousands of crowns he had funneled north over the years were never recovered.

Another one of the king's closest lackeys—though lackwit is perhaps a more apt title—was the Royal Architect, Goseph Greene. As Royal Architect, Lord Goseph did remarkably little in the way of actual infrastructure projects. In fact, over the course of the 350s and 360s, many roads, bridges, dams, castles, moats, walls, turrets, and portcullises fell into severe states of decay. Near the beginning of his tenure as Royal Architect, Goseph Greene did attempt the construction of a new road between the villages of Fort Price and Yellowstone; however, the project was haphazardly planned and considerably under-manned. Much of its resources were stolen by bandits, and most of its workforce deserted its construction to go seek new employment in Feldin—or joined in the banditry themselves. With the project abandoned in 356, there still remains no road between Fort Price and Yellowstone to this day. With that failure, Lord Goseph did largely abandon his responsibilities as Royal Architect. It was, after all, a title better suited for House Rohe—as was formerly precedent—and perhaps he knew it.

Instead, Lord Goseph's role on Oliver II's Glorious Council was as a personal protector, or perhaps *enabler*, of the king. Any project that the king set his mind to, whether it be the establishment of a new law known as the Lord's Right—enabling the lord of any holding throughout the Glorious Realm to be the first to take any newly married bride to bed before their groom—or any other of his deplorable ventures, was first vouched for by Goseph Greene. For Lord Goseph delighted in the fact that he would be permitted to join in the spoils of whatever schemes his king was concocting. History suggests that there was never a more lecherous man in the Realm's entire history;

Lord Goseph Greene enjoyed more luxuries and privileges than most who ever lived and died in the Glorious Realm, and he obtained it all with neither work nor sacrifice of any kind.

When Goseph Greene died in 369 of a stab wound in Chastity Manor,[19] his death was met with collective indifference from the commonfolk and celebration from the nobility. As Greene had done so little to justify his title, the king had come to consider the position of Royal Architect irrelevant, and so no replacement was chosen for the rest of his long reign.

Additionally on the council was Orson Oxer, the Royal Defender since the end of the Third Tungish War. Orson was a brutish, simple man whose greatest source of entertainment in this world was to hit things with his sword until they broke. His father Abus believed that Oliver II was his "friend in Arcanan," and so was delighted when the Keeper of the Keys, Lupin Hylar, arrived in Oxcommon to request his firstborn son be brought to Arcanan in service of the king. It is perhaps obvious that the true intention of the king was to keep Lord Abus' firstborn as a ward, for Oliver II was not a trusting man.

Lord Abus passed away in 371, and, hesitant to allow the succession to pass on to someone as dim and violent as Orson, the king and the Keeper bypassed him as they had Orion, instead planting his much more capable, though still malleable, younger brother Alfred

---

19   Reportedly, Lord Goseph had been following a woman home after every night of the king's festivities for weeks leading up to his death and would stand outside her window watching her sleep. He was so determined to keep her as his own that he even used his power on the king's council to have her followed and all of her other patrons beaten bloody in the streets of the Nobles' Quarters. When one day, he kidnapped her in an elaborate plot to gain her hand in marriage, she blindsided him with a hidden dagger and ended his life. It was not a slow death, as the blade struck his groin; it is said that he bled out in a puddle of his own blood, weeping and calling out her name until his final breath.

in charge of the Prairielands. Orson served on the Glorious Council until 385, when he started a barfight he could not win.

Throughout Oliver II's reign, there was another who, despite not holding a title on the council, held considerable influence over matters of the Realm. This was the king's own sister and queen, Sarah Pike. Despite having married her brother, it is believed that she never held any great affection toward him aside from the familial; while she did her duty at least three times, bearing the heirs Jacob, Murth, and Ashar[20] in 361, 362, and 370 respectively, she always kept a throng of loyal concubines at court. This was a revolving cast of thirty men—and half that number of women—who did her bidding and would present themselves at her chambers upon a simple summon. It is said that Queen Sarah had about her an alluring presence; that all were putty in her hands when she spoke. The presence of her many favourites at court did not in the least upset the king, for his carnal urges were satisfied and then some weekly at Chastity Manor.

Therefore, the infidelity of the king and queen proved to be impervious to scandal or scorn from the public, as it was an open secret all but acknowledged by the council and court. Condemnation ought to have come from the Church of Gutenberg, though with Dorj'hepktii as the High Elder throughout Oliver II's reign, any dissent or objection toward his or his sister-wife's promiscuity was swiftly silenced by the clergy—and by misuse of the newly founded Order of Holy Clerics of the White Daisy.

It is believed that Queen Sarah was instrumental in the passage of new laws regarding the taxation of nobles. For hundreds of years, each

---

20   It is a curious thing to note that King Oliver and Queen Sarah would name their third son after the last of the line of Alexander III, when the two sides of the family had been at war so prominently throughout the bulk of the fourth century. Perhaps it was a way to cement the annihilation of that line by the seizure of everything they held, even their names. Though perhaps the reason was simply that the king and queen believed the name sounded good.

noble was able to be taxed differently depending on circumstance, but in the year 366, Queen Sarah did away with that convention and instead instituted a flat blind tax upon all nobles Great and Small throughout the Glorious Realm. This was majorly controversial, especially in the poorer provinces, such as the Cornerstone and Arcane, where income was substantially lower than in Hylete, the Prairielands, and the Lakelands. This became known as the Harlot's Tax, and while House Rohe did rebel against it—and successfully, as Oliver II could not be bothered to start a war over taxation in the Cornerstone Province—the law remained until the reign of Reese I, when the majority of the incumbent laws were overturned in favour of the Glorious Constitution.

Another of the major reforms pushed by Queen Sarah was judicial in nature. Since the age of King Jacob I, in the absence of witness or evidence, all trials had been settled with a duel with Gutenberg as witness. High Elder Dorj'heptkii instead introduced the Trial by Ordeal, in which the accused would undergo a series of harsh, difficult tasks, often involving physical pain or torment of some nature. Upon completion of said tasks, if their wounds should heal, then they would be declared innocent—for Gutenberg would have judged them as such. But if their wounds should fester instead, then Gutenberg had declared them guilty, and they would be put to death, or whatever their sentence demanded, which was often death. This Trial by Ordeal was endorsed heavily by Queen Sarah; in her eloquent manner of speech, she argued that this method was legally preferable to "two men passionately slapping and stabbing one another with their sticks to see who submits first."

Trial by Ordeal was written into law in 370, and remains there to this day, for it was one of the few articles of judiciary law to remain during the drafting of the Glorious Constitution in 442. Trial by Duel did still remain alongside it, however, and was enacted in cases when the accused would surely die under Trial by Ordeal, or when a member of the Church of Gutenberg was under trial—for in those cases, the High Elder carried his own sovereign judgment.

The Lord Commander, Samwell Leon, remained on the council for the remainder of Oliver II's reign. A timid and soft-spoken man, Lord Samwell knew when to lower his head, and rarely balked. His subservience to the Crown can largely be explained by the manner of his appointment; following the execution of Lord Grant Leon for treason in 350, the House of Leon had believed they would never see themselves as Lord Commander again. The Leons were, after all, enemies of the Line of Avery, having aided the kings Jacob II, Oliver I, and Ashar I faithfully throughout the Royal Schism and the Second Tungish War. Therefore, when Lord Samwell, son of Grant, was chosen in 353 to succeed Lord Earl Voyant, House Leon knew that in order to retain their status, they would need to tread carefully.

And thus, we turn to the last councillors of note: Archwizard Lamentius Simon, and the Keeper of the Keys, Lupin Hylar. Both had been instrumental in the king's victory over his enemies during the Third Tungish War.

Following the demise of the Archwizard's chief rival Jaremius Simon in 353, the Archwizard largely kept to his studies, governance over the College of Sorcery, and the chronicling of history. He was occasionally met by enemies who revered Jaremius and sought revenge, but during this age, there was no wizard as experienced and as powerful as Lamentius Septimus. Lamentius would continue to serve the Line of Avery until his death in 386.

As for Lupin Hylar, there was never a more cunning, devious man to serve as Keeper of the Keys. Despite having been on both sides of the Royal Schism during the Second Tungish War, he managed to stay ahead of any plots directed his way. His seizure of the Zehiram cemented his power within the White Keep, the City of Arcanan, and across the Glorious Realm at large, for the secret power of the Crown remained at his beck and call.

Following his death in 381, his protégé, Lord Petras Plume, took the reins thereafter. It is unknown if Lord Lupin was aware of the schemes Lord Plume would one day enact during his tenure as Keeper of the Keys, though it ought to be acknowledged that any true understanding of Lupin Hylar's actions remains a mystery for all who study this history. Suffice to say that few men who lived to gain such power and influence over so many were granted the luxury of dying peacefully in their own bed at the age of sixty-eight.

The matters of the Church were of great importance during the reign of Oliver II. Its continued endorsement of the king, queen, the council, and the court were of great controversy to the people of Arcanan and the Realm at large. Ever since the Holy Schism of 264, the High Elder in Farcross had governed the East Church in the Prairielands and Feldin, while the High Elder in Arcanan governed the rest. Naturally, the High Elder in Farcross, a man named Bib'murzbo, detested the "deplorable impunity" of Oliver II and his entire court, deriding them for the revelry that went on "without a single damn given by the Church in Arcanan."

This High Elder desired action, and while he could not legally hold sway over the Church in the West, he did have the authority to create his own Holy Order of Clerics. It was established in Farcross in 373, and so as to avoid confusion, was named the Clerical Order of the Holy White Daisy.

Now, House Rohe of the Cornerstone Province remained an enemy of the Line of Avery—in particular Queen Sarah for the Harlot's Tax. And so, when the Clerical Order of the Holy White Daisy marched west in 373, Stone Haven provided shelter, amenities, and weapons for the Clerical Order, and even offered a fleet of ships to sail them across the Mouth and invade the Arcane Province. They landed not in Arcanan, but along the southeast coast of the Borderland Hills. Heading north toward Arcanan, one thousand clerics from the Prairieland Province made camp about a day's march from the city. In honour of the last of the Line of Alexander III, and in open rebellion against the Crown, High Elder Bib'murzbo named this camp Fort Ashar. In the years since, it has become a small holding in its own right, despite attempts by Oliver II to raze it or otherwise destroy its name.[21]

However, before the Clerical Order of the Holy White Daisy could march upon Arcanan in protest of Oliver II, they were met in the field by the Order of Holy Clerics of the White Daisy—two thousand strong, armed with maces and clad in pure white cloaks to contrast the Clerical Order's green stripes.

A battle was waged in the fields north of Fort Ashar, and was thereafter dubbed The Trampling of the Daisies. The Order of Holy Clerics of the White Daisy were the clear victors, having taken their foes by surprise in the early morn. Following the battle, High Elder Dorj'heptkii announced, "Gutenberg's Guiding Hand Favours Our Holy Cause," and reaffirmed King Oliver II as righteous.

After decades of whoring, eating, more whoring, and more eating, by the 380s, Oliver had swelled to a gargantuan size. None of his royal garb could fit—not even the Crown of Yellow, which he had stopped wearing by 381—and when he sat the throne, his flesh filled the seat so thickly that it drooped over the edges.

The reign of King Oliver II finally came to an end in the year 384, for his sordid lifestyle eventually caught up to him.

---

21   Upon the seventh attempt, in 382, when Oliver II sent forth the Royal Armies to sack Fort Ashar, he found it repopulated and rebuilt once more three fortnights later. Finally conceding defeat, he instead decided to tout Fort Ashar as being named after his third son, also named Ashar, instead of King Ashar I as it was undoubtedly intended.

The Fair and The Mad: The Sons of Oliver II

(384—386 AA)

COMPILED FROM THE CHRONICLING WORKS OF ARCHWIZARDS LAMENTIUS SEPTIMUS SIMON AND PHINEAS DUOS SIMON

When the grossly obese king Oliver II was found expired upon the Arcane Throne in a heap that stank of wine and urine, the throne was desperately in need of a new king—and a deep cleaning.

The crown naturally passed to Oliver's firstborn son and heir, Prince Jacob Pike. The name Jacob was imbued with a hopeful omen, for the first King Jacob had been the one who founded the Realm in its dawn days. While the second King Jacob's reign did bring great civil unrest with the Royal Schism and the dreadful Second Tungish War, the name Jacob Pike still held a hopeful ring. The people of the Glorious Realm were holding their breath to see what sort of king Jacob III would turn out to be.

King Jacob III Pike was crowned in 384 in Arcanan, by which time the Royal Crowns had at last been recovered.[22] The Crown of Blue inlaid with sapphires was placed upon Jacob III by Archwizard Lamentius Septimus Simon. The audience present at the Royal Coronation of 384 were astonished by this choice, as its last wearer was none other than King Oliver I—perhaps the greatest adversary to the Line of Avery.

But the new king reminded the Realm of the Crown of Blue's original significance: to represent peace, wisdom, and stability. The Old King Alexander and Tomas the Root had also been past wearers of the Crown of Blue, after all. It is said that on his coronation day, the sight of its gleaming sapphires resting upon Jacob III's curly golden locks was a spectacle for all.

Of Oliver II's sons, Jacob had been the fairest, the kindest, and the most beloved since the early days of his childhood. He was polite, jovial, and well-mannered—in great contrast to his father. Oliver II's other two sons, Murth and Ashar, were quite different in their own ways; Murth was more like his father, but perhaps more sinister yet.

---

22   Rolph Leon, the Royal Accountant who stole the Crowns following the ascension of Oliver II, had a change of heart when he travelled to the Port of the Setting Sun to pawn them off for riches and wealth beyond measure. It is believed that he changed course upon pondering the significance of these Crowns to history, and could not bring himself to sell them to common merchants and traders of the Port. Instead, it is believed that he returned to Arcanan under a new name, where he lived with the rest of the Leons in Pendlebury Manor as their "butler." The Crowns, he smuggled in with him and placed in a secret vault beneath Pendlebury Manor that was constructed in secret by Rolph and perhaps even Grant Leon before his arrest and subsequent execution at the hands of Oliver II.

Finally, when Oliver II perished, Lord Samwell Leon saw fit to unearth the Crowns and bestow them upon Oliver II's sons under the belief that, following the Bloated Reign, a new era was upon the Glorious Realm, and that the line of Avery should be given another chance with the coronation of Jacob III.

From the moment he could conceptualize what it meant to be a Royal Prince, he had held a high opinion of himself. He was a relentless bully to other children at court, and in particular his younger brother Ashar. The third and youngest son of Oliver II and Queen Sarah, Ashar was timid, small, and weak; he was constantly attacked for his short stature and feminine nature, and largely spent his youth being coddled by the queen.

Let us briefly diverge from the story of Jacob III's early reign to illustrate Prince Murth's cunning, ambitious nature, which was on display even at a young age. It was the year 381, and Murth was at this time fifteen years of age. He joined the lists at the Royal Tourney held at Arcanlodge in the year 381 in honour of the sixty-second birthday of Oliver II, who was carted in to witness the festivities firsthand. Neither the king nor the rest of the audience in attendance expected the young Prince Murth to enroll, as many thought it folly for a boy his age—and of such high birth—to risk his life in a joust.

Regardless, Prince Murth rode against the others in the listings and outperformed many. Among the defeated were Sir Rohl Rohe, Sir Adam Oxer, Sir Herman Hylar—nephew to Lord Humphrey—Sir Sylviar Hunter, and Sir Bartimus Stock. The final joust was between the prince and the Lord Commander's eldest son, Sir Samuel "the Silver Star" Leon, reigning champion of the previous three Royal Tourneys.

During the joust, Murth's beautiful chestnut stallion stumbled when one of Sir Samuel's lances struck his shield. The young prince was thrown off his mount and into the dirt. The crowd was aghast, as King Oliver II himself was witness to the scene. Stricken with the worry that he might have seriously wounded a Royal Prince, Sir Samuel dismounted and rushed toward Murth's side. To his relief, he saw the prince was unharmed save for a bruise upon his arm where the lance had struck. The prince's stallion was another matter entirely. It had fallen so poorly that it had broken its leg, and would regrettably never walk again. The prince immediately called for his mount to be taken from the tourney grounds and put out of its misery.

Now, the rules of an Arcanian Tourney state that if a rider's horse should be the reason for his fall, his opponent's victory is moot. As it stood, Murth required only a victory against Sir Samuel Leon to be declared champion of the Royal Tourney of 381. Remembering his father's words of warning in regard to the Pikes, Sir Samuel prudently yielded the match to Prince Murth. The crowds cheered exuberantly as he knelt in apparent humility before the victor.

Little did the young knight know—nor did anyone else present at the tourney in 381—that they had been played for fools. For Prince Murth was well aware that he would likely not defeat the Silver Star in a fair match, and so administered poison to his horse before the final joust. The crimes committed by Murth in future years were far more grievous than this.

During the dawn of his reign, King Jacob III almost immediately established himself as the polar opposite of his father. While Oliver II had spent the majority of his reign enjoying the delights of rule in all its hedonistic splendor, Jacob got right to ruling proper. He called the Glorious Council to session—which happened to be the first time in nearly four years—and together, they discussed the state of the Realm in the wake of Oliver II's passing.

The aging Lord Commander Samwell Leon was loyal to the Crown as ever, and Jacob III was delighted to keep him as leader of the Royal Armies. The sprightly Royal Admiral Drayton Dunn was one Jacob knew to keep at an arm's length, but he did not doubt his commitment to the Crown; House Dunn's prestige depended on it, after all. Archwizard Lamentius had served Jacob's father since 350, and swore to serve Jacob III as fervently as he'd served Oliver II.

The Realm was currently at peace, as uncertain as it was, since the greatest sources of division in the Realm these past hundred years were the Royal Schism—resolved when Keeper Lupin Hylar ended the Line of Alexander—and the Tung Empire, which had kept its distance since the 350s.

Due to Queen Sarah's reforms, such as the Harlot's Tax, taxes had been raised exorbitantly high—to fund King Oliver's great festivities, no less—and the burden upon the average Arcanian peasant was enormous. King Jacob III sought immediately to correct this, lowering taxes tenfold from fifty percent to five,[23] though he did keep the flat tax instituted by his mother.

Also during the Bloated Reign, due to the many failings of Royal Architect Goseph Greene, much of the Realm's infrastructure had fallen into shambles. By 384, there had been no Royal Architect for fifteen years—and by all accounts, Lord Goseph was one in name only before then. As such, many of the Realm's roads, bridges, and fortifications were in dire need of repair to provide safe travel. King Jacob III appointed Mohsen Rohe, twin brother to Lady Malina Rohe and grandson of Lady Falisha, who had passed in 367, and sent him off forthwith to work.

Another matter was in regard to Royal Subsidiaries. The peasants of the realm were in desperate need of aid in order to maintain their farms or the Realm would scarcely survive the coming winter. The Royal Accountant, Lord Ernest Stock, who had served since 383, informed the king that due to the previous king's lavish "festivities"—

---

23   He also lowered the rate of the Royal Orgies tenfold—they were happening nearly five times a week by the end of Oliver II's reign, despite the fact that the enormous king could not physically partake, much less leave his throne, for he was content to watch. Jacob III wanted to end all such frivolities from taking place behind the walls of the White Keep immediately, but they had proven to be quite popular among the nobles, so he was forced to come to a compromise: there would be an orgy held once bi-weekly, and at Chastity Manor—far out of Jacob's sight. It was enough to appease the nobles' appetites, which had been lavishly indulged during Oliver II's long reign. Alas, it was not to be, for they continued five times a week—outside of King Jacob III's knowledge.

which Lord Stock himself surely did not partake in whatsoever—the Royal Treasury was in dire need of replenishment. The cutting of Royal Taxes would require another source of income for the Crown, but Jacob III was adamant he would not raise taxes. "Not even by half a copper piece!" Therefore, the Royal Accountant was forced to seek alternative methods to procure such funds.

All in all, the young King Jacob had already shown himself to be wiser than his father, for he listened to the advice of his elders, sought solutions even in the event of compromise, and settled any disagreements with a steady mind and clear judgement. The reign of King Jacob III was off to a promising start, and the peoples of the Glorious Realm—nobles and commoners alike—collectively sighed in relief. The long and dreadful reign of Oliver II had ended, and it appeared as though the Realm was now in good hands.

As the years went by and many more shortcomings held over from King Oliver II's reign were amended by his son, the question of Royal Marriage began to arise. In 386, the Glorious Council urged the twenty-five-year-old Jacob III to choose a highborn lady as his queen. Many options were spoken unto him: Fiora Voyant, Penelope Felix, Bertha Oxer, Gretchen Dunn, and even the homely niece of Lord Ernest Stock, Sylvia—a maiden of thirty-five-years-old.

Many expected the Royal Accountant to vouch for his niece—but he instead proposed that the king choose a different woman as his queen, for he had at long last found a solution to the restoration of the Royal Treasury, as unsavoury as it was. Lord Stock did not want to sell off further territory to the Stronghold Bank as his treasonous predecessor Salem Finch had, and so instead, he looked to the Great Houses for aid.

The Hylars of Hylete Square were well known to be the wealthiest House at the time, and for most of history, save for the scant few times they were eclipsed by House Oxer. Lord Ernest discussed matters of coin at great length with Lord Humphrey Hylar, who was eager to expand his House's influence, as many Lords of Hylete had tried before. The abundant mines of silver and gold still flowed during the 380s, so there was much they could loan the Crown. Lord Humphrey elected to accept the Royal Accountant's offer: enough gold to satiate the Royal Treasury for the next ten years—but Jacob III must wed Lord Humphrey's daughter Laura.

Upon hearing this news, King Jacob III resolved to do his duty; one of the many great compromises he was wont to make. The other councilmembers could not argue with the king's decision, though many were concerned with this debt the Crown now owed House Hylar—and how it might affect their own influence at Court.

That year, King Jacob III travelled west with an entourage of the Crown's most loyal knights—and Lord Ernest Stock, for negotiations—to visit Lord Humphrey Hylar and his daughter Laura in the Checkered Hall of Hylete Square. Lord Samwell Leon sat the Arcane Throne during the king's absence.

One month later, the king returned to Arcanan with a great Host of Hylete knights behind him, their checkered sky-blue banners fluttering in the winds, and announced that he would be taking the stunning Laura Hylar as his queen. The wedding was to be held as soon as possible, as during his visit, he had fallen deeply in love, and wanted to "waste not a day before saying [his] vows!"

The king ordered the Council to make haste and prepare at once so that his union with the Hylar girl could be officiated in three days' time. He then announced to all peoples of Arcanan that they would *all* be invited to attend his Royal Wedding. Evidently, the people could hardly wait to partake in such a joyous occasion, as attendance was barely manageable by the Royal Accountant. It was shaping up to be a truly wondrous occasion.

Alas, it was not to be.

For when Jacob III brought his betrothed to Arcanan, the young Prince Murth was overcome with envy and plotted to steal her for himself. On the night of the king's grand wedding, Prince Murth stole into his brother's chambers to wish him a message of goodwill from Gutenberg. The king was not overly fond of his brother; they had quarreled much in their youth, and Jacob was well aware that Murth deeply envied him.

None were present in the king's chambers that night other than the prince and the king, so none can truly say what the circumstances were—but one thing was certain. King Jacob III was murdered in cold blood by none other than his younger brother, Prince Murth.

When the king's personal guards turned to arrest the prince, they were challenged by a legion of Zehiram hiding in the walls. In minutes, the sworn protectors of the late King Jacob III were slain in the hallways of the White Keep, and their blood seeped deep into the castle's ornate Tungish carpets.

When morning came, and the people of Arcanan and beyond gathered to bear witness to this most celebrated union between Pike and Hylar, they were all greeted by a most devastating sight: instead of their beloved King Jacob III, King Murth II presented himself as the groom, and beckoned for the sweet Laura Hylar to come stand before him and speak her vows. The audience was a gallery of ghosts, for none dared challenge Murth. The Zehiram were visible in the rafters, their crossbows aimed at the council. Laura sobbed through the vows she had written for her beloved Jacob, as she was wed to King Murth II.

Deeply outraged, Lord Ernest Stock stepped forth in protest and scolded Murth with scorn in his voice. "For years, your father sat upon the Arcane Throne and lusted after every such thing! Women, gold, food, incense, spices, and clothing! You have only just crowned yourself king and already have outdone him! You demonstrate your lust for all the Realm to see! But your lust is of a more deplorable kind: the power and titles rightly granted to your elder brother. But you did not stop at kinslaying—no! You hath stolen his love as well!"

The furious lord was barely given a moment to breathe after speaking his words, for with a dark glance from Murth and a slight raise of his left hand, an arrow shot through the air and lodged itself in Lord Ernest's right eye. The crowd was horrified, yet they could neither run nor hide, for the Zehiram were watching their every move. It was at this moment that King Murth II took the sobbing Queen Laura in his arms and sealed their union with a forceful, binding kiss.

That evening, when all had settled down, King Murth II sent out his Royal Guard to announce to all of the Realm that he was their lawful king. He then journeyed down to the dungeons to greet his Archwizard, Lamentius Septimus Simon. The Archwizard had been there overnight and had endured much torture at the hands of Warden Ulgar. Being one hundred and fifteen—elderly even by Simon standards—he had broken quickly under Ulgar's scalpels and declared Murth the new King of the Glorious Realm the morning of the wedding.

It took but a few signings and a stamping of the Archwizard's seal for Murth to officially become King Murth II, unbeknownst to anyone but himself, the warden, and the wizard. But now, as the news spread swiftly across all the Realm, Murth paid a visit to Lamentius once again. The wizard was thoughtfully informed that he would now be left to languish in the dungeons until he died.

Upon himself, King Murth II bestowed the Crown of Red—being the first king of the Glorious Realm to wear it since his namesake, Murth I.

After his public coronation, King Murth II returned to his wedded wife to show her something "special." He brought her to the tallest tower of the White Keep, where he bid her glance out the window. To her horror, she bore witness to the grisly sight of her betrothed Jacob III, impaled upon a spire, the Crown of Blue still visible upon his pale head.

And then, in that furnished tower, King Murth II and Laura Hylar consummated the marriage.

The next day brought forth an era of great darkness upon the Glorious Realm, for the reign of King Murth II was underway, and his ambition knew no bounds.

The War Under the Sun

(386—393 AA)

COMPILED FROM THE CHRONICLING WORKS OF ARCHWIZARDS PHINEAS DUOS SIMON AND SILAS OCTAVIOUS SIMON

Jacob III was dead. It was the blistering summer of 386, and the Glorious Council was in disarray. Archwizard Lamentius languished in the dungeons of the White Keep and King Murth II sat the Arcane Throne. The Realm anxiously awaited what was to come.

King Murth confidently strolled into the Council Chambers the night after consummating his wedding and greeted the councillors. There were two empty seats at the table: those belonging to the Archwizard and Royal Accountant. Murth II was in need of suitable replacements.

The title of Archwizard was hereditarily passed down to the next in line of House Simon's seniority. As it stood, the heir of House Simon was Valerius Onus Simon, who was bestowed the Amulet of the Archwizard, a brilliant, eight-sided, blood-red ruby that had been carried and displayed around the necks of each Archwizard since the days of Ethzar. However, a mere three days after his elevation to the title, he stole away into the night, never to return. Regrettably, the Amulet of the Archwizard was lost with him—and to this day, neither the Amulet nor Valerius himself have ever been recovered.

Thus, Valerius' younger brother—still ninety-one, mind you—Phineas Duos Simon was thereby granted the title in his place, though he was notably ambivalent about taking his father's position. "Where is my father? Where is Lamentius?" he asked King Murth II before the other councillors.

Murth gravely looked to the ground, and in lamentation, declared, "The Archwizard is no more, for he died suddenly during the night." This, by all accounts, was not a lie.

With Phineas Duos staring on in shock, it was decided—although with tensions thick in the air—that Phineas Duos Simon would be named the Fifteenth Archwizard of the Glorious Realm.

Next, a new Royal Accountant was to be chosen as, regrettably, Lord Ernest Stock had received an arrow through the eye and could not attend the Glorious Council at this time. The Keeper of the Keys, Lord Petras Plume—who had served in that office since the death of Lupin Hylar in 381—proposed that a certain Dirk Dreggs should be considered due to his "unmatched skill in procuring new and prosperous avenues of income."

Murth II entertained this proposal. Then, before the council was officially adjourned, King Murth declared that under *his* rule, he meant to see the Glorious Realm emboldened. "The Gornak Ranges, with their mines overflowing with ores, gems, and riches, have remained sovereign for nearly *four hundred years* of Glorious Kings—governed only by hard-headed dwarves who follow the most violent among them! I, Murth II, vow to change this. The vast mountains to the north shall see the new sunrise at last—and be welcomed into my kingdom. In fact, the preparations are already in order."

The Council was aghast. Not since King Murth's namesake had any king of the Glorious Realm attempted to conquer the Mountain Dwarves—and that king's efforts had been swiftly ended by his own Lord Commander. Phineas Duos timidly inquired, "What of the seal required by the Lord Commander designating his approval of such an act of war? Do you mean to suggest that you do not require such a measure?"

The king smiled and glanced towards the Lord Commander's seat, which was currently occupied still by Lord Samwell Leon. Lord Samwell curtly nodded to the Archwizard. "The king has my support. I have already signed the papers and given them my Lordly Seal. His Grace has the right of it; preparations *are* already underway."

The councillors were wise enough to hold their tongues. The death of Lord Ernest Stock still lingered in each of their minds as a reminder that this new king was not to be questioned.

Later that summer, as the winds of autumn were beginning to blow from the Mouth into the streets of Arcanan, King Murth II sent four legions of the Royal Armies north into the Gornak Ranges, heralding his Conquest. They were led by Sir Sylviar Hunter—the finest knight of the Prairieland Province, a proven warrior, capable commander, and heir to Wolfdale. The city of Arcanan watched apprehensively as the Royal Host rode out from Arcanan's gates.

Meanwhile, the king's marriage was under considerable strife. As one might expect, Queen Laura was disgusted by Murth II's very presence. "Bile in the form of a man," she wrote. That did not do much in the way of stopping the king's forthright advances, and the guards of the White Keep—many of them either Zehiram or loyal to Lord Dirk Dreggs—turned a blind eye to her suffering.

Throughout these years, as perplexing as it may have been, the West Church of Gutenberg remained adamantly in support of the Crown and its actions. Dorj'hept'kii, still High Elder of the Faithful at the start of Murth II's reign, was seldom seen outside the walls of the Sanctum, mostly keeping to himself in the twilight of his life. However, during his rare public appearances, his message remained the same: the House of Pike was anointed by the Holy Hand of Gutenberg, and that the king's word is *His* word. To make matters worse, the Order of Holy Clerics of the White Daisy were commanded by the High Elder to stand behind the king as stalwart guardians of his rule. They were to keep the King's Peace and ensure a secure—and uncontested—transition of power. Naturally, the elder's fellow clergymen did take issue with this. A certain High Priest of Gutenberg known as Shepherd Cage to many—and L'iuk'jibar'bnorskii to few—spoke outwardly of the king's impiety and avarice. His words were well received by the people of Gutenberg, as many were still reeling from Murth II's tumultuous coronation. The understanding as to why their beloved Jacob III had perished was shared in their hearts. But when Shepherd Cage found himself on trial for indecency by the West Church, his name besmirched and his rank stripped from him along with his robes, those remaining in dissent of the High Elder's positions held their suspicions and bowed their heads. And thus the madness continued.

As the autumn gave way to harsh winter winds and Arcanan froze over, the Northern Conquest was proving to be quite fortuitous, for in that winter, the lands betwixt the Vokmar Pines and the Takkar Hills were seized by the Royal Armies. Sir Sylviar Hunter's signed and sealed letter was read aloud by Phineas Simon in the throne room: "The Dwarven savages have given up the fight. With nearly two-thousand dead on their side of the conflict and merely four hundred on ours, their blood runs cold upon the crimson snow. I, Sir Sylviar Hunter of Wolfdale, declare a victory for the Crown!"

Murth II was elated. He bade the Archwizard send a reply to the Northern Host at once, with mention that the king was pleased, and that all who fought bravely in the Battle Where the Blood Runs Cold would be rewarded greatly upon their return to Arcanan. But that day would wait, as their next orders were to lay siege to the Dwarven city of Holm Tagor.

As springtime returned, King Murth II set in motion a Royal Command for Lord Terrance Tals to gather his banners and march for Hildar to conquer the land of the Hill Dwarves for the Crown. It was unknown to the council—save for Keeper Petras Plume—that

Terrance Tals and the Tagdornat of Hildar had cultivated an amicable trade friendship in the years since Tal Taro's founding. Naturally, the king was informed. One could surmise that Murth II's decree was not merely to further his Conquest, but also served as a test of loyalty for Lord Tals.

While these plots were underway, the king's marriage continued to chafe. Murth meant to keep the queen not only as his lawfully wedded wife, but also as a ward to keep Hylete Square in check. He also meant to produce an heir in order to secure his line, intending to name it Murth if a son, and try again if a daughter, for after the culling of the Line of Alexander during the Royal Schism and Tungish Wars, it so happened that the sons of Oliver II were the last true remnants of House Pike. Fragments of Royal Blood existed in many of the Great Houses, especially due to the many daughters of King Tomas the Root, but nary enough to ever claim hold to the Arcane Throne.

While Murth II found great success in his Northern Conquest and had complete control over the Council, he could not say the same with regards to his queen. On a tragic day in the spring of 387, when the queen learnt she was with child—a secret kept by the Archwizard who had performed the required tests—King Murth II wandered up the winding steps of the King's Tower to find her absent. This immediately sparked his ire. The king tore apart his chambers in search of her, even rending his own Royal Tapestries in a fit of rage. However, once his gaze drifted to the window, he found her.

One spire over from where the remains of Jacob III were still displayed, was the body of the sweet young Laura Hylar, joining him in impalement. The king shed nary a tear, one of the castle guards tells us, but was "angered beyond reason"—for his hold upon Hylete had leapt from his window. Now he would be forced to reckon with the wrath of Lord Humphrey and all the strength of the West.

It did not take long for news of the queen's tragic death to travel across the Realm—though the manner of her passing was cause for great controversy. The official declaration was that Queen Laura had been tragically murdered by a jealous castle guard who had routinely listened by the door during their intimate moments.[24] The Royal Executioner, Spliggins, was brought to the City Square forthwith to carry out the King's Justice and execute the accused, who had already been declared guilty before the sun had yet to rise.

Rumours began to circulate through the cobbled streets of Arcanan—in the Dregs, the Mudpits, and the Windmaker Inn—that it was not this guard who had murdered their queen, but rather, that the ignoble treatment of her husband had led her to take her own life. Others yet whispered of an even more grievous tale—that the king himself had disposed of her in the same manner as he had his brother King Jacob III.

Regardless of the truth, the West was in a fury. Lord Humphrey Hylar received the tidings with a great sorrow that grew into a raging storm by morning's end. He strode into the Checkered Hall and declared, "Hylete will not suffer this treacherous usurper any longer! As in the days of my forefathers Hector, Harris, and Harrison, Hylete shall be a Province no longer, but a Kingdom in its own right. We shall have our *own* king, not this monstrous fiend ruling over us! Gather our banners at once, and mobilize our armies! We must defend our land and secure our independence!"

And so it was that in the year 387, while King Murth II had four legions fighting far from Arcanan in the Northern Conquest, Lord Humphrey became King Humphrey Hylar, and the Kingdom of Hylete was re-established for the first time since the reign of Old King Alexander. King Murth II was so furious that he rode down the King's Road swinging his sword at anyone in his path. When he was done, he returned to the White Keep and decreed that any and all Arcanians sharing the name of Laura must be seized and burnt in a heap.

---

24   This guard happened to be none other than the one who had given his testimony of the king's reaction to finding his queen dead.

However, as much as the king wanted to avoid it, a Hylar Rebellion was a reality he would have to reckon with. After a fortnight stewing in hatred, Murth graced the Council once again with his presence.

As if on cue, Lord Plume proposed a strategy that the king might be inclined to entertain—one that would not only crush their separatist enemies, but also inspire fear in the Crown once again. Murth II had lent his ear to the Keeper of the Keys many times before, and here, once again, he heard Lord Plume's carefully considered plans.

By midsummer of 387, the king was prepared for war.

One month and a day after King Humphrey declared Hylete's independence from the Realm, he received an urgent message from the Baron of Fort Unity. Apparently, a great Royal Host had been spied approaching from the east. The baron bade King Humphrey to send reinforcements at once to secure the Bridge of Unity. Pleased by the news that Fort Unity had taken his side, King Humphrey gave his commanders the order to march east. One of the commanders, Sir Ronald Rooker, suggested that this may be a ruse. The King of Hylete considered this for a moment, but then changed his mind. "If indeed your suspicions ring true, then regardless, the Bridge of Unity must be held strong! Let us march forthwith!"

And so it was that a Hylete Host of eight thousand strong, with four hundred knights among them, marched toward the Bridge of Unity. Upon their arrival, they were greeted by a legion of the Crown's Royal Armies suspiciously numbering less than a quarter of their own. Commander Rooker took this as evidence of his hunch. He knew he must send a message to his king post-haste, and so a courier was dispatched westward. Rooker then awaited an envoy from the Crown's Host to parley in his camp.

None came. The Royal Host waited patiently in the town of Alexander.

After a fortnight of fruitlessness, Rooker announced to the Hylar Host that they would cross the bridge; their enemy's host was small, and he meant to carry out the King Humphrey's orders without tarrying a day longer, for he was wary that another, more grievous attack might be imminent upon Hylete Square.

Once the entirety of the Hylete Host had marched onto the Bridge of Unity, being only at the halfway point, there appeared a lone mage standing before them. "Begone!" shouted the Commander. "We are here to fortify the eastern border of the Hylete Kingdom, and we will not stop, not even for the College!"

The mage cackled. "You mean to fortify your traitors' land by marching onto *our* soil and warring against the Crown? Do so at your own risk, sir knight, for *I* am not of the College."

Commander Rooker replied, "The declaration of war was already made when Murth murdered our sweet Lady Laura! Move aside, mage, or you will be trampled underfoot by this great host!"

"As you will," smiled the mage, before he vanished in a cloud of sapphire smoke.

The Bridge of Unity collapsed.

The Hylete Host was swept away by relentless rapids or crushed by debris. All four hundred of King Humphrey's noble knights perished under the waves of the Father's River where countless Hyletian nobles had been laid to rest, their armour too heavy to permit them to swim. Some less heavily armoured soldiers found their way to the riverbanks and sought refuge in the Tower of Departure or Fort Hylar. But regardless, the battle was won by Murth II before it even began, and the Bridge of Unity was no more. None in the Western Kingdom understood what caused the Bridge's fall on that dreadful day, though the Dark Wind was on everyone's lips.

Thereafter, the king was known to all as Murth the Mad.

But alas, the Crown's *true* attack was already underway, just as predicted. At the end of the first watch, a great fleet of ships appeared upon the horizon of Providence Shore. They bore the moon-and-sun banners of House Dunn, and by the time King Humphrey ascended his castle's battlements, it was already too late.

The King of Hylete bore witness to the destruction that Murth's
Royal Fleet had wrought. As many could attest, great fires had already
swallowed up the fertile lands of the Vale. Overcome with deep sorrow
for all his subjects, King Humphrey announced he would personally
lead a sortie out upon the shore to "drive [their] great enemy back out
to sea!" Whether Humphrey was referring to the Crown or House
Dunn, none can truly say; it was likely both. His son Prince Lorn
protested his involvement, but those words fell on deaf ears. The King
of Hylete could not bear to see his kingdom in pain for a moment
longer.

King Humphrey Hylar emerged from his armoury clad in sky-
blue-and-silver armour. His ancestral sword, a beautiful blade inlaid
with sapphires, was already in hand. Humphrey then bade his son
Lorn a sorrowful farewell. "Should I not return, know that you are the
heir to this Great and Independent Kingdom. It will be upon *you* to
oppose the tyrant who sits upon the Arcane Throne. Make my spirit
proud!"

And with that, King Humphrey rode into battle upon a stallion
so white it seemed to glow beneath the silver moon.

Prince Lorn never saw his father again.

The Raid of Providence Shore raged on through the night, but
as the rays of morning graced those desolate shores, the Royal Fleet
took to its return to Arcanan, its task completed. Hymphrey Hylar's
rebellion was in shambles.

Prince Lorn was greeted later that day by a breathless messenger
bearing an urgent letter from the late Commander Ronald Rooker.

The remaining nobles of Hylete all congregated in the Checkered
Hall to discuss what ought to be done. Following the triple blow of
the Bridge of Unity's fall, the desolation of the Hylete Host, and the
death of King Humphrey, there were many calls for Prince Lorn to be
crowned King of Hylete.

The young Lorn refused this mandate. "I do not mean to suffer
the same fate as my father. While his intentions were admirable, his

cause was doomed. Compared to the might and strength of Arcanan, Hylete is a mouse to a great cat. My father thought himself a dog and bit the cat's tail. I mean not to repeat his mistake. I shall bide my time and rule this *Province* as a lord, not as a king. And when I *do* act, it will not be without allies."

Meanwhile, the Royal Fleet returned to the Port of Arcanan bearing news of victory. King Murth II was pleased—and even more so when Royal Admiral Drayton Dunn presented King Humphrey's rotted head before the throne. Murth took the grisly token in his hands, and with a dagger, he sheared it of all its white hair and placed a crown of barbed thorns upon its scalp. He then gave the order to Royal Defender Marsden Mudpitts to place "this symbol of avarice" in the Kingsroad Marketplace for all to witness the consequences of rebellion.

Murth the Mad did not stop there. His next decree was to order the City Guard to lead an inquisition upon the people of Arcanan and root out any remaining support for Hylete. Nobles of the White Keep's Court fell prey to the Zehiram who stalked its shadowy halls. Not even the city's bards and fools were spared, as the utterance of a word that defamed the king—even in jest—was met by cold steel and certain sorrow.

Thus, the year 387 ended with the Great Purge of Arcanan. By the end of it all, the city had surrendered so many corpses that the cemeteries were overflowing, and bodies were instead burnt in the streets. The Kingsroad Marketplace was thick with the putrid stench of burning flesh, rot, and death, and had become home to swarms of black flies and writhing maggots. Finally, with the coming of spring in 388, the Great Purge reached its end. The name of Murth the Mad was etched into the bitter hearts of all.

But for King Murth II, things were proceeding fortuitously. He now ruled with certainty that none would dare to stand up to him as long as he lived. When he received an epistle from Lord Terrance

Tals that the Hill Dwarves had been subdued and Hildar had been conquered for the Crown, his spirits were raised further.

However, there remained an urgent matter for King Murth II. The Northern Conquest, while successful thus far, utilized a great portion of his Royal Armies, and the king was too distrustful to call on the Great Lords for their banners after what had happened in the West. As such, Murth was in need of a *new* army. Further idolizing his namesake, the king sent for Archwizard Phineas Duos Simon, for he had a wicked idea.

As snows layered softly upon the White Keep in 388, Murth II inquired as to the location of the Sworn Swords. The Archwizard was ambivalent in carrying out the king's request, as it was his ancestor Roswell Trinius, the Second Archwizard who sealed them away in the first place.[25] But alas, he could not protest, for the Great Purge had claimed the lives of many of his friends and fellow mages, and those wounds stung fresh in his mind.

Later that year, King Murth II was stricken by a special flavour of madness when he read Sir Hunter's latest letter regarding the Northern Conquest. It appeared that the siege of Holm Tagor was nearing completion, meaning the land of the Mountain Dwarves was nearly his. As such, the king made an announcement. "I have newly set my sights upon a land that not even my namesake did aspire for. I mean to conquer the Elden Wood and bring it under my rule. I shall be forever known as the king who conquered not only the Dwarves, but also the Elves. Soon, I will claim all their lands for *my* Glorious Realm!"

Much to the Council's surprise, the Royal Architect, Mohsen Rohe, spoke up angrily in protest. "No king has set their sights upon

---

25   He did not mention the atrocities committed by King Murth I that led Archwizard Roswell to seal away the Sworn Swords, as he was well aware that Murth II likely did not care, or worse yet, *agreed* with his ancestor's actions.

the Wood, aye, because—forgive my bluntness—it is folly! The most we know of the Elves has come from the Hunters of Wolfdale, and even their tales are mired in mystery. With all due respect, my liege, such a venture is a fool's errand!"

The rest of the Council was so silent one could have heard a brooch drop—the rest, that is, save for the Keeper of the Keys, whose words always pleased the king. "Your Grace, while our Lord of Rohe does speak out of turn, I believe a grain of truth lies therein his words. There is indeed a reason why no king before you has ventured out to claim the Elden Wood for the Realm. Simply spoken, there has not yet been a king so brave and so ambitious."

The Royal Architect's face went a ghastly white. "My liege," he stammered, "your armies are still occupied in the North. With what Host do you mean to do battle against the Elves?"

"Silence!" declared the king. "I have heard enough of this fool's blabbering tongue. Does he think that I have not already made such preparations with the Lord Commander?"

Lord Samwell Leon nodded, as always, and softly replied, "It is true. The king came by my chambers on yester-eve and divulged to me his plans to conquer the Elden Wood. All is already signed and sealed, and a muster in Oxcommon is at the ready."

King Murth grinned—"a sickening sight," as Archwizard Phineas writes. He then summoned forth Warden Ulgar. The haggard, rat-faced man stepped into the Council Chambers as silently as a ghost. "Why don't you take our esteemed Royal Architect for a tour?" said the king. "Let him inspect the dungeons, perhaps?"

And so it was that the Glorious Council found itself in need of a new Royal Architect. The replacement was chosen—like all the rest—by Keeper Petras Plume. This time, the king did not even have to ask. Lord Stefan Shanksworth had likely never seen a silver goblet in his life, yet out of one he drank fine Dunnish wine many times throughout that summer of 388.

At this point, the king occupied himself with updates on the Northern Conquest and the muster in Oxcommon, for he was very eager to see his Eastern Conquest come to fruition as well. As for the Archwizard, the king was growing impatient, but Phineas Simon insisted that the investigation of the Sworn Swords was not to be rushed. "The notes left behind by Archwizard Roswell are cryptic and inscrutable."

One night when a chill hung hesitantly in the air, the king was staring out upon the city from atop his lone tower. The skeletons of his brother and wife had finally been removed and buried next to Oliver II. As for the Crown of Blue that had adorned the fair head of Jacob III, it was given back to the Archwizard and the Collegiate to await its next wearer.

The king received a knock upon his door. It was none other than the Keeper of the Keys, Lord Petras Plume. The king was intrigued as to why the Keeper would visit him at such an hour. The Keeper bore tidings of a grievous scandal pertaining to the Council. Chastity Manor had secretly reopened and its members were engaged in clandestine nocturnal activities. To hear that members of his *own* Glorious Council were squandering the Crown's gold upon such degeneracy— that, he could not abide. According to the Keeper, frequent patrons were Warden Ulgar, Royal Admiral Drayton Dunn, Executioner Spliggins, and even Lord Samwell Leon.

Murth II immediately sent for Lord Marsden Mudpitts to round up the City Guard and surround the manor. The king and the Keeper of the Keys stood at its faded white doors and looked on as their guards broke them down, revealing many nobles in the act. Nearly two dozen immodestly clad noblewomen were about Executioner Spliggins, who was completely, undeniably, and without a shadow of a doubt in the nude.

To Spliggins' horror, King Murth II strode inside to survey the scene with fiery eyes. The king declared that, "Under [his] reign, such lascivious frivolity shall not and will not be tolerated." He ordered the

Royal Defender and his City Guard to "give this unholy place to the flames," and it was done.

That night, many a noble could glimpse flaming, naked forms fleeing from the furnace formerly known as Chastity Manor, though the Royal Executioner did not go far. His charred remains were scrounged from the manor's ruins days later.

Through the weeks to come, as the last remnants of summer burnt out, the Council saw great reform—naturally, all at the recommendation of the Keeper of the Keys. Warden Ulgar was sent to the very dungeons he had overseen since the time of King Oliver II. The new Warden was a man so vile the king could barely look upon him, though Lord Plume insisted he was "just the sort of fellow who you *want* in the dungeons, lest his proclivities find their way to the streets instead." His name was simply Arse.

As for the new Executioner, Lord Plume brought in a man who the king initially suspected to be the Keeper's own brother, given how similar they appeared. Lord Plume laughed, though he did make note of their "uncanny resemblance." He was called Petre Plum. The Keeper declared, "the man [could] swing a sword as if it were a stalk of grain."

Next, the position of Royal Admiral was in question. Lord Drayton Dunn had caught wind of the king's crackdown and promptly fled the city upon his *Eclipse*. He returned to Dunnland and out of the Crown's reach.

So, King Murth once again turned to the Keeper of the Keys. "I could inquire into the Port of the Setting Sun, my liege," the Keeper replied. "I have many friends down there who are savvy where the sea is concerned, and who may be of aid." The king grumbled, giving Lord Petras leave to make the necessary arrangements.

By this point, it was clear to the Council that the king was weary of politics and merely wished to observe his Conquests. He had recently been assured once again in a letter from Sir Sylviar that the Northern Conquest was going splendidly, with the siege of Holm Tagor ending in victory for the Crown. However as things currently stood, the Port of Arcanan was wide open and completely vulnerable.

Finally, there was the matter of Lord Commander Samwell Leon, who had vehemently denied any accusations regarding himself and Chastity Manor. For his insolence, he was sent to the dungeons, though now the king was bereft of both a Royal Admiral and a Lord Commander. Still, he would have a purpose for Lord Samwell soon enough.

As winter came and went, and scant progress was made of the Sworn Swords, King Murth's gaze turned eastward. As the recent letters from Lord Adam Oxer mentioned, the Eastern Conquest was proceeding in a manner both slow and costly to the Prairielands. The Rangers of Wolfdale were reluctant to do battle with the Elves directly, as they feared it would invoke the destruction of their city. The bannermen of House Felix remained in Feldin to protect it from bandits, whose numbers were rising. And those of Oxcommon who had answered the call were utterly unprepared for the style of warfare the Elves waged.

As such, the king moved to release Lord Samwell Leon from the dungeons and restored him to the status of Lord Commander. He had forbidden Warden Arse to lay a finger on him, ready for an occasion where he was required for battle. In the Council Chambers, which were often unoccupied as of late, Lord Samwell's silver armour, blue cloak, and ancestral sword of House Leon were all returned to him.[26]

The king then informed Lord Samwell that he was to lead what remained of the Royal Armies into the heart of the Elden Wood. He was to slay the Elven King Helios Aphelion and claim victory for King Murth II. The Lord Commander accepted this task—for he had no choice—though he did ask the king a favour. The king

---

26 However, when Lord Samwell donned his armour, it was noticeable that his stature had considerably thinned during his time in the White Keep's dungeons, so padding was required to fit it to his new form.

entertained his request. Lord Samwell humbly requested a visit with his son Samuel so he might say his farewells. The king obliged on the condition that it be done behind the walls of the White Keep, where the Zehiram were always listening.

Lord Samwell met with his son on the eve of his departure. He was unable to express all that raged inside him—for he was wary of spies—but he hoped that his son understood how dire matters had become, for he was certain that this venture would be his last. Stifling tears—a fool's errand, by all efforts—the Lord Commander embraced his only son and bestowed upon him the ancestral sword of House Leon, the Silver Star. "You will soon need it more than I, my son."

With that, he went off to fight King Murth's vainglorious war.

And so, in the spring of 389, three legions of the Royal Armies clad in steel and wielding swords fresh from the forge disappeared into the Elden Wood, never to return.

Samuel Leon read the news one day while breaking his fast with his dear wife Lara Tals. A messenger with a grim expression had knocked upon his door at Pendlebury Manor and delivered the letter. When Samuel read the words, he was beyond sorrow. Not even the sight of his infant son Reese could bring him joy.

After a night spent in lamentation, Samuel Leon took up his father's sword and left the city. He led his family to the Port of Arcanan clad in unassuming brown cloaks, hoods draping over their heads. Young Reese was bundled safely in his mother's arms. The Keeper of the Keys, disguised as a fishmonger, concealed them in a small vessel that stank of chum and sent them on their way westward.

When the king learnt of his Lord Commander's death, he im-mediately sent the Royal Defender to summon Lord Samwell's heir to the White Keep, but Pendlebury Manor was already abandoned. Enraged, Murth II had Defender Marsden flogged, and when that did not sate his fury, the Royal Defender was strung up in the centre of the marketplace as a feast for the crows.

The king then summoned the Keeper of the Keys. As he had been doing now for weeks, Murth inquired into the status of the Keeper's friend from the Port who was to fill the still-vacant post of Royal Admiral. Lord Plume replied that this friend was on his way, but that raiders in the Mouth had proven themselves to be a considerable obstacle in his travels, what with the lack of a Royal Fleet to keep the peace.

The king, growing restless, then asked Lord Plume if he additionally knew of a suitable candidate for the newly vacant position of Lord Commander, as the natural successor had seemingly fled. The Keeper replied to this dreadful news by offering to send another inquiry to the Port of the Setting Sun. King Murth II impatiently asked if there were any such candidates within Arcanan, to which the Keeper replied—with a slight smirk, "Alas, there *were*... but my liege has unfortunately killed them all."

The king dismissed Lord Plume and retired to his chambers to observe the city once again from atop his lone tower.

To the east, dreadful events had come to pass. In a bloody conflict known later as the Slaughter of Wolfdale, the city was stormed in the night by a host of Elves from the edge of the Wood. They fell upon the people unleashing arrows steeped in poisons so fierce that one pleaded for a swift death rather than suffer the agony they wrought.

By the time news of the harrowing attack reached Lord Adam Oxer, Wolfdale had already fallen. Few were spared—and those who were, namely Half-Elves—were stolen away into the Elden Wood.

The Elves had delivered swift retribution in retaliation to the king's attempt to conquer their demesne and the result ought to have been enough to dissuade anyone from stirring the Elden Wood ever again. But when news of this slaughter reached Murth II, his resolve was not shaken. He immediately dispatched orders for the Lake and Prairie Lords to continue the Eastern Conquest despite their losses. "It will require more than the savagery of Elves to dissuade me from excellence!"

That summer in 390, the king once again received news from Sir Sylviar Hunter, this time that the Northern Conquest continued with great success. The Royal Armies had reportedly captured the Dwarven settlements of Holdarim, Thernum, Kimterolwaak, Vahkrim, Mornduhn, Nongaruhm, and Moldim, and were headed towards the Great City of Garm, home to the King Under the Mountain. However, Sir Hunter did appear to be more troubled than usual, mentioning depleting supplies and low morale, as well as an offhand remark regarding the "barbaric Grey Dwarves" who would pull his men into the earth at night.

Regardless, King Murth sent a reply commanding them to keep fast to their plans and make their way to Garm post-haste, for he could feel at last his Conquests were reaching their resolution. He awaited the day he could rest in the knowledge that both the Realms of the Dwarves and Elves were secure in his enlightened rule.

In the dawn of 391, a great alliance was forming in Hylete Square, unbeknownst to the king, for Samuel Leon and his family had arrived safely in the West, and were promptly admitted to the Checkered Hall for an audience with Lord Lorn Hylar. The Lord of Hylete heard Samuel's woes and found common ground with him over the deaths of their fathers—both direct results of Murth's tyranny. However, when Lord Samuel made mention of vengeance, Lord Lorn was hesitant. "My father sought vengeance against the Crown for the death of his beloved daughter Laura, but it was an ill-fated errand."

Lord Samuel then unsheathed the blade of his forefathers. "In the past, it was indeed true that Hylete could not stand against the might of Arcanan. But times have changed. The Crown has spread its armies thin, what with these conceited attempts to conquer both the Dwarves to the North and the Elves to the East. Murth sent his own Lord Commander to his death. His council has become a pigsty of scoundrels from the foulest of Arcanan's gutters. He is without a Royal Fleet and an Admiral to lead one. If there was ever a time to strike against Arcanan, it is *now*. For you have it right: one House alone cannot hope to defeat the strength of Arcanan, but Hylete is not alone. You have an ally in House Leon, and many more will heed our call, for Murth the Mad has made many enemies, and the time of his demise draws nigh."

A bond was formed that day between the houses of Leon and Hylar—one nigh-unbreakable. The chance to act that Lord Lorn had awaited all these years had finally come. Dozens of letters were sent out from Hylete Square, calling all its banners. Hundreds of new knights were trained across the Hylete Province, and battle strategies were devised in Castle Hylar to aid them in the coming war.

While the king was yet unaware of both the alliance and the muster, time was of the essence. The Men of the West prepared as much as possible before news inevitably reached the White Keep. They did not have long.

King Murth II received the news from his Zehiram while on a stroll through the White Keep's beautiful, though overgrown, Queen's Gardens. Upon learning of his enemies' pact, he was so furious that he set flame to the gardens, watching them curl and twist in the heat.

As the king had no more men of the Royal Armies to muster, he summoned the Keeper of the Keys at once. "It is time to call upon all the Great Houses who have not chosen treachery in order to crush this foolish Lord of Hylete, just as I crushed his father!"

With that, letters were sent out to the Rohes of Stone Haven, the Wayns of Westerton, the Voyants of Stathmore, and even the Dunns—with a pardon of all charges set against their lord. These letters carried a simple order: to capture Hylete Square and destroy the traitorous lords of Hylar and Leon, extinguishing the fires of insubordination.

But there was further strife for King Murth II within his city, for at long last, Dorj'hept'kii, High Elder of the West Church of Gutenberg since 352, breathed his last breath. It was scarcely known at the time that the High Elder's health was waning, though, any who caught a recent glimpse of him could have surmised. When he finally passed, he was seventy-seven years old. Sitting in his bedchamber surrounded by sheets of white that glowed under the winter sun, his eyes had gone pale and his mind had all but faded away. The last soul to speak with Dorj'hept'kii before he died was an errand boy who routinely brought him soup, though, in his final moments, answer to that Holy name he did not. "Murth! My name is Murth!" [27]

And so a new High Elder was named. This successor, a proud and forthright man named Mar'tornian'dzangrir—or Stout Heart by the people by which he was dearly beloved, made clear that the West Church of Gutenberg would no longer endorse Murth the Mad. He declared that the Church would do all in their power to resist the king's tyranny, which "[went] against all that is Good and Holy under the sun!" Thus, the Order of Holy Clerics of the White Daisy were turned against the Crown, united with the multitudes who hated the king like a blister on the sole of their foot. Few in the Prairielands dared declare it out loud, but for perhaps the first time since the Schism, the two halves of the Church had been in alignment. However, the king's final reckoning would not come just yet.

That spring in 391, a great battle loomed over Hylete Square—an event for which the lords of Hylar and Leon were not yet prepared. As the Bridge of Unity had been demolished in the previous Hylar rebellion, any means of passage across the Father's River was severely compromised, and many still recalled the ill-fated journey of Grayson "the Grey Wolf" Leon during Brendan Dunn's occupation of Hylete Square. The Rohe Host had no choice but to sail by sea, as the Bridge of Unity still lay in rubble. After dropping anchor within the Bay of the Twisted Canyon, the host embarked, marching on Hylete Square. In the north, a legion of Sentinels was dispatched, marching south

---

27   Over the years, many scholars have mused over Dorj'hept'kii's final words. While he had denounced the name of Murth to join the ranks of the Church, this may have been his way—and *only* way—to ever hold authority of his own. The Line of Alexander kept the throne until their utter destruction, but Murth remained uncontested upon his Throne of Piety.

in silent reply to the king's decree, for the Wayns of Westerton still harboured deep resentment for the House of Hylar.

Lord Drayton Dunn, afeared of the king's wrath, was relieved to see mention of a Royal Pardon, for he wanted nothing more than a return to the king's good graces. He rallied his Host and boarded his *Blight of Providence* to lead the Dunnish Fleet toward Providence Shore once again.

With the hosts of four Great Houses approaching the city, Lord Lorn and Lord Samuel readied their defences and braced for the worst, for they knew that failure would mean their rebellion would fare no better than what King Humphrey's had. Despite the odds, Samuel Leon was confident that they would succeed; he believed support for King Murth II among the Great Lords was waning, and that anything could happen.

Less than a fortnight later, the armies were visible from atop the walls of Hylete Square: The Sentinels approaching from the north, the Starsworn of Stathmore from the east, the Meshiran of Stone Haven from the south, and the familiar crescent-moon banners of Dunnland upon the horizon of Providence Shore. The settlements upon the shores were once again put to flame as the Dunnish Host raided them. The other three armies, meanwhile, had set up camps surrounding the city to the north, south, and east. There was no escape for the people of Hylete Square, for the siege had begun.

But Lord Lorn had prepared. The city's stores were filled to the brim, and much of the population had been sent to the towns and villages beyond the Vale, so there were fewer mouths to feed. The defending garrison was stationed along the walls to defend them from siege infrastructure such as ladders or towers, as well as to survey the lands and loose arrows upon any approaching forces.

Lord Samuel donned his silver armour, fastened Silver Star at his hip, and rode out to parley. He met with Lord Valar Voyant, Lady Rayna Wayn, Sir Amir Rohe—son of Lady Malina Rohe—and Sir

Dennis Dunn, as Lord Drayton had resolved to remain aboard *Blight of Providence* for the time being.

Lord Valar declared to Samuel Leon that there were no terms to discuss. "We have been summoned to answer a call from the king himself! You, Lord of Leon, are a traitor, and my army will not back down until you and that foolish son of a fool are put in your place! The stars have revealed to me that if I should fail, the Glorious Realm will see a tumultuous upheaval the likes of which has never been seen before!"

Lady Wayn was more thoughtful in her approach. She listened to the talks and responded sparingly, with much wisdom in her words. She recognized that King Murth oft overstepped his bounds and abused his power. "Ultimately, he is our king, whether we Lords and Ladies like it or not. It is not our place to defy his rule; we should be working together to bring our grievances to Arcanan instead, not going to war like impetuous youths."

The representative from Dunnland, the young Dennis, threatened Lord Samuel instead. "If you do not surrender the city and concede your ill-conceived rebellion *tomorrow*, the raids will not stop with Providence Shore. You can tell your friend Lorn that Dunnland is fierce and ready for war. Our fighters are restless and prepared to burn as many Hyletian towns and villages as it takes. Tell him so that he may choose *wisely* and not be a fool like his father was."

Sir Amir did not speak, but merely observed.

Lord Samuel responded in turn. "You have all presented your positions thus to me, and I have heard them. It saddens me that you all express such unearned devotion to the tyrant Murth, who has done nothing but serve his own vainglorious ambitions since the day he stole his brother's crown. Lord Voyant, you claim the stars have guided you to make this decision, and I do not doubt your conviction. I only ask: what if this upheaval your dreams speak of is a good thing? What if such an event is precisely what the Realm needs in order to truly thrive? For not all change is woe; like the fires that burn the forests, ashes bring forth new, healthier soil. Perhaps Murth II's heir will be a kinder, fairer king? I bid you ponder the question: what if the future the stars hath foretold is one you ought not forestall?

"And to the Lady of Wayn, I see in you a wise and tempered leader, but at the same time, I believe you grant the king too much benefit. My father served the king to the day he died in vain and described to me firsthand the cruelty of it all. To Murth, his subjects are his pawns, his means to an end. If they fail to serve his ambitions, he discards them like rotted grains. I admire your optimism, my Lady, but I fear that with Murth as our king, there is no hope for reform. That man serves only his ambition: to rule over all.

"To the Lord Rohe, who has remained silent, I bid you remember what happened to your father. As my own father hath divulged to me, the old Royal Architect was sent to the dungeons to be tortured until death—and for speaking out against the Western Conquest, no less! He simply spoke the truth and was put to death. *That* is the kind of king you serve. I suggest you let that weigh heavy on your mind tonight, and maybe then, you will have something to say.

"And lastly, Sir Dunn, I am saddened by the enthusiasm with which you speak regarding the destruction of lives. Are the innocent peoples of the Hylete Province to you naught but insects beneath your feet? Shame on you, Sir Dunn. If I were your lord, I would strip away your titles; a knight with such bloodlust and avarice is no true knight. I will inform Lord Lorn of all you have said, as well as mention how your lord father was too afeared to leave his galley and parley with us."

Without a further word, Lord Samuel bade the leaders farewell and rode back through the gates of Hylete Square. And that night, all who remained behind the walls of the city slept with one eye open, wary of what the dawn would bring.

Come next morn, the horns of battle were blown, and the hosts of the Great Houses of Wayn, Voyant, Rohe, and Dunn descended on Hylete Square. The garrison responded in full force, standing strong to protect the city from the incoming forces. Ladders were toppled and siege towers were burnt by hot coals flung from wall-mounted catapults, but inevitably, their enemies scaled the walls. From there, melees were fought man-to-man, and the Hylar garrison was overwhelmed by the sheer number of their opponents. Lord Samuel led a sortie atop the walls to smash the enemy forces attempting to lower the drawbridge—an act that would surely spell defeat for their rebellion—and with Silver Star in hand, he kept the soldiers at bay for as long as he could.

But from atop the parapets of the castle, Lord Lorn witnessed something greatly unexpected: a turn in the tide of battle. The armies of House Rohe descended upon the Voyant Host from the rear and scattered their ranks. At the same time, two hundred Meshiran clad in brass tore through the Sentinels, sending them into disarray. More Meshiran rushed the Providence Shore and set the Dunnish fleet aflame.

Within hours, the enemy forces were crushed. The defending garrison took advantage of the chaos to oust the invading forces from the city and once again secure the walls. The battle finally met its end when Sir Dennis Dunn was struck down by the blade of none other than Sir Amir Rohe, by which point the Starsworn and the Sentinels had already routed their foes.

And so it was that the Battle of Hylete Square in the year 391 was unexpectedly won by the rebel allies of Hylar and Leon—joined by House Rohe.

As the other Great Houses returned to their family seats with their tails between their legs, the Meshiran remained. Sir Amir was admitted into the city. He rode upon a woolly Rono to the Checkered Hall and bowed before Lord Hylar and Lord Leon, pledging himself to their cause. "The words thou hath spoken unto me, Lord Leon, reminded me of the great injustices delivered unto my people. As we speak, the waters surrounding my home are swarming with raiders and pirates—a direct consequence of the king's mishandlings. The Crown's duty to the Realm is to protect us, and it has failed in that.

So, let me join you; let me join this cause against the Crown, for Stone Haven shall not abide this tyranny a day longer!"

It was upon that day in 391 After-the-Arrival that a historic three-way alliance formed in Hylete Square between the Houses of Leon, Hylar, and Rohe. It was the Star Resistance.

King Murth II ought to have been frightened.

When the king heard of the failure at Hylete Square, his first action was to descend below the White Keep, where Archwizard Phineas laboured endlessly. The king demanded one final time that the Archwizard procure the Sworn Swords at once. Phineas bowed graciously and promised yet again that preparations were underway. "You shall have your army soon enough, my liege."

The king was wroth. "How soon? You have been given *ample* time, and so far, I have seen nothing. I will speak plainly, Phineas: If the Sworn Swords are not in my employ by the year's end, I shall have you flayed and killed." With that, he left the Archwizard with his work and retired to his tower, frustrated in the knowledge that no progress had been made.

As the year met its end, all other wizards of House Simon had gone missing. When the king sent the City Guard toward a place he was certain another Simon's tower stood, his guardsmen found naught but empty plains.[28] Phineas could not be replaced. Embittered and without recourse, Murth resolved to let him continue his work into the year 392.

Meanwhile, in the west, the Star Resistance made its first move. In retaliation for Hylete Square, Lord Lorn struck Dunnland in the spring. Its lord had sought refuge in Sharktooth Keep and was drowning himself in drink. He was alerted by his chamberlain that Swordfish Harbour was ablaze and that his *Blight of Providence*

---

28   There most definitely *was* a tower in the place the king designated the Guard to search, but a tower built by a Simon is more than your average pile of stone.

had been not spared. Alarmed, Lord Drayton rode out toward the shores, and was stricken by the sight of the Hylar banners. A battle was waged that saw the proud Dunnish fleet torched and sundered, ending when Lord Lorn crossed blades with Lord Drayton himself. As his son had fallen before him in the Battle of Hylete, the Lord of Dunnland was slain—though unlike his son, he met his end by the blade of a Hylar, whose enmity against Dunnland had been forged over centuries of bitter strife. Victorious against their enemies nearby, the Star Resistance sailed back home, now looking ahead toward enemies afar.

With the beginning of 393, the Eastern Conquest had come to an end, though not by the King's command. The Lord of Oxcommon, Adam Oxer, had withdrawn, citing the ruins of Wolfdale as reason enough. Lord Adam dispatched a messenger to Feldin bearing news of his decision and urging Lord Morgan Felix to withdraw as well. Upon personally riding north to Feldin, he was able to secure a mutual agreement. Lord Morgan was ambivalent about betraying the Crown, but that changed when the Lord of Oxcommon revealed his plan to join the Star Resistance and end the Conquest that "drained the Prairieland's coffers faster than a puncture in an oxen waterskin."

And north of Feldin, Tal Taro was so moved by the news of the Star Resistance that Lord Terrance decided their mummer's farce was long overdue its end. For these past few years, the knights Murth II had stationed in Hildar to oversee its occupation had grown complacent. All the while, Lord Terrance assured them, "the Hill Dwarves [were] being thoroughly subjugated."

On the night of the new moon, after a long evening of festivities shared between Lord Tals' men and the Hill Dwarves, the king's knights were captured and gaoled in a single swift maneuver. By the next morning, the occupation had been lifted, and following some lighthearted banter with the Dwarves, Lord Tals and his men departed home to Tal Taro as if it were nothing more than the end of a long, exhausting party.

Just as the king received belated news of the Lake and Prairie Lords' treachery, a new predicament appeared upon his doorstep. The Port of Arcanan was suddenly home to an ominous fleet of ships, their sails emblazoned by fiery phoenixes. There was a mouthful of Rygar ships in the port. In a day, Arcanan was effectively blockaded.

The king immediately summoned forth Lord Petras Plume—as he always did—but this time, his summons were fruitless. To make matters worse, all of the councillors appointed by the Keeper could not be located. When Murth stormed into the Council Chambers in search of Lord Plume, he found instead a goblet upon the table by the place Lord Plume sat. On its own, it was nothing extraordinary; it was the same goblet Lord Plume drank from during most Council meetings. Yet, it was what lay *inside* the goblet that mattered. No drink to be found, but a feather the colour of embers.

King Murth II, at his wits' end, bounded down the steps of the White Keep until he reached Phineas Duos Simon. The king drew his sword and pointed it at the old wizard's throat, demanding that he present the Sworn Swords to him now, or die. The Archwizard pleaded for his life and assured the king that he had at long last solved Roswell's riddle. King Murth reluctantly lowered his sword. The Archwizard then sauntered over to the sealed stone wall, and with a flick of his hand, it erupted into an explosion of blue flames, incinerating his notes and himself. As the underground chamber began to collapse and crumble, the king barely escaped with his life. When he turned around to inspect the damage, he saw that the entrance had utterly caved in.

Without any armies to speak of, any Council to deliberate with, and any support from the people, Murth the Mad was entirely alone. And to further his anguish and rage, his last letter from Sir Sylviar Hunter had been well over a year ago. The Star Resistance marched on Arcanan and the Mad King, its host bolstered by nearly all Great Houses.

But alas, Murth would not concede. He had come too far to lose it all. In his mind, one option remained to him if he were to make his mark upon the Realm: he needed to do what no king before him had even dreamt of. He needed to conquer the Elves.

It was at this point, late in the year 393, that King Murth II visited his younger brother Ashar. Ever since they were children, Murth had tormented Ashar unceasingly. Growing up, he would destroy Ashar's toys and shove him into the dirt, or practice swordplay with steel while his brother wielded a prop. As they grew to manhood, Murth's treatment of Ashar simply grew graver and more insidious. During a practice joust, he knocked his brother off his steed with such force that he landed in a way that nearly crippled him. With intense aid from the Collegiate and the Archwizard, Ashar's legs were saved, but ever since the incident, he had suffered from convulsions and shakes that wracked his entire body.

When Murth became King of the Glorious Realm, he put Ashar under permanent watch by the Zehiram and forbade him to leave his room. Over the years of Murth's reign, Ashar had grown ever more frail and brittle. By 393, his hair had grown down past his hips and was flecked with premature streaks of grey, despite the fact he was only twenty-two. He spoke little and left his bed even less, and his only companions were the Zehiram who stalked his chambers and enforced his imprisonment. Why the king kept his brother in this state during his reign is not truly understood, but some believed that Murth the Mad feared on some level that his frail brother might yet somehow rise up and snatch his throne out from under him, just as Murth had done to his elder brother Jacob.

It was Prince Ashar who Murth II relied upon in 393 before he ventured into the Elden Wood, for while the White Keep was bereft of the king's presence, someone was still needed to watch the throne in his stead, and nobody remained for this task save for his younger brother.

The feeble young prince was carried from his chambers by an escort of Zehiram and brought to the Throne Room, where he was laid upon the Arcane Throne. He was to sit there until King Murth II returned victorious from his Conquest. For the king was convinced that with his Royal Presence in the Elden Wood, his armies would crush the Elves at last.

Alas, it was not to be.

King Murth II was not even an hour past the Wood's edge when he found himself and his entourage ambushed by Elves. His retinue immediately turned tail to flee in vain, abandoning the king to his own devices. Once again alone, and surrounded by enemies, King Murth II is said to have suffered a "death by one-hundred arrows."[29] The Crown of Red was stripped from him and stolen away into the Elden Wood, never to be recovered. Murth the Mad's ill-fated conquest, later referred to as the War Under the Sun, had reached its end.

When the Star Resistance finally arrived at the gates of Arcanan in the autumn of 393 with a Host twelve legions strong, they were joined by multitudes of peasants, merchants, nobles, and commonfolk, all led by High Elder Stout Heart of the West Church of Gutenberg. Blood was hot and spirits were high, for the king's reckoning was finally at hand. But Murth II was absent. In his stead sat the newly crowned King Ashar II. During a small and sparsely attended coronation, the Crown of White had been placed upon his head by the new Archwizard, Silas Octavius Simon, who had arrived not even a day after Murth's departure.

When Lord Samuel Leon and Lord Lorn Hylar arrived atop Jacob's Hill, the gates to the Outer Courtyard were wide open. Ashar II's men bid them welcome to visit the king in the Royal Cemetery.

---

29   Many scholars of the College have combed through the old parchments that document these events to find no mention of the king's death actually being by exactly "one-hundred arrows." If it was more or less, we may never know, but this much is certain: the Elves had indeed delivered death unto King Murth II.

Intrigued, the two lords entered. They found the thin young king kneeling before the gravestone of his eldest brother, Jacob III. He had lain a single white rose upon the dirt. When Ashar noticed the lords, he congratulated them on their victory against his brother. "You won this war without a single life lost in the City of Arcanan. When my brother received news of your march against him, he fled to the Elden Wood in a vain attempt to claim victory there instead, for he knew he would find none here. Remnants of his small sortie returned one week before today and reported that he was killed. So that makes *me* king. Isn't that a cruel jest?"

The lords did not know what to make of this news. They had gathered up nearly all the Great Houses and mustered a massive Host with the purpose of laying siege to Arcanan, but their victory had seemingly been handed to them without issue. They went to bow before their new king, but Ashar II bid them pause. "No, my lords, there is no need."

Then, shaking violently, as if he were likely to collapse at any moment, Ashar removed the Crown of White from his head and placed it upon the soggy ground. "While it is indeed true that my ancestor King Jacob I founded this Glorious Realm, and while it is true that since his reign, every king has been born of his Line, I believe that our sun has finally set. Let the Realm witness the dawn of a *new* dynasty! I leave this choice to the two of you."

Ashar—"the Last Pike"—then retired to the Manor, the ancestral seat of his House, where he lived out the rest of his days as he had lived thus far: in solitude.

With the Arcane Throne now vacant, all of the Pike banners, flags, and tapestries were thereby removed from the White Keep for the first time since its construction. Not even a single guard stood sentry upon Jacob's Hill. A curious quiet prevailed in the Nobles' Quarters.

Lord Rudolph Rygar emerged from the Rygar Fleet in the Port of Arcanan and attended the first session of the Silver Council of

393, during which the Lords of the Star Resistance congregated to deliberate upon which House the next king would emerge. While Lord Rudolph's name was entered into the discussions as early as possible, the general sentiment among all present was thus: "No Rygar shall ever be King of the Glorious Realm, or so help us Gutenberg!"

Sir Amir Rohe announced that he had spoken at length with his mother, the Lady of Stone Haven, and that House Rohe would pledge its support for Lord Samuel Leon, who had inspired Sir Amir to recognize their true enemy. Lord Adam Oxer put his name forth for candidacy, and Lord Felix announced his House's support, but many more lords and ladies such as Terrance Tals were throwing their lot behind Samuel Leon, including, to much murmuring, the West Church of Gutenberg, when High Elder Stout Heart knelt before him. Many recognized Lord Samuel's outstanding leadership and more yet bore witness to his anointing by the Church.

The last of the lords yet undecided was Lorn Hylar, who all others expected to vie for the throne himself. Lord Lorn once again refused this mandate, as he had in Hylete Square.

"I have known no greater leader, nor a more inspiring friend than Samuel Leon. Without him, I would likely have taken refuge behind the walls of Hylete Square until the day I died, all while tyrannical kings such as Murth the Mad desecrated this Glorious Realm we all cherish so dearly. So I say look not to me! Look to King Samuel Leon, who shall surely lead us into a Golden Age the likes of which has never been seen before!"

Appendix A: Kings of the Glorious Realm

(1—393 AA)

AA: After-the-Arrival

1—49 AA	Jacob I, King of the Setting Sun
49—78 AA	Jared I, The Conqueror; grandson of Jacob I
78—84 AA	Murth I, The Menace; son of Jared I
84—153 AA	Alexander I, The Old; son of Murth I
153—163 AA	Christopher I, The Cursed; grandson of Alexander I
163—236 AA	Tomas I, The Root; son of Christopher I
236—237 AA	David I, The Abomination; left no issue
237—253 AA	Alexander II, The Tourney King
254—276 AA	Samuel I, Killed during a riot
276—278 AA	Jared II, The Frail; son of Samuel I
278—294 AA	Alexander III, The Explorer; lost at sea

294—306 AA   Grant I, The Just; son of Alexander III

306—342 AA   Jacob II, Second son of Alexander III

343—343 AA   Alexander IV, Usurper during the Royal Schism

343—349 AA   Oliver I, Son of Jacob II

349—350 AA   Ashar I, Last of the line of Alexander III

350—384 AA   Oliver II, The Spurner; ended all Tungish Wars

384—386 AA   Jacob III, The Fair; son of Oliver II

386—393 AA   Murth II, The Mad; usurped the throne

393—393 AA   Ashar II, Last of the Pike Kings; abdicated

Appendix B: The Pike Family Tree

FROM SAMUEL I TO ASHAR II

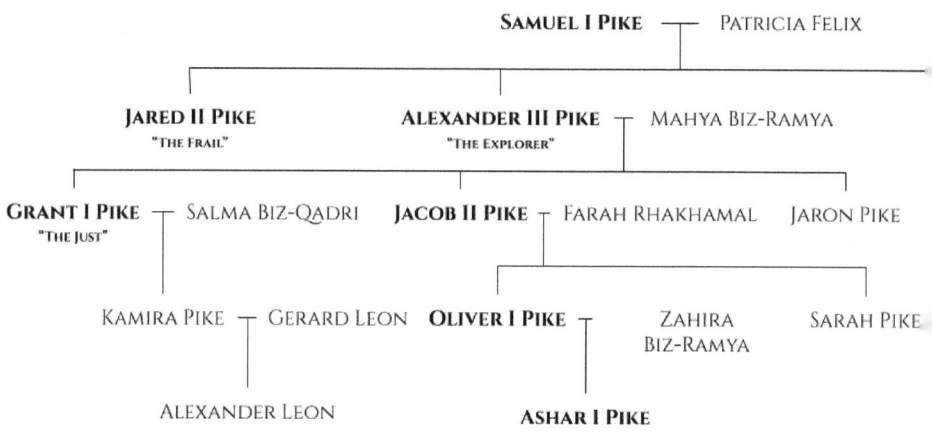

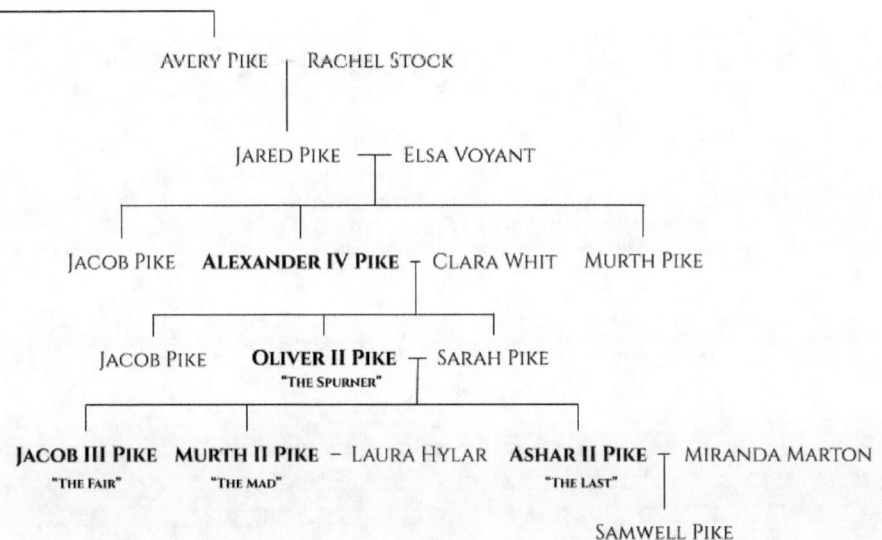

AVERY PIKE — RACHEL STOCK

JARED PIKE — ELSA VOYANT

JACOB PIKE   **ALEXANDER IV PIKE** — CLARA WHIT   MURTH PIKE

JACOB PIKE   **OLIVER II PIKE** — SARAH PIKE
              "THE SPURNER"

JACOB III PIKE   **MURTH II PIKE** – LAURA HYLAR   **ASHAR II PIKE** — MIRANDA MARTON
"THE FAIR"   "THE MAD"   "THE LAST"

                                                         SAMWELL PIKE

About the Authors

Brighton Greet was born in White Rock, British Columbia in 1998. He grew up with *The Lord of the Rings* and later embraced *Dungeons & Dragons* and *A Song of Ice and Fire* in his teenage years. Brighton began formally writing in 2020, and is the author of the *Tales From the Wilderness* series. Outside of writing he is a computer engineer and musician. He lives in Edmonton, Alberta with his wife Brie.

Joshua Hillman was born in Calgary, Alberta in 1998. He took dance lessons for most of his life; his favourites being tap and ballet. *The Legend of Zelda: A Link to the Past* was his first introduction to the realm of fantasy along with *RuneScape*. Joshua started writing in 2021 and enjoys passing the time with an engaging video game. He currently works as a controls technologist and lives in Edmonton, Alberta with his wife Robyn.

Thank you for reading *The Setting Sun.*

*We would love if you could help by posting a review at your book retailer
and on the PageMaster Publishing site. It only takes a minute and it
would really help others by giving them an idea of your experience.*

Thanks

PM Store
https://pagemasterpublishing.ca/

To order more copies of this book, find books by other
Canadian authors, or make inquiries about publishing your
own book, contact PageMaster at:

PageMaster Publication Services Inc.
11340-120 Street, Edmonton, AB T5G 0W5
books@pagemaster.ca
780-425-9303

catalogue and e-commerce store
PageMasterPublishing.ca/Shop